DANCE
OF THE
INNOCENTS

*To my new friend
Shannon*

A NOVEL BY

TODD R. LOCKWOOD

iUniverse, Inc.
Bloomington

Dance of the Innocents

iUniverse books may be ordered through booksellers or by contacting:

iUniverse
1663 Liberty Drive
Bloomington, IN 47403
www.iuniverse.com
1-800-Authors (1-800-288-4677)

Cover photograph by Dick Luria

ISBN: 978-1-4620-2570-1 (sc)
ISBN: 978-1-4620-1184-1 (hc)
ISBN: 978-1-4620-1185-8 (e)

Library of Congress Control Number: 2011909950

Printed in the United States of America

iUniverse rev. date: 08/10/2011

ONE

JEROME ROBERTS AGONIZED OVER how he'd break the news to Catherine, the flight attendant he met online. They hadn't met face to face yet, but Jerome knew it was only a matter of time. Sooner or later, he'd have to come clean. Catherine knew practically everything about Jerome—his taste in music, his favorite foods, his hobbies. She'd even seen his picture. The problem was his job. Jerome told Catherine that he worked for the *Centers for Disease Control* in Atlanta, which was true. What he neglected to mention was his job description: janitor. Jerome's pager let out a shriek, and a new message appeared:

Prepare Room 99 for 9:00 a.m. meeting

Jerome parked his floor polisher and hustled to the elevator. Instead of selecting a floor, he inserted a pass card and punched in a six-digit code. It was a long ride. Room 99 resided in a hollowed-out cavern, several hundred feet below the CDC basement level. Only a handful of people outside the CDC even knew it existed. Jerome remembered only one other time Room 99 had been used: during the anthrax attacks.

Room 99 resembled the Situation Room at the White House, only larger. It could accommodate several dozen people, and it included support facilities to house and feed them for extended periods, if

1

necessary. This high-tech crisis center dealt with catastrophe head on. From deep within the earth, decisions would be made, actions implemented, and millions of lives might be saved.

At Robins Air Force Base in nearby Macon, a phalanx of helicopters lifted off the tarmac, headed for Atlanta. The cargo included officials from the National Institutes of Health and the Pentagon, as well as physicians from Harvard, Yale, and other elite medical institutions.

Jerome stepped off the elevator to find a dozen CDC personnel already at work. Blue-suited maintenance workers cleaned and vacuumed. AV technicians checked their equipment. "This is a test, check, one, two," a voice boomed through speakers in the ceiling. Blue and white CDC logos filled each of three large plasma displays. The logo on the center display then disappeared—replaced by the seal of the president of the United States. Jerome tried his best not to stare at it.

"Jerome, check the supplies in the restrooms," his supervisor barked.

"I'm on it." Jerome pushed a supply cart to the women's restroom and cracked open the door. "Maintenance," he shouted. No response. Jerome went inside and checked the soap, paper towels, and toilet tissue. Everything looked fine, so he headed to the men's room. The last stall in the men's room needed tissue. Jerome grabbed a fresh roll from his cart. He extended his janitor key ring, unlocked the holder, and slid the new roll into place. Then he locked the stall door, dropped his blue coveralls, and lowered himself onto the seat. "Man! The president!" Jerome whispered. "Something big must be goin' down." *Could this be the big one everybody's been worried about,* he wondered, *a dirty bomb or bioattack?*

"Attention," a voice blared from a speaker in the men's room ceiling, "all persons without high-security clearance must vacate Room 99 immediately."

"Oh, shit. Are you are doggin' me?" Jerome heard a two-way radio outside the men's room. He lifted his feet up against the back of the stall door. The men's room door opened, and a security guard walked in. The guard eyed the restroom, but didn't notice the last stall was locked. He gave the all clear on his radio and left.

Up in the CDC main lobby, physicians, researchers, and military brass rushed through security and descended to Room 99. At the White House, the president and his senior staff assembled in the Situation Room, where they were connected to Room 99 via secure satellite video link.

"We are live with the White House," a CDC aide announced. "The president is online."

Dr. Charles Miller, CDC's executive director, took his seat, and a hush fell over the room. Miller's imposing form sent a clear message about who was in charge. "Mr. President, esteemed doctors, members of the security, military, and intelligence communities …"

Jerome sat quietly on the toilet as Dr. Miller's words emanated from the men's room loudspeaker.

"I'm going to cut right to the chase. We have a crisis."

— — —

In Minneapolis, the morning parade commenced. Cell phone commuters and minivan moms dominated the streets. Makeup was checked in rearview mirrors, coffee juggled. Necktied guys and smart-suited women vied for position. Everyone had a place to go and a reason to be there—everyone except David Peters.

Peters sputtered along in his venerable Honda Accord, trailed by billows of blue smoke. He practically had the northbound lane to himself. He scanned the faces in the oncoming cars. He could just imagine their upscale homes and widescreen plasma TVs. In the rearview mirror, he caught a glimpse of himself—forty-five years old, a guy who built a career on selling other people's ideas, a guy who needed a haircut and a job.

Things had gotten a little rough around the edges for David Peters since he was let go. His former tidiness had given way to a sidewalk-cowboy patina, featuring a tattered motorcycle jacket from his twenties. Wiry stubble played at the corners of his mouth. Salt and pepper hair crept over his collar like a relentless clock, counting the days until the next mortgage payment. The gym membership and the BlackBerry were history. David plummeted in a back-to-basics spiral, with no end in sight.

The steering wheel felt sticky in David's hands, likely from the coffee spill a few days before. Candy wrappers and month-old newspapers lined the floor. The Honda needed a good cleaning inside and out, but David thought it more logical to deal with the car's mechanical issues first. He knew what the car needed, but couldn't bring himself to spend the money. Consequently, neither the repairs nor the cleaning was likely to happen anytime soon. The belching Honda was a rolling tribute to indecision. To David, the car embodied one of the great ironies of being unemployed: that you need to *look* prosperous to get a job that will *make you* prosperous. His life had become one great chicken-and-egg conundrum.

While he tried to look forward, David couldn't help looking back. He'd had a promising and successful marketing career, and then one day he didn't. The plain truth of it was, he'd been *outsourced*—replaced by a young marketing guy in Pakistan named Raj Nabi, who no doubt worked for a fraction of David's salary. For David, it was hard to believe it had come to this. Marketing jobs were supposed to be immune to the scourge of outsourcing. It was long believed that only Americans could sell products to Americans. But the Internet and satellite television changed everything. Now there were young English-speaking people in Pakistan and India who knew quite well what was on the minds of Americans. These outsiders had become the new, hip marketing paradigm, and corporations were eating it up.

David and Raj Nabi had traded a couple of polite e-mails right after the axe came down. David knew he couldn't very well hold Raj Nabi responsible for the situation. He lived in a rich country and Raj did not. It was a simple matter of economics. Nonetheless, David felt a twinge of antipathy when he thought about how his life had changed. It'd been five months already, with no real prospects.

David's life teetered between comfort and oblivion. Just *getting by* in America was no small feat. Gone were the Kerouacian days when you could survive on the edge, taking in the street-level view just for the adventure of it. Inflation had changed everything. The distance between a roof over your head and homeless was approaching six figures. People were slipping through the cracks everywhere. Where do they go, David wondered, those people who lose their grip on the American dream?

Belching blue clouds, David navigated his customary route to Max's Diner: eleven blocks north, past Crystal Lake, past North Minneapolis High School where his wife Julia taught, and then over to Broadway. Max's was a well-maintained relic of the sixties. So was Sue, the waitress, her platinum hair spray-sculpted into a Petula Clark throwback with bangs jutting out like an awning. Coors beer can earrings dangled at each side. Sue was in remarkable shape for her years, packing her figure impressively into the two-tone uniform. She'd been working at Max's since the eighties, earning herself the honorary title of head waitress. Over the years, Sue had developed a bartender-like wisdom. She'd seen all kinds.

Through the front window, Sue saw David climb out of his car. She primped herself and grabbed the coffeepot. David's cup awaited him at his usual spot at the counter, with cream and extra sugar. Johnny Cash wafted from the Seeburg, its translucent red buttons aglow. "Hey there, good lookin'," Sue chirped—her standard greeting for any guy under sixty.

"Hey, Sue." David swung onto the stool and leaned into his coffee. He scanned the diner on the unlikely chance there was someone there he knew. Most of the customers were old enough to be retired, or if not, they were out of work or worse. A postman who never said a word occupied his usual stool at the other end of the counter.

"So, how's the job search going?" Sue's beer cans jangled.

"So far, so good. I've got the shrubs planted and the windows washed. Next, it's the lawn."

"You sound pretty handy to me. I bet the wife is happy to have you around."

"Well, that can be a double-edged sword. Let's just say I'm operating on borrowed time."

"You and me both, honey," Sue confided.

David took another sip of coffee.

"You know, I bet there's somebody out there looking for a guy just like you."

"A forty-five-year-old marketing guy? Don't count on it. Jobs like mine are going to Pakistan and India. It's the new global marketplace. The American dream turns out to be the American nightmare."

Sue opened up the newspaper. "Let's check your horoscope."

David sipped his coffee and listened.

"What was your ...?"

"Aries," David muttered.

"Hmmm. Aries ... 'You have a gift. You can see what no one else can see. While most see only trees, you see the forest. A discovery could change your life forever.'"

David shook his head. "Can you believe this bullshit? Excuse my French, but can you believe people actually take this stuff seriously?"

"You're not a horoscope guy, huh?"

"How about a horoscope that says, 'A job awaits you at 111 Main Street, includes private office and full benefits.' It's all part of a government mind control plot anyway, these horoscopes."

"Mind control?" Sue chuckled.

David's voice took on a humorless tone. "I saw it on the Internet. The feds won't admit to it, but you can see what they're doing, playing with people's minds, moving the masses. Nobody knows exactly how they do it, but believe me, they're up to something."

Sue raised her eyebrows and stepped back from the counter.

David changed his tone. "Okay, okay, I know this must sound a little bit out there, but not everything is what it appears to be. Believe me, I know. I'm a marketing guy."

"You had me worried there for a minute," Sue said. "I thought you were another one of my nutcases."

"Talk to me in a few months. I'll be communicating with aliens."

"Being out of work can change people. I've seen it." Sue folded her arms in front of her. "Somethin's gonna happen for you," she said. "I can feel it in my bones."

— — —

David's wife, Julia, stood in front of her tenth-grade biology class. She had a well-maintained look—precise and youthful, and if it were not for her confidence, she might have been mistaken for a student. "Today, we're going to discuss *biomass*. Can anyone tell us what biomass is a measure of?"

Several hands went up. Julia motioned to one of them.

"Biomass is a way to measure the density of living things within a given area."

"That's right," Julia said. "When we talk about a biomass of sharks in the ocean, we mean the average number of sharks in a certain area multiplied by the average mass of one of those sharks. Species of very low mass, such as insects, must exist in much greater numbers to achieve the same biomass as larger animals. Greater biomass can give a species a competitive advantage within its territory, but if that biomass becomes too great, the species can become a victim of its own success. We saw this in the 1930s with the dramatic rise and fall of locust populations across the Great Plains."

A hand went up in the front row.

"Yes?"

"Wouldn't a species be able to see this coming?"

"Good question. Very few species have the ability to step back and see the big picture, to see beyond their own individual needs, to plan for the future."

Another hand went up. "What about honeybees?"

"A honeybee colony is what we call an *intelligent biomass*. Each honeybee has a very simple job to do, but the colony as a whole is capable of complex tasks, such as hive building. The colony appears to have intelligence beyond that of an individual honeybee. How can that be?"

"Are the bees' brains connected together somehow?" a student asked.

"For years, there have been theories about groups of insects or animals acting as if they were a single organism, combining their brain power to create a singular being known as a *superorganism*. Superorganisms are more fiction than fact. While it's true that a honeybee colony appears to have more intelligence than an individual honeybee, it's not real intelligence; it's pseudo-intelligence," Julia explained. "It's also known as *swarm* or *flocking behavior*. When a group of organisms gather together, they respond to each other in predictable ways. These responses are based purely on instinct. In a honeybee colony, individuals are born to fulfill particular roles in the colony. By simply responding to each other and doing what comes naturally to them, a colony of honeybees can build a complex hive. None of the bees has the ability to step back and say, 'Gee, what a nice hive we're building here.' They're oblivious to the big picture."

A hand went up in the front row. "What makes them stay together then?"

"Nearly all species have found that there is safety in numbers. So one of the most basic instincts of all organisms is to stay near the group."

Julia chalked a horizontal line across the blackboard. "If this line represents the range of biological complexity—from single-celled creatures to human beings—you will notice that, as organisms become more complex, they rely less on flocking behavior for their survival. Human beings are the most autonomous creatures on the planet. Evolution has pushed us in a direction that favors autonomy. Can anyone think of an example of flocking behavior in humans?"

— — —

David tugged on the lawn mower starter cord. The mower sputtered and died. He pulled the cord again. Nothing. The grass was long, almost too long to mow. Soon he'd have to call in the professionals, which was something he didn't want to do. "Why do we have to mow the damn grass anyway," David muttered. "Where is it written that grass has to be mowed? It's unnatural for grass to be mowed. It probably all started as a marketing gimmick, just like diamonds."

David heard a turbine-like sound down the street and swung his head around. A black Porsche convertible slithered down the block. It was Mike Stewart, a neighbor from two blocks down. He slowed to a stop in front of David's house. "Hey, lookin' a little shaggy there," Stewart called. It was an attempt at humor, but David wasn't amused.

"My Porsche mower is in the shop," David retorted.

"I'd get a couple of goats, if I were you."

"Thanks, I'll try that."

The Porsche rolled on, and David resumed pulling the starter cord. "Start, you son of a ..." David threw his whole body into it. The engine coughed a mocking reply. He pulled the cord again and again, working himself into a sweaty frenzy.

Julia pulled into the driveway. She climbed out of her car and stood a few yards away.

"This lousy piece of crap," David growled.

"Maybe you should get it fixed," Julia said.

David responded with a steely glare and gave the cord another yank. "If I take it back to where we bought it, they'll replace a thirty-nine-cent part and charge us seventy-five dollars."

"Well, it's either that or we get the mowing people over here." Her voice had an administrative tone—fitting, given her smart work suit that contrasted with his coffee-stained T-shirt and jeans.

A honeybee flew by David, and he swung at it. The bee plunged its stinger into David's forearm. "*Yeoow!* What did I do to deserve *that?*"

"We're not alone in this world, you know," Julia said, as she walked toward the house.

So much for sympathy, David thought. He pondered his options and decided to postpone the lawn mower decision. *There's always tomorrow.* He followed Julia inside.

"Did you get a chance to edit the block party video?" Julia asked. "I promised copies to several neighbors."

"It's on my list," David replied, relieved that he had yet another reason to put off the lawn. "I'll take a look at it after dinner."

The family ate around the wooden kitchen table, the dining room being reserved for company or holidays. The two kids ate across from one another. Jamie was thirteen, tall for his age, not much of an athlete, president of the chess club. He still made cards for David's and Julia's birthdays. Nine-year-old Katie was smart beyond her years. She had taken to reading several books at a time. Books, in various degrees of completion, could be found in practically every room in the house.

"Let's put the book down, Katie," David said. "We're at the dinner table."

"Did you get a job yet, Dad?" Katie asked.

Jamie threw her a glare.

David didn't answer. It was a sore subject.

"We had to tell our class what our parents do," Katie continued, "so I said my dad was a consultant. Isn't that what out-of-work people say they do?"

"Some people really are consultants," Julia pointed out.

"I'm just looking for the right job," David explained. "It takes time to find a good job, one that you really love and one that pays enough money."

Jamie had an I-told-you-so look on his face.

"Well, I'm going to be a writer when I grow up," Katie continued. "Then I'll be able to be anyone I want to be, just by writing it."

"That's very nice, honey," Julia said. "But for right now, let's eat your broccoli. That's good brain food, you know, and the first thing a writer needs is a good brain."

Katie stared at her broccoli. "They look like little brains," she said.

David noticed that Jamie was quieter than usual. "How were things at school today, Jamie?"

"Okay, but the bullies are still beating up kids, usually at recess when the teachers aren't around."

Julia winced. "That's terrible!"

"It's just the way things are, Mom."

"I'm going to call the principal."

"I'm not sure about that, Mom."

"He's right, Julia," David interrupted. "We don't want to stir up a bees' nest here."

"Well, somebody should teach those kids a lesson. Which kids were they?"

Jamie didn't answer.

"I don't think we should get involved," David said. "It has nothing to do with us. Katie, eat your broccoli."

— — —

The kids slept while David and Julia watched TV from their bed. The blue glow of the screen played on the framed wedding photos on the wall. Julia positioned herself near the edge of the bed, whereas David lay closer to the middle.

"Are things okay?" he asked.

"Things are fine," Julia replied, without taking her eyes off the TV.

"You just seem a little distant lately."

"I just get too hot when I'm right up against you."

Remote in hand, David scanned the channels. The news channels brimmed with the latest uprising in the Middle East. Angry faces leaned into the television camera. American flags went up in flames; western governments were denounced. David gazed at the mayhem. "How are we ever going to make friends with the Middle East?"

"When we stop backing anti-Islamic governments," Julia replied.

"I just wish there was a way for us to connect with them, one to one, without governments involved."

"We already have three million Muslims in the United States. That might be an easier place to start. Perhaps we should invite a few of them over to dinner."

"Look, I'm serious here. I like Muslim people."

"David, do you have any idea how ridiculous you sound? That's like saying you like black people."

"You know what I mean."

"Are you forgetting? A Muslim in Pakistan now has your job."

David was lost for words. He gazed at the violence on the screen—the blood on the pavement next to the twisted metal that was once a car. Men standing nearby seem pleased with the outcome, as if some abstract debt had been avenged. Children climbed over the smoking wreck, looking for something to hawk. "I can see why nobody reads fiction anymore," David lamented. "It's been completely trumped by reality." A commercial for Levi's jeans came on. A computer-generated teen model shimmied across the screen, a boy's reflection caught in her sunglasses. Electric sitar punctuated by a hip-hop backbeat filled the room. A chorus of female voices oozed words that were unintelligible, but it didn't matter. The overall effect was undeniable. David watched in amazement. "Can you believe that?"

"What?"

"They put one of those Levi's commercials from Pakistan right after the Middle East news segment."

"I'm sure no one was keeping track."

David pointed at the television. "That could be Raj Nabi's work."

"Even Pakistanis can make nice commercials," Julia said.

"Well, it wasn't *that* nice." David grabbed the remote and changed the channel. The screen changed to black and white.

A vintage narrator spoke in haunting tones … "Ordinary people just like you and me. Good, wholesome, hardworking people. And little do they know, as they go about their daily routines, they blindly participate in a master plan of which they are completely unaware. This is the will of a master race, a race so intelligent that they play with us—as if we were pawns on an immense chessboard. Those who think they are living their own lives, think again!" The music swelled.

Julia buried her head under her pillow. "David!"

"Had enough?"

"I'm exhausted—long day."

David killed the TV. "Good night."

"Good night."

TWO

A CACOPHONY OF BIRDSONG yanked David out of his slumber. Julia was long gone. The kids were already at school. Were it not for the racket, David could have slept for at least another hour. It had been months since he'd had that jump-out-of-bed-and-tackle-the-day feeling. As soon as his feet touched the floor, life resumed the state of limbo he'd been in the day before. *What was the point of rushing into the day?* he thought. That would just lead to expectations, and expectations would invariably lead to disappointments. David lumbered into the bathroom. In the mirror, he saw a former version of himself from his post-college wanderlust, except now the packaging was less forgiving. He climbed into the shower and stood motionless while the hot spray pelted his back. He wished there was a way to simply stop the clock, to take a nice long vacation from it all. But time just kept marching onward.

Julia had left a note on the kitchen table:

David,
Don't forget the video!
Julia

"Oh yeah, the block party video," David recalled, realizing this might be a decent morning after all. He headed into the den where the computer resided. Julia had left the camcorder right there for him. David connected the camcorder to the computer and began watching the raw video footage on the computer monitor.

The block party video, supplied by a neighbor, was even worse than he expected. It was shot from an unmanned tripod, giving one the impression the camcorder had been left on by accident. The lens captured a wide-angle view of the entire party, with no particular point of reference. Children raced chaotically across the frame. Adults milled around, drinking beer. A few of them tried to get a softball game started. "Well, this is confusing as hell," David groaned. "What am I going to do with this?"

Then he got an idea. "What if there was a way," he mused, "to uncover the fundamental movement in this scene—to make the chaotic parts disappear?" The problem reminded him of the film *A Beautiful Mind,* which was about mathematician John Nash, who was able to reduce complex trends to mathematical formulas. "I need to compress time. That's what I need to do. Where's Einstein when you need him?"

David loved these challenges. He had always thought of himself as a closet inventor. He had a pretty good understanding of science and mathematics and knew his way around computers. He just lacked the academic credentials to make it official. "Not to worry. Don't forget that Apple got started in someone's garage," he reminded himself. "A good idea can come from anywhere."

The block party video indeed presented an interesting challenge: how to distill complex motion down to its fundamentals—to see order within chaos. Time-lapse photography allows us to see motion that is either too slow or too fast for our brains to process, such as a plant growing or a bullet leaving the barrel of a gun, but David knew this was a different sort of problem. This was a case of putting on the Superman glasses and seeing into a different dimension. He needed to take time and twist it around sideways and see through its layers.

The clock on the desk gave David an idea—a perfect analogy to the problem. He began talking himself through it … "Suppose you shot a video of a clock, and you want to eliminate the movement of the second hand, but keep the minute and hour hands moving at their normal speed. How would you do that? How would you make the second hand stand still, yet keep the other hands moving normally?"

David leaped out of his chair and gesticulated around the den. "I could shoot a time-lapse video—one frame per minute. That would stop the second hand." He paused. "But then the minute and hour hands will move too fast when I play it back. Somehow, I have to slow those hands back down without affecting the second hand. I need a way to add frames, to synthesize time." Then it came to him.

The solution was elegant. "Shoot a video of a clock for, say, ten minutes. Delete all the frames of the video, except the frames that periodically show the second hand pointing straight up. Then synthesize new video frames to replace the deleted ones, using video morphing software to do it." Typically, morphing is used to transform one image into another, like a baby's face into an adult's face, but David had a very different application in mind. He would use morphing to synthesize time. "All I need is the first and last frame of each minute of video, and I can synthesize what goes in between. The morphing software will recreate the correct movement of the minute and hour hands and leave the second hand where it is. Hell, I think it might work!"

"But what about the block party video?" To hide the chaotic movement in the block party video, David knew he needed to use a different time interval, something shorter than he used in his clock example. "Two seconds seems about right. Theoretically, anything moving quickly will stop or disappear, while slower moving objects should continue to move normally."

David set to work. First, he copied the video to the computer's hard drive. Then he opened the video-editing software and created a set of instructions that the computer could repeat over and over. To change the parameters, he would simply have to revise the instructions. The computer crunched through the data, creating a new video file that was time compressed and then was morphed back to its original length. David opened up the new file and clicked play. The video flashed onto the computer screen.

The block party took on an entirely new dimension—as if performed in ballet. People floated like magic. Motions became mercury-like; smiles melted into one another. The children's movements, instead of being random and chaotic, now looked choreographed. Suddenly, there was order where before there had been confusion. The chaos had all but disappeared.

In the midst of this surreal scene, David noticed something he hadn't noticed before. Mike Stewart, the Porsche guy, floated toward Julia whenever David moved away from her. Each time David strayed more than ten feet away, Stewart reappeared at Julia's side and her smile blossomed. "What the hell is going on here?" David whispered. "Am I seeing what I think I'm seeing?"

— — —

Julia heard a familiar voice behind her—Marsha Reeves, the school librarian.

"Hi, Marsha. Glad I ran into you."

"Hi, Julia."

Julia leaned a little closer. "We need to talk."

"The science department under siege again?"

"No, actually, it's David."

"I guess we do need to talk. Where are you headed?"

"The principal called a special meeting of the science teachers.

Probably another disgruntled parent or a PTO mandate about too much homework."

"How about after that?"

"In your office?" Julia suggested.

"Sure, I'll be there."

"See you then."

"Looking forward," Marsha said.

Julia entered the faculty lounge and took a seat at the conference table. Several members of the science faculty were already there, as were the principal and two other people Julia didn't recognize.

"Thank you all for being here," the principal began. "I'd like to introduce Patricia Jones of the Minnesota Department of Education and Reverend Robert Blanchard of the Minneapolis Christian Coalition."

"You can call me Bob," Blanchard added.

"I'm going to let Patricia fill you in," the principal continued.

"Thank you," Patricia Jones began. She closed the manila folder in front of her and folded her hands on top of it. "As you know, there has been considerable discussion in Washington regarding the teaching of evolution in our schools. Congress has made it clear that they wish to see a counterpoint to Darwinism added to science curriculums. The counterpoint they have suggested is the theory of intelligent design."

"There's nothing intelligent about it," Julia broke in. "Intelligent design has absolutely no scientific basis."

"Please, Julia," the principal interrupted, "let's hear what they have to say."

"At some point in the future," Jones continued, "teaching of intelligent design could be mandated by federal law. The state board of education feels that we should begin to develop our own intelligent design curriculum, or later we may be forced to accept the federal version."

Julia shook her head in disbelief. The other science teachers sat in a state of shock.

"Now I'd like to turn the discussion over to Reverend Bob," Jones added.

Bob Blanchard gave her a little bow and began. "For many years, the theological community has been searching for a way to bridge the gap between creationism and Darwinism. There is such a vast desert between these two schools of thought. With intelligent design, we have found an oasis in that desert. Intelligent design presents a credible, modern explanation for the extraordinary biodiversity found in our world. And, I might add, it fills some of the gaps found in Darwin's theory."

"What gaps?" Julia blurted.

"Certainly, there are many creatures whose ancestry has never been determined," Blanchard continued, "creatures with such unique qualities that science has not been able to explain them."

"With all due respect, Reverend, I just can't believe this is being discussed with the science department."

Patricia Jones broke in, "The board of education has already mandated that science teachers will present an alternate theory along with Darwinism. Again, we are looking at this as an opportunity to develop our own curriculum before one is forced on us."

"I thought this was a science department," Julia said, "not a philosophy department."

"Unfortunately," Jones continued, "our educational system is not a democracy. As you know, the federal government pays 30 percent of our budget, so we have no choice but to listen to them."

Julia stood up. "I've heard all I need to hear."

The other science teachers remained uncomfortably glued to their chairs. Julia went to the library.

— — —

Marsha Reeves licked her lips when she saw Julia, anticipating a juicy story that only she was privileged to hear. "Let's step into my office," Marsha said with mock urgency, and she closed the door. "Now then, I want all the details. Before you say anything, just let me say that I've been there. We've all been there. He's having an affair, isn't he? They all do it eventually."

"Well, no, I don't think he is, actually. In his present state, it's hard to imagine anyone would want to be with him. He's looking more like a street bum every day."

"Oh yeah, I forgot he's been out of work."

"The money is going to run out at some point, and he's looking less employable by the day. I'm getting worried."

"How is he doing, you know, otherwise?"

"You mean sex-wise?"

Marsha nodded.

"I can't remember the last …"

"You know what they say. Everything starts there."

Julia shook her head. "At this point, it's hard to even imagine it."

"Well, I would not completely rule it out. He might just be trying to get you off the scent."

"It would certainly be ironic," Julia said.

"Why's that?"

Julia looked at her watch. "Oh, I don't know. I've got to run. I'll talk to you later."

"Anytime," Marsha replied. "See you soon."

— — —

When Julia opened the kitchen door, she found David rummaging through the refrigerator.

"I checked out the video," David blurted. "There's really nothing useable in it."

"And the lawn?"

"Oh yeah, the lawn … the lawn."

Julia got herself a glass of water and stared out the window at the shaggy backyard. Her crisp white blouse caught the light from the window. David still wore the T-shirt he spilled coffee on the day before, his hair splayed like something washed up on the beach.

"I'm taking the mower down to the shop in the morning," David said. "That's what I've decided to do." He made it sound like a major corporate decision. David's words sounded pathetic and only added to the wall of contempt Julia felt for him. She resented being the breadwinner and the homemaker while David degenerated into an embarrassment of a husband.

Julia dropped a pile of mail on the kitchen counter. The monthly credit card bill sat on top. David recognized the envelope immediately and slid it under the pile. "So, how was work today?" he asked.

Julia was in no mood for small talk. "David, you have got to get a haircut."

"There are only so many hours in the day. It's on my list."

"Perhaps you can fit it in between meetings," she said. "And while you're at it, do you think that you could change that T-shirt?"

"I've had things on my mind, many things."

Julia could no longer conceal her contempt. The brilliant, successful guy she married was looking like an indigent. They hadn't had company over in ages. Julia suspected that her girlfriends were avoiding her for fear that their husbands might catch David's malady. "Do you have any idea how pathetic you're looking these days?" she said. "Who would possibly hire you looking like this?"

"Do you expect me to get dressed up to mow the lawn?"

"But you didn't mow the lawn."

"I was inventing something."

"Inventing something?"

"It doesn't concern you," David said. "And it was not fashion-critical."

"We can't afford to go on like this forever. The bills are piling up. You've got to get back to work."

David flipped through the mail pile. One of the envelopes was a bit larger, and David picked it up. "Hey look, I'm an instant winner." The envelope had the familiar Publishers Clearing House logo on it. David opened it up and spread the contents across the counter.

"You can't be serious." Julia winced.

"We only need to sign up for six magazines. Then we get our million dollars." David held up the mock certificate. "See, we've got the winning number."

"Please tell me you're not doing this in lieu of getting a job."

David scanned the cover letter and began reading the fine print at the bottom. "'Winners agree to allow PCH to use their name and likeness in advertising and promotional materials.'" David shook his head. "That'll never work," he said, collecting the contents of the envelope.

"Thank God."

"Once they have your name and picture, then you've got every Tom, Dick, and Harry on your doorstep looking for a handout. I've always suspected that it might be a government surveillance plot anyway."

"A what?"

"Think about it. It makes perfect sense. Those Publishers Clearing House envelopes make it into everybody's home, right? Well, just add a little RFID radio tag transmitter—you know, like the ones they're using at Walmart—and bingo, you're tracking the whole nation."

Julia rolled her eyes.

"I was reading about it online," David said.

Julia had had enough. "I'm going out for a run. Why don't you take the kids out for dinner tonight. It's been a while since they've gone out."

"I'll pay for it. I really will," David said.

Julia knew full well she'd be picking up the tab. "Whatever. Just get them back here in time to do their homework."

— — —

For a Tuesday evening, the Minneapolis traffic seemed heavier than usual, even in the neighborhoods. Traffic lights were backed up ten cars deep.

Katie fidgeted with the window button. "Do we have to go to Deegan's?"

"But you love Deegan's," David said. "And we're only a few blocks away."

When they arrived at Deegan's Restaurant, the parking lot was full, and a line of people extended out the door.

Jamie pressed his nose against the car window. "Wow, what is going on here?"

"It's weird for a Tuesday," David said. "Could be a private party or something. You kids wait in the car while I have a look."

"It's just a coincidence," the hostess explained. "A lot of people must have decided to eat out tonight. Right now, it's about a thirty-minute wait."

David and the kids squeezed onto two barstools and ordered Cokes. David eyed the crowd.

"I bet they're giving something away for free," Jamie said.

Katie had an alternate theory. "Maybe they're all just hungry."

David peered at the line at the hostess stand. "Or, it could be mind control."

Katie put down her Coke. "Dad, I think that's just in the movies."

"I wouldn't put it past them," David said. "Might be something the government is experimenting with."

"Dad? Should we start worrying about you?"

"Probably just a coincidence," David said, altering his posture. "Just a coincidence."

The host escorted them to a booth in the back of the restaurant. Jamie and Katie sat on one side and David on the other.

"My name is Christie, and I'll be your server," chirped the waitress. "Have you had a chance to look at the menu?"

"I think the kids already know what they want. What do you recommend tonight?"

"Well, most people are ordering the honey chicken. We've had a real run on that. It's made with real honey."

"Okay, honey chicken it is," David replied. "And my daughter will have pasta with butter, and the big guy will have …"

"Two plain pizza slices, please."

"And what do you make of the situation tonight?" David asked.

"You mean the crowds?"

"Yeah."

"Kinda weird, isn't it, especially for a Tuesday. The boss says we've already broken a record."

"Probably just a coincidence," Katie said. "Right, Dad?"

"Right," David replied, as he peered out the window at the line of cars waiting to get into the parking lot.

— — —

The kids went upstairs to work on their homework, and David flopped into his easy chair. The situation at the restaurant still captivated him. *What the hell was going on there?* he wondered. Could it really be a coincidence that so many people decided to go out to Deegan's on a Tuesday night? How could this happen? It just seemed too weird. He couldn't let go of it. He rethought his steps earlier in the evening, trying to remember what it was that caused him to decide to go out to dinner in the first place. "It was Julia!" he recalled. "She came up with the idea to go out to dinner. Something must have put it in *her* mind."

David got up and marched to the kitchen. He reached into the trash and removed the Publishers Clearing House envelope. Piece by piece, he held the contents of the envelope up to the kitchen light, looking for a telltale sign of an RFID radio tag. Nothing. If there was a radio tag, it was damn well hidden. David put the envelope and its contents back into the trash.

"What we have here," David said to himself, "is a classic example of behavior modification. A large number of people independently decided to go to Deegan's on a Tuesday night for no particular reason. Big brother is up to something here, and I intend to get to the bottom of it."

Then David recalled the heavy traffic. "Maybe it was more than just Deegan's." He grabbed the telephone directory and flipped to the restaurant listings. "It's only seven-thirty. I should try to get a table somewhere, just to see if I can." David scanned the ads, looking for restaurants that wouldn't require a reservation. He grabbed the kitchen telephone and dialed the number for the Capital Grille.

A lady answered, "Good evening, Capital Grille."

"Hello, I was wondering if you might have room for two people this evening?"

"I'm very sorry, sir, but we are completely booked for tonight. Usually Tuesdays are not a problem, but tonight, we've been turning people away. It's really quite unusual."

"I see," David said. "Well, thanks anyway." *Could it be?* he wondered. He ran his finger further down the restaurant listings and dialed the number for Morton's Steakhouse.

"Morton's. May I help you?"

"Yes, I need a table for tonight for two people."

"We are absolutely booked tonight, and I have a line out the door. Could you try us another time?"

"Sure, thanks anyway."

David ran to the stairs. "It wasn't just Deegan's!" he yelled.

Julia came to the top of the stairs. "Please, David, the kids are trying to study."

"I know, I know, but we witnessed some sort of mind control experiment tonight at the restaurant," David stammered. "It affected restaurants all over the city!"

"Oh God. Did you actually wear that T-shirt out to dinner?"

"Deegan's was absolutely packed on a Tuesday night, and so were other restaurants all over town. Doesn't that strike you as strange?"

"It strikes me as a coincidence," Julia said. "And please don't mention these mind control theories of yours to our friends. I have enough to explain as it is." She turned and went back to the bedroom.

David returned to the kitchen. The newspaper sat on the counter, still unread. A small headline toward the bottom of the front page caught his eye. He unfolded the paper and began reading:

Public Access Granted for Secret Satellite

Today, the federal government began allowing public access to a previously classified satellite. The BIOSAT satellite detects population density using infrared imaging technology. Developed originally for the military, BIOSAT can identify the presence of human beings by detecting their infrared heat signatures. The decision to declassify the satellite was made in the interest of offering more powerful tools to urban planners. Access to the satellite's images can be found on the web at www.biosat.us.

David carried the newspaper into the den. He sat down at the computer and entered the BIOSAT web address. The website requested his zip code. Slowly, an image filled the screen in shades of deep blue and purple. Rows of tiny rectangles aligned themselves along a grid of streets and avenues. Against the deep blue backdrop, clusters of tiny yellow dots appeared across the image like swarms of fireflies. "Wow. Those must be people down there," David marveled. Across the bottom of the image it read:

MAY 15 - 4:34 PM CST - IMAGE UPDATED EVERY 60 SEC

David looked at his watch. "It's seven-thirty-five. They must be delaying the satellite feed by a few hours." He studied the image, trying to find his own street in the deep blue matrix. "Got it." He clicked the mouse, zooming in on his block. Two dozen houses now filled the screen. David recognized his house by the two cars in the driveway. He clicked on his house and the image magnified further. Four glowing yellow dots appeared through the roof—two in the kitchen end of the house, and two in the den. "That must have been before dinner. Julia and I are in the kitchen, and the kids are in the den. Wow, it's like X-ray vision!"

The video camera next to the computer gave David an idea. "What if I made a video out of this? I could download a bunch of these satellite images and transfer them to a video file. Who knows what that might look like?" For David, the challenge was irresistible.

He set to work. First, David zoomed the image out so that the entire city of Minneapolis came into view. Then he clicked the capture button to download the first image. The clock on the desk served as his timekeeper. Every sixty seconds, he clicked the capture button again, downloading a new image from the satellite. After two hours, he had enough images to try his video experiment. He opened up his video-editing application and loaded the images into a new video file. David sat back and clicked play.

The deep blue image came alive with motion. Thousands of tiny yellow dots buzzed around like a giant swarm of fireflies. David's simple time-lapse video had made the chaotic pulse of the city visible. Only people on the highways moved in a somewhat orderly fashion; the rest of the city seemed caught in complete chaos.

David adjusted the video playback speed downward to one half and then to one quarter normal speed. The movement slowed down, but the city's population still moved randomly. "I guess that's the way people live their lives—chaotically. We're as chaotic as insects."

Julia's voice arose from the doorway. "Were you talking to somebody?"

"Uh—no."

"Don't forget to say goodnight to your children."

"Yeah."

"Loser," Julia muttered as she climbed the stairs.

David paced the den. "Something is missing. There has got to be more to this video." Then he remembered something—the block party video. "What about *time synthesis?* At some level, there's got to be order within this chaos," he reasoned. "If you boil complex motion down far enough, eventually you're going to see the order in it. It's just a matter of degree."

David sat down at the computer again. "I'll squeeze it down by increasing the time interval from one minute to ten minutes, and then stretch it back out with some heavy-duty morphing."

David began downloading satellite images again. Every ten minutes, he downloaded another one. He used an egg timer to alert him. Image after image, the satellite shared its infrared bounty. David completely forgot about Julia and the kids upstairs. An hour turned into several hours, midnight passed, and the images kept on coming.

— — —

Julia smoldered in the darkness of the bed. She starved for physical affection. Her legs pressed against the sheets. She clutched the pillow against her. Had things been different, she would simply call down to David in that sweet voice reserved for such occasions, and he would drop whatever he was doing and come up and make love to her. But somehow, that ritual didn't seem in the realm of the possible now. Julia had built a wall around David. She couldn't remember enough of his positive qualities to outweigh the negative. She had him in a perpetual doghouse.

Julia put David out of her mind, replacing him with a vague muscular visage of a man, someone she might have seen somewhere in passing. She could feel his weight pressing against her, the moistness of his skin, the heat of his breath. She luxuriated in the moment, feeling feminine in the presence of this masculine fantasy.

The room was no longer her room. He lifted her off her feet and onto his bed. Her breath became shallow with anticipation. She felt his hands moving across her. She tasted his scent. The more he pressed, the more she yielded. This was the place she longed for, to be a complete woman again.

THREE

JULIA AWOKE TO FIND herself alone. She assumed David got an early start so he could get the lawn mower to the repair shop. She showered, dressed for work, and headed downstairs. David was asleep in the den, light on, snoring like an old accordion in his easy chair. The den emitted a locker room fragrance that extinguished Julia's appetite. She rolled her eyes and marched to the kitchen.

"What's with Dad?" Katie asked.

"He must have been working late," Julia replied, barely hiding her contempt.

"When's Dad going to get a regular job?"

"That's a good question, a very good question." Julia took out bread, peanut butter, and honey, and began making sandwiches for the kids' lunches.

"I want extra honey on mine," Jamie said.

Katie protested. "He always gets extra honey."

"So?"

"You're gonna turn into a bee," Katie said.

Jamie chased Katie around the kitchen with his index finger stinger at the ready. "Well, then I'll be able to sting you!"

"Okay, let's get everything together for school," Julia said. "I'll be at the doctor's office when you get home, so I want to see some homework done when I get here."

Jamie and Katie grabbed their backpacks and headed for the

door. Julia followed, briefcase in hand. She pulled the front door shut with a bit more force than necessary. David jerked to life with a snort and fell out of his easy chair. Blinded by the morning sun, he slowly grasped his whereabouts. His T-shirt clung to him like an oily rag. He climbed onto the computer chair and squinted at the screen. There were thirty new satellite images—enough to make a one second–long video. With maximum morphing, he figured he could stretch it to about thirty seconds. He loaded the satellite images one by one into a fresh video file, being careful to maintain the correct order. Then he fired up the morphing software and entered the settings. David leaned back and clicked play. The computer digested the data for a few seconds, and the video appeared.

David's jaw dropped. Amid the chaos of yellow fireflies, a ring-like pattern emerged, stretching from one side of Minneapolis to the other. The ring rotated clockwise, like the lights of a Ferris wheel. The motion didn't simply follow the city's street grid. No, this was bigger than that. It was as if someone had orchestrated a behemoth circle dance, and tens of thousands of people were participating. David sat motionless. "What the hell is this?" The image in front of him was astonishing. The ring seemed to have a pulse, the way it rotated in discrete steps, as if the dancers were all moving to the same beat.

David stood up and paced the den. "What we have here are human beings involved in a huge dance." He paused for a moment. "But they don't know they're part of it. This is too frigging weird." David looked out the window at the passing cars on his street. "Something is making people move around in an organized pattern, and they don't even know they're doing it. Holy shit! This is *bizarre*." Then he remembered what put him on this track in the first place. "Deegan's—the restaurant madness! Oh my God, I caught it on video."

David could barely contain his excitement. He ran back to the computer and watched the video again. "Something is definitely going on here. This could be proof positive the government is messing with us, making us do things without our knowledge, making the innocent dance."

David felt a wave of fear wash over him. "What if this is part of a secret government operation? What if this is something I wasn't supposed to see?"

David stared at the telephone on the desk. He'd read that the government could eavesdrop through a typical home telephone anytime they wanted—without even taking it off the hook. Deftly lifting the receiver, he listened for any unusual clicks or beeps. There was only dial tone. He peered out the window to see if someone might be parked outside. There were just a couple of empty cars. He tiptoed into the kitchen and spied into the backyard—nothing there either. "How could something this big be kept secret? Sooner or later, people would have to notice the pattern. People must be altering their routines to accommodate it. They just don't realize that's *why* they're altering their routines. I've got to talk to somebody about this." David ran out the door, jumped into the Honda, and billowed his way toward Max's Diner.

The morning hubbub took on an entirely new appearance. The movement of every car and pedestrian was suspect. *Are they part of the dance?* David wondered. A gaggle of first graders crossed in front of David's car at a light, the teacher in front and an assistant behind. *Where might they be going—and why—on this particular day?* he wondered. They could be part of the dance without even knowing it. A group of cyclists pedaled down the right-hand lane. David inched past them, watching with sideways glances until they peeled away at an intersection. On the surface of it, the morning looked like any other morning. But David knew there was something more going on. He just didn't know what it was.

— — —

Sue saw David pull up outside Max's and grabbed the coffeepot. David waved his way through the oily blue cloud and stepped inside the diner.

"Hey there, good lookin'." The moment Sue's words came out, the irony was apparent: David looked like hell. His stubble had crossed the line from manly to street bum. She knew the job search was going to be a sore subject.

"Hey, Sue." David combed his slept-on hair with his hand and slid onto his usual stool.

"What have you been up to, honey?" she asked.

"Oh, the usual stuff."

"Get the lawn mowed?"

"The damn mower wouldn't start."

"Hey, you should've seen this place last night," Sue said. "Packed, absolutely packed, a line going right out the door. I've never seen anything like it."

"Really?"

"We were running out of things by eight o'clock."

"Well, you weren't alone. The whole city was going out to eat. Places all over town were packed."

"You don't say."

"I took the kids out last night, and I couldn't believe it."

"What do you suppose …?"

David looked around to make sure no one was within earshot. He waved Sue to come closer. "Something's going on," he whispered. "I don't know what it is, but there is something going on, and it's huge."

"Maybe everybody just needed a night out," Sue said.

"I saw it, Sue, in the satellite photos. Something is making people go places without their knowledge."

Sue pulled away. A sympathetic smile came over her. "Everything's gonna be just fine, honey."

"There's some kind of alternate reality that we can't see," David stammered. "Something is controlling people."

Sue had seen this before, out-of-work men slipping over the edge, talking about alternate realities and government conspiracies. "How about some more coffee, honey?"

"You think I'm crazy, don't you?"

"Well," she said, choosing her words carefully, "you've been under a lot of pressure."

"I swear to you, Sue. I saw something. I really saw something!"

"I bet you did, honey." Sue smiled and busied herself wiping down the counter.

— — —

David turned on his stool and looked outside. The traffic in front of Max's had slowed, maybe a car every five seconds. A few pedestrians dotted the sidewalk but not so many that they would get in each other's way. There was a leisurely pace about it. Then David noticed something.

At first it seemed like an illusion, but the longer he watched, the more puzzled he became. The traffic was all moving in the same direction, even though Broadway was a two-way street. Not a single car had passed the other way, even after several minutes. The pedestrians were doing the same thing. David watched and sipped his coffee. "Is there something going on this morning?" he called to Sue, keeping his eyes fixed on the street.

"Like what?"

"I don't know, anything."

"Just like any other day, I think," Sue replied.

"Come take a look out here and see if anything seems strange to you."

Sue gazed out the front windows. "What am I looking for?"

"Nothing in particular."

"There's an old man with a cane. Is that it?"

"You really don't see it, do you?" David said.

Sue shook her head.

"Watch the traffic and the people on the sidewalk. Notice anything strange?"

"Nope."

"They're all moving in the same direction."

Sue watched for a moment. Then she resumed wiping down the counter. "They probably just got the other lane closed for construction," she said.

"What about the people on the sidewalk?"

"I don't know. Maybe they like to have the wind on their backs."

David kept his eyes fixed on the street.

Sue folded her arms in front of her. "Honey, you really need to find yourself a new situation. All this time alone is not doin' you any good at all."

"Don't worry about me, Sue. Everything is under control." David stood up, put a couple of dollar bills on the counter, and walked toward the door.

"You take care," Sue called.

David gave her a wave and stepped outside. His car was already pointed in the direction the traffic was moving. He got in, started the engine, and proceeded down Broadway. He could see cars ahead of him and others in his rearview mirror, but the opposite lane was still empty.

David stopped at a traffic light where a dozen pedestrians waited for the light to change. He called out to a couple on the sidewalk, "Excuse me. Where is everyone going?"

"We're just out for a walk," the man said.

"But why in this direction?"

The couple looked puzzled. "We like walking this way. It's a free country, isn't it?" the man declared. The woman noticed David's dishevelment and pulled the man away. The light changed, and David drove on.

"This is getting ridiculous. There has got to be a reason for this. I wonder if it could be related to the dance? Is there some kind of supernatural force at work here? Or is the government doing something to manipulate the masses?" David's mind wandered. He had visions of radio telescopes and lasers and space-based weapons of all description. He had read on the Internet that the military had developed technologies beyond our wildest dreams. "Maybe they were testing something, or maybe it wasn't a test at all. Maybe we're beyond the testing stage."

Then something caught David's attention. In the opposite lane, there it was, just as Sue had predicted: construction.

— — —

Julia approached the reception desk at her doctor's office. "Julia Peters," she said to the nurse. "I'm here for my annual checkup."

"Oh yes, Dr. Austin will be with you shortly. Please take a seat, and someone will call you."

"Thank you." Julia found an unoccupied chair in the waiting area. The room seemed crowded. She took a quick inventory of the faces around her. *Can't be the flu season*, Julia thought. *That's six months away.* A *TIME* magazine beckoned from the table in front of her. The headline on the cover read, "Breast Cancer: Are We Winning the Battle?" Julia was reminded that she would soon be discussing cancer in her class, a subject she wasn't sure her students were ready for. She lifted the magazine off the table and then heard her name.

"Julia Peters," a nurse announced.

"Yes, that's me."

"Dr. Austin will see you now."

Julia put the magazine back on the table, and the nurse escorted her down the hall to a small white examination room.

"Please remove your clothing and put on this gown. The doctor will be with you in a few minutes."

"Thank you."

Julia changed into the hospital gown as requested. A minute later, there was a knock at the door. "Come in," she said.

Dr. Austin extended a warm handshake. "How are you, Julia?"

"Hi, Ted. Hard to believe it's been a year already."

"How's your family doing? That son of yours must be another foot taller."

"Everybody's fine."

"And David?"

"Well, he's been out of work since January."

"I'm sorry."

"He got laid off and hasn't found anything yet."

"How have you been feeling?"

Julia ran her fingers through her hair. "A little run down lately— probably just stressed out over David's situation."

"Why don't you take a seat up there on the table, and we'll have a look at you."

Julia slid onto the paper-covered examination table, and Dr. Austin began checking her vital signs.

"How's your teaching going?" he asked.

"Pretty well. I mean, I enjoy it, but the board of education has managed to create some new hurdles."

"That's their specialty."

"Ain't that the truth. But I love my class and the challenges of opening them up to new ideas. We're just starting a unit on cancer."

"That's pretty serious stuff."

"Yeah, I guess it is, but they need to hear about it. Maybe it will make them think twice about making dumb choices."

"Kids do tend to think of themselves as unbreakable. Let's have you lie down, and we'll give you a quick breast exam. You know the routine: hands behind your neck. That's perfect. We'll do the left side first."

As Dr. Austin's latex fingertips probed Julia's breast, her mind wandered to David and how long it had been since they'd made love. *Was it three months?* she wondered. *No, maybe four.*

"No obvious problems there," he said. "Let's have a look at the other side." He continued probing.

It certainly isn't because my boobs have dropped, Julia thought. *They're still pretty damn perky for thirty-seven years old, thank you very much.*

Dr. Austin's fingers came to a halt. "I'm going to check the right side one more time."

Why is he doing this? Julia wondered. *He's never had to check twice before.* "Is everything okay?"

Dr. Austin probed a bit more before answering. "Well, Julia, you seem to have a mass in your right breast, just large enough to detect with my fingers. I recommend we do some tests right away to determine how serious it is."

The air left Julia's lungs. She felt as though the body she occupied wasn't her own. She distanced herself from it, the same way she did when she picked up the *TIME* magazine. "Oh my God."

"These lumps can be caused by a variety of things, but knowing your healthy lifestyle, I can assure you it was nothing you did or didn't do. Let's wait and see what the biopsy says before getting too concerned about this. Sound like a plan?"

Julia forced a smile. "Okay. I'm just in a bit of shock."

"I'd like to get you in for a mammogram and biopsy as soon as possible."

"I guess I could come in tomorrow, before my two o'clock class. I could be there by noon."

Dr. Austin lifted the telephone. "Oncology, please … This is Dr. Austin. I wonder if you might have room for a mammogram and biopsy tomorrow at noon. The name is Julia Peters. Thank you. I'll let her know."

Julia's mind raced. "This is all so sudden."

"Better to be on the safe side, Julia. You're all set for tomorrow at noon. In a few days, we should know what we're dealing with here. Please, don't worry."

"Thank you, Ted."

— — —

Jamie walked alone past a long row of lockers. The middle school hallway looked deserted, except for a couple of snickering eighth graders headed his way. Jamie knew these two boys should be avoided. He hung close to the opposite side of the hallway, hoping to pass by them unnoticed.

"Hey, Murphy, look who we have here," one of the boys said, swaggering.

Jamie avoided eye contact and kept walking.

Murphy stepped right into Jamie's path. "Hey, Jamie-boy, I hope you're not givin' us the brush-off."

"Yeah, we don't appreciate the brush-off," the sidekick said.

Jamie trembled, his eyes fixed on Murphy's shoes.

"I heard his dad's getting kinda wasted," Murphy cackled. "Out a' work and goin' off the deep end. I guess Jamie-boy better start lookin' for a job, so he can support his family."

Jamie didn't make a sound. His shoes felt like concrete blocks.

"They're lookin' for somebody to clean the halls around here," said the sidekick.

Murphy grinned. "Oh yeah, that would be choice. When Margo sees Jamie-boy pushin' that broom around school, she'll be history. Jamie-boy has got a thing for Margo, don't you, Jamie-boy?"

Jamie didn't answer.

"You never asked my permission to go out with Margo, did you, Jamie-boy? You know what that means?"

The sidekick winced. "Oh, this is bad."

"Well, I'll tell you what it means, Jamie-boy. As far as I'm concerned, you've earned yourself a swirly. Know what a swirly is? That's where we stuff your face in the can and give it a power flush. You better hope we don't crap in it first."

Jamie heard the sound of adult footsteps behind him. He spun on his heels and walked briskly away from Murphy and company.

"Better keep an eye on your back, Jamie-boy."

— — —

Julia fumbled with the buttons on her cell phone. "Please be there. Please be there," she cried.

"Hello, library," Marsha Reeves answered.

The air left Julia's lungs. She couldn't get a word out.

"Hello?" Marsha repeated.

"Marsha," Julia whimpered.

"Julia?"

"They found a lump," Julia said, choking back tears.

"Who found a lump?"

"My doctor."

"Where?" Marsha asked frantically.

"In my—breast," Julia stammered.

"Oh my God, Julia. I'm so sorry."

"This, on top of everything else." Julia shook her head in disbelief. Was this really happening to her?

"I'm in shock, Julia."

"They're going to do some tests tomorrow."

"To tell if it's …?"

Julia knew what Marsha wasn't saying: *cancer.*

"Well, let's not go there until you have some results. And even then, I'd get a second opinion. Sometimes I think they make these things up just to get billable hours."

"There really is a lump, Marsha. I felt it."

"Well, it might be nothing, Julia. So don't get yourself all worked up about it."

"You're right. I have more important things to worry about right now."

"If I were you, I'd be looking for lipstick in places where it doesn't belong."

"Thanks, Marsha. I'll see you tomorrow."

"Bye, Julia. And don't worry."

— — —

David pulled into his driveway and climbed out of the car. Above him, he heard the sound of high-pitched applause. He looked up. A cape-like shroud darkened the sky above him. The shroud folded back on itself and skimmed across the treetops like a giant sea skate. They were blackbirds—several thousand of them—performing giant double helixes and moving like one whale-sized organism. David tried to identify the leader. "One of them must be calling the shots," he reasoned. But when they reversed direction, the tail of the group became the head. "There must be something that's keeping them organized, some sort of brain link." The mass of birds landed in a large tree, weighted down its limbs for a few breaths, and then, for no apparent reason, they took off instantly. "They must be connected somehow—like a neural network." David had a vague recollection of the term *neural network*. He remembered it had something to do with connecting multiple computers together to solve complex problems.

David went into the house and made his way to the den. He sat down at the computer, typed the words *neural network*, and clicked search. Several web links appeared, and David clicked on one. A web page opened describing a book written by two British professors. David scanned down the text, and something caught his eye:

Neural networks, with their remarkable ability to derive meaning from complicated or imprecise data, can be used to extract patterns and detect trends that are too complex to be noticed by either humans or other computer techniques.[1]

To David, this sounded oddly familiar. Extracting patterns and detecting trends is exactly what he had done with his video time synthesis. "If the birds do have their own neural network, they could be linking their brains together to achieve some sort of higher intelligence."

David read another link: "Neural networks have the potential to predict collective behavior in humans, although this potential has not yet been realized. Only the most basic group behaviors have been synthesized with neural networks, such as the group behaviors of insects."

David read the passage in front of him again. This time, the words *collective behavior* seemed to float right off the screen toward him. "Collective behavior. Oh yeah, I remember that one from sociology 101. Show them a race on Sunday and watch them buy cars on Monday. From Pavlov to Clorox, the makers of collective behavior are proud to bring you mob lynchings, race riots, and soccer stampedes." Ever since high school, David had avoided large crowds because he believed the mentality of the crowd tended to match that of its least common denominator. The "idiot president syndrome," he liked to call it. *Yes, indeed*, David thought, *some of humankind's darkest moments were the result of collective behavior.*

David tapped his fingers on the desk. The blackbirds were still a mystery. *The answer to the blackbird question might begin to explain what's going on in the dance,* he thought. "Time to talk to somebody who knows about this stuff. When in doubt, call a professional." He grabbed the telephone book and began looking through the yellow pages under the letter *c*.

"What the hell am I thinking? They're not gonna have a yellow page listing for collective behavior." He put the telephone book down and typed *collective behavior* into his web browser. Next to it, he typed the word *Minneapolis* and clicked search. Only one web listing appeared:

J. Wilson, PhD, Advanced Studies in Collective Behavior, University of Minnesota, Minneapolis (612) 625-2818

"Well, this guy must know something about this stuff. What the heck. Let's give him a buzz." David dialed the number. The phone rang several times, and then a faint voice answered.

"Hello."

"Is this Doctor, ah—Wilson?"

"Yes, it is."

"My name is David Peters. I noticed that you're involved in the study of collective behavior, and well, I need to talk to someone about collective behavior. Can I ask you a couple of quick questions?"

"Excuse me, what did you say your name was?"

"It's David Peters."

"And who are you with?"

"Well, I'm not really with anybody. I mean, I was with a marketing company."

"So you're looking for behavioral marketing advice. I don't do behavioral marketing work."

"No, that's not it at all. I just need some information."

"Of a personal nature? If that's what it is, then you should call a behavioral psychologist."

"No, it's not that kind of thing. I just have a couple of questions about things I've seen."

"What sort of things?"

"Well, for one, I've been watching a large flock of blackbirds over my neighborhood. They seem to be moving as if their brains are linked together somehow. Is this some kind of neural network?"

There was silence on the line.

David looked into the receiver. "Hello?"

"Mister—"

"Peters."

"Yes, Mr. Peters. What you have witnessed is an example of flocking behavior. Although it looks like the birds are following a common command source, in fact, the individual birds are simply following rules they were born with."

"Really?"

"Those rules include how close one should fly near other birds, and which direction to turn when the group changes direction. Technically, there is no leader. The group is governed by chance as much as anything."

"But they look so organized."

"From a great distance, just about any group will appear organized. We tend to perceive groups as unified, when in fact they are not."

"There's just one other thing," David said, thinking now of the dance in the satellite video.

"I really must be going," Dr. Wilson said. "There are some good books on this subject. I suggest checking the library."

"Okay, I'll do that. Thanks for your time."

David hung up the phone. "So much for that idea. Of course, it still doesn't explain what's going on in the dance, unless it's just one of those group illusions he's talking about."

— — —

At a traffic light, Julia took a moment to look at herself in the rearview mirror. It felt as though a year had passed since she'd left the house that morning. She was still dazed by her doctor's discovery of a lump in her right breast. Nothing was concrete yet, just a lot of questions until the results of the biopsy. She decided to keep the whole situation under wraps until the results came through. *No sense getting everybody else on edge about it*, she thought.

David sat in the den, staring at the dance video. He zoomed in on a small part of the dance, so the yellow dots were as big as pencil erasers. Behind him, Katie stood in the doorway, trying to see what he was working on. "It's the honeybee dance, isn't it, Dad."

"The honeybee dance?"

"We saw a video about honeybees at school. They dance like that."

"Really." David hid the dance video. "I think it's time for dinner."

Clinking flatware filled the silence at the dinner table. David didn't see much point in making small talk. Julia might as well have been sitting at a dinner table in China, as far as he was concerned. David thought he might throw out an innocent question about Mike Stewart, the Porsche guy, just to see what her reaction might be. But he decided to hold off, realizing his evidence was still a bit thin.

Finally, Julia broke the silence. "So, how are things going at school, Jamie?"

"Same as usual."

"Any more problems with the bullies?"

Jamie kept his eyes down as he spoke. "No. No problems."

"Groups can bring out the worst in people," David said. "I remember when I was in school, the greasers ran everything. The smarter kids stayed out of their way, so the greasers got to do what they wanted. Of course, that all comes to a quick end in college. You'll see."

"I wanna be in the army," Jamie said.

David sat back in his chair, dumbfounded.

"What would make you want to do something like that, honey?" Julia asked.

"I dunno. I just want to."

"The army is a better place for those jock types," David said, "not the brainy types like you, son."

"I wanna shoot some guns."

Julia dropped her fork.

"Machine guns."

"Well, you don't have to go into the army to shoot guns," David pointed out. "Lots of people shoot guns for a hobby."

Julia threw David a disapproving look.

"Though it's not something I would recommend," David added.

Jamie seemed unfazed. "I wanna blow some things up, maybe blow some people up."

Julia winced. "Don't talk like that, Jamie. You sound like a nut."

David stared at Jamie, trying to get a fix on his behavior. The din of clinking flatware returned.

"Dad's got the honeybee dance on his computer," Katie announced.

"What?" Julia cringed.

"The honeybee dance, like we saw at school, only he has it on his computer."

Julia gave David a you-better-explain-what's-going-on look.

"It's nothing," David explained. "Just a little project I've been working on, nothing really."

"Perhaps it will help pay the credit card bill."

"That's really not fair."

"How many months has it been now?"

"This is not the time or place to bring that up, Julia."

"Well, when exactly did you have in mind?"

David stared out the window.

"What do you do with yourself all day, anyway? Nothing is getting done around here. The lawn looks like a field. You've been living in the same clothes day after day."

Jamie's fingers began to wrap around the handle of his dinner knife.

"Our savings are drying up, David. We can't go on like this much longer."

"Are we going to be poor, Mom?" Katie asked.

Julia kept drilling David. "I can't see any indication that you're plugged into reality. We have a serious situation here, and you're missing in action."

On Julia's last word, Jamie sank the knife blade into kitchen table with a guttural scream.

Julia shrieked and leaped from the table. Katie cried with fright. David wrapped his arms around Jamie and held him close. "It's okay, Jamie. It's okay. Everything's going to be okay."

— — —

The bedroom curtains billowed. A wispy fog obscured David's view. He felt a breeze against his back, as if to guide him in the proper direction. In the distance, he could see a walking figure. He recognized the unmistakable body language. It was his grandfather, Albert. "Granddad, how are you?" David beamed.

Albert turned in his dignified way and extended a warm hand. "It's been a while."

"Too long," Albert replied, "much too long."

"I have so much to tell you about. There's been a lot going on."

Albert gently removed his glasses, breathed some moist air on each lens, and wiped them clean with a handkerchief. "No need," he said, "I've been keeping an eye on you."

"So you know I got married."

"Yes, she's quite beautiful."

"And Jamie and Katie?" David asked.

"That Katie is a real crackerjack, and Jamie is going through some changes, isn't he."

"Yes, he is," David replied.

"But how is your life going, David?"

"I've had a great job with a marketing company."

Albert smiled. "The future is much more interesting than the past."

"Well, it wasn't that great of a job," David admitted.

"You have made a discovery."

"Yes, I have. And I don't have any idea what it means."

"In good time," Albert cautioned.

"Can you tell me anything?"

"Yes. Your wife needs you more than you realize."

"But was she, you know, fooling around?"

"That will be the least of your challenges," Albert said.

"Can you give me any advice about the future?"

"Embrace life. Everything is connected."

"You look really good, Granddad. It was great to see you."

Albert placed a hand on David's shoulder and smiled. "Remember the buffalo," he said. Then he walked away like an aging diplomat. The breeze swept the fog away, leaving only darkness and silence. David slept.

FOUR

RAJ NABI'S E-MAIL CAUGHT David by surprise. It had been months since he'd heard from the young Pakistani marketing guy.

> David,
> I hope this message finds you well. I think of you from time to time and wonder how you are doing. I hope you have found a suitable job by now. Looking back, I feel bad about what happened. Allah says I will get a chance to make amends. I guess that is why I am writing. I want you to know that you have a friend in Pakistan. No matter what you see on TV, the violence, the hatred toward Americans, you still have a friend in the Muslim world.
> Peace,
> Raj Nabi

The words engraved themselves into the computer screen. David recited them over and over. It had never occurred to him that Raj Nabi might harbor remorse over David's job. The e-mail was like a desert rain, and David soaked it up. The blood and the bombings on the television would appear differently now. David wondered if there might be a fourth dimension to the world, a dimension that cut through the rights and wrongs of politics and religions, a dimension that had a pulse all its own.

— — —

David located the Behavioral Sciences Department in a sprawling four-story brick building. He approached the reception desk.

"May I help you?"

"I'd like to see Dr. Wilson."

"Do you have an appointment?"

"Well, not exactly an appointment, but we did speak on the telephone."

"And your name?"

"Peters. David Peters."

The receptionist lifted the telephone receiver. "Dr. Wilson, there's a Mr. David Peters here to see you." She asked David, "Are you a student?"

"No, not exactly."

"No, he's not a student. He said he spoke to you on the telephone." The receptionist asked David, "What was this regarding?"

"Something of great importance to the city of Minneapolis."

"He says it's something of great importance." She said to David, "He's awfully busy right now."

David grabbed the telephone receiver. "Dr. Wilson. This is David Peters. I spoke to you about the blackbirds."

"And I told you—"

"Yes, and I really appreciate that. But this is something much more important, something that could affect the whole city."

"Yes—"

"And, if you have a DVD player in your office, I can show you what it's all about."

Dr. Wilson hesitated. "I can only spend a short time with you."

"Thank you, Doctor." David handed the receiver back to the receptionist. "He says it's okay."

"Room 109 on the right," the receptionist said.

"Thank you. Thank you very much."

David hastened down the hall to room 109. A sign on the door read,

J. Wilson, PhD
Advanced Studies in Collective Behavior

David knocked. The door opened and David found himself face to face with a portrait of American history. Deep fissures divided the man's face, like the symmetrical stones of an old monument. His coal black hair parted in the center and flowed into twin shoulder-length braids, tied off with strands of rawhide. An eagle feather hung on one side.

"I'm here to see Dr. Wilson," David said.

"I'm Dr. Wilson. Were you expecting someone different?"

"Well, it's just that I—"

"Don't mention it. People are often surprised to find a Paiute in my line of work."

David followed Wilson into the office. Native American rugs covered the floor. Animal skins and Indian memorabilia crowded the walls. "You have five minutes," Dr. Wilson said, taking a seat behind an old wooden desk.

David sat on a nearby chair. "First, I really appreciate your taking the time—"

"Get on with it!"

"Yes, well, this whole thing started when I took my kids out to dinner Tuesday night. It was one of those off nights when you wouldn't expect to see anyone out. Well, we were more than a little surprised to find our favorite restaurant packed to the gills. There was a line of cars waiting to get into the parking lot. It was as if everyone independently decided to go out to dinner at the same time, on a night that few people usually go out."

Wilson drummed his fingers on his desk.

"Now, I chalked the whole thing up to coincidence, until I got home and called a bunch of other places. Turns out, restaurants all over the city had the same thing happen Tuesday night. They were all packed."

Wilson raised an open hand. "My friend," he began, "Mister—"

"Peters."

"Mr. Peters. Are you familiar with the concept of a *tipping point*?"

"I'm not sure."

"That is when various conditions build and build, until, at a certain point, resistance gives way to allow an event to occur. What likely caused this miracle you speak of was a tipping point. Perhaps many people missed an opportunity to go out to dinner last weekend because of some other event, such as a game on TV, and this contributed to their collective desire to go out on Tuesday. Since many restaurants are not open on Mondays, Tuesday was the next best option. There could be additional factors that would become clear with a thorough study of the event."

David felt a wave of disappointment. "Hmmm. You've got a point there."

"Most of these kinds of things have a cause, when you dig into them."

"I guess I've wasted enough of your time." David stood up and walked toward the office door. "Thank you, Dr. Wilson. I really appreciate your—"

"*Enoohta*." (Leave.)

David closed the door behind him. A few paces down the hall, he stopped. Something didn't add up. A tipping point could not be responsible for the mysterious dance in the satellite video. No way. David did an about-face, marched back to Wilson's office, and opened the door.

"What in God's name is it now?" Wilson barked.

"I'm sorry. There's something I must show you. It's a short piece of video."

Wilson's eyes burned. "I have a stack of student papers to read. I'm a professor, remember?"

"Please?"

"I can't believe I'm wasting my time with this. Make it quick."

David slid into the office and located the DVD player. "I have to show you a very short piece of video, less than a minute long."

Wilson drummed his fingers on the desk.

David put the disk into the player. The television screen turned deep blue, and the dance commenced.

Wilson scowled at the screen. "What the hell is that?"

"That would be the city of Minneapolis on the night of the restaurant madness, photographed from six hundred nautical miles up, time-lapsed at ten-minute intervals, and then slowed back down using time synthesis. Oh yeah, and shot in infrared."

Wilson's eyes stayed fixed on the television. "How did you do this?"

"Well, I saw an article in the newspaper about a military satellite that was recently declassified. It's got thermal imaging capability, so humans show up as little yellow dots. They have a website where you can download still images of various cities, so I got thinking, what if I made a little movie out of some of those images?"

"My God," Wilson whispered, his tone changing entirely.

"But the first time I tried it, my time reference was all wrong. The video was just a jumbled mess. So, I went back to the drawing board and figured out a way to do it with time synthesis. What do you make of this?"

Wilson got up from his desk and knelt on the Indian rug in front of the television. His breathing became deep and deliberate. Tears streamed down his cheeks like rivers. He held his trembling hands together in front of him and spoke in his Paiute tongue, "Wovoka, Wovoka, Wovoka."

— — —

David stopped the DVD player. "Perhaps I should leave now."

Wilson wiped away the tears. "No, you must stay. Wovoka has sent you here."

"Who's Wovoka?"

Wilson motioned to a spot on the native rug. "Sit."

"Well, I guess I can spare a few minutes."

"Wovoka was a Paiute shaman—a medicine man—who grew up in the late 1800s. When he was young, his father died, and a white family took him in. The family thought Wovoka might pass as one of their own, but eventually he returned to his tribe. Years later, during an illness and fever that almost killed him, Wovoka had a vision that he died and went to heaven. There, he spoke to his dead ancestors and to God himself."

"Where does the video come into the picture?"

"Listen, please. God instructed Wovoka to organize a round dance, a spiritual dance to welcome a new era of peace and restoration for the Indians. Wovoka believed that it was not the Indians' place to fight the white man—that God would determine the white man's fate. The dance was performed in a large circle, lasting through the night for five nights. The dancers trembled and sometimes fainted. Many described visiting the Happy Hunting Ground and conversing with dead relatives."

David gazed at the Indian artifacts, mystified at the turn things were taking.

"Wovoka never left his reservation after that, but word of the round dance spread to the Arapaho and Cheyenne. Many chiefs came to visit Wovoka, and he taught them how to do the dance.

The Plains Indians named it the ghost dance. Within two years, the ghost dance was being performed by nearly every tribe west of the Mississippi." Wilson handed David an old sepia photograph. "That's a ghost dance, right there."

"Do they still do this?"

"No. Ironically, the ghost dance—which was supposed to bring peace and harmony—was perceived as a threat by white settlers. They didn't understand it and were spooked by it. This happened at a time when the US government was intent on moving all the tribes onto reservations. The ghost dance interfered with the government's plan to convert Native Americans to Christianity and to adopt the white man's way of life."

David shook his head. "You can believe in any God you like, as long as it's the Christian one."

"The government blamed two people for the ghost dance: Wovoka and Sitting Bull, chief medicine man of the Lakota people. The government was worried about Sitting Bull, given his stature among the Lakota. They ordered tribal police to arrest Sitting Bull, and he was killed when some of his own people tried to defend him. Two weeks later, army troops attempted to relocate the Lakota people away from the Pine Ridge Reservation. The Lakota ignored them and continued their ghost dance—a dance of peace. Under the command of General Nelson A. Miles, the Seventh Cavalry opened fire. The dancers wore sacred ghost shirts that they believed would protect them from the bullets. Sadly, the ghost shirts didn't work. Two hundred ninety men, women, and children were killed, along with thirty-three soldiers. It was the battle of Wounded Knee."

"Oh yes, I remember hearing of Wounded Knee," David said. "So much for justice."

"It is not for us to judge—only to understand and to keep from making the same mistakes again."

"What happened to Wovoka?"

"Wovoka became a shadow of himself in the white man's world. He used the name given to him by his adopted family—Jack Wilson. He made a living by displaying himself at county fairs and sideshows. He even appeared in a few silent westerns, a shell of an Indian pretending to be a real Indian. The ghost dance was all but forgotten. By the time he died in 1932, Wovoka was forgotten—even by his own people."

"That's a very sad story," David said.

"I just want to see Wovoka's legacy given the light it deserves, to be taken seriously—not as a circus act, not as religious fanaticism. You see, Mr. Peters—"

"Please—David."

"You see, David, I came into this field of collective behavior to learn the science behind the ghost dance, to show my people and the white man that Wovoka was more than a dreamer, that the ghost dance is as real as the clouds in the sky. You see, my name is also Jack Wilson. Wovoka was my great-grandfather."

— — —

Julia made it back to school just in time for her class. She felt a bit sore from the biopsy but was glad to have it behind her—one less thing to worry about. A hush came over the classroom after she wrote one word on the chalkboard: *CANCER.*

"Today, we're going to discuss one of the most feared and misunderstood illnesses, one that affects many thousands of people every year: cancer. Billions of dollars have been spent on cancer research, yet we still don't understand exactly how cancer gets started." Julia's words flowed with cool detachment, distancing herself from her own situation like a flight attendant on a doomed airliner. "Let me see a show of hands of those who have known someone with cancer."

Ten of the thirty students in the room raised a hand.

"Now, let's see a show of hands of those who have had cancer in their family."

The same ten students continued to hold their hands up.

"And how many of those have had cancer in the last year?"

Not a single hand came down. Julia's train of thought derailed. She opened a door she wasn't supposed to open. Her mind jerked her back to the doctor's office, his latex fingers probing the lump in her breast. A shadow rushed through her like a raven winging through a snowstorm. The air left her lungs. Julia stood helpless, gazing into the sea of young faces in front of her.

The hands came down. "Mrs. Peters? Mrs. Peters?"

"Sorry, I guess I forgot my coffee this morning. Now, where were we?"

"Cancer."

"Oh yes, of course. Cancer." Julia regained her composure. "What exactly is cancer?"

A few hands went up.

"Michael."

"It's when your body turns on itself and becomes its own enemy."

"Yes, that's partially true. Who else has an idea? Susan?"

"You get cancer when God decides it's time for you to die."

"Let's limit ourselves to scientific explanations. Peter?"

"It's the government's secret way of reducing the population."

"Well, we have a conspiracy theorist among us. If that was true, I'm sure we would have overthrown the government by now. Jessica?"

"Cancer is what happens when we get chemicals in our bodies."

"There is only a small shred of truth there. Problem is, what affects your body might not affect Susan's body at all. Cancer is a complex problem. There are many things that can trigger it and many different parts of our bodies that can be affected by it. What all cancers have in common is the uncontrolled replication of cells." Julia turned toward the chalkboard.

"Our bodies are made up of many different types of specialized cells. Brain cells, skin cells, liver cells, hundreds of different varieties. We constantly produce new cells to replace older worn-out cells of the same type. This process is carefully regulated so that we always have about the same number of cells. Older cells are killed off to make room for new ones. This process happens slowly and under very tight control. Enzymes inside our cells contain the instructions to make it all work smoothly. When chemicals or radiation interfere with these enzymes, the replication process can become unregulated and spin out of control. Can anyone tell me what the result would be? Peter?"

"You'd get more new cells than you really want?"

"Exactly. Without older cells being killed off, the bundle of fast-growing cells would form into a clump, also known as a tumor. Now what's potentially hazardous about a tumor? Susan?"

"Might affect your figure?"

The class laughed.

"Well, perhaps in an extreme case. The danger with tumors is that they can start getting in the way of other normal functions, such as circulation. Can anyone tell me what a malignant tumor is? Jessica?"

"A tumor that can spread?"

"Yes, that's right. In a malignant tumor, the new cells that are created carry the same defect as the cells that started the tumor. If some of these new cells break away from the tumor, they can travel to other parts of the body and start new tumors. To grow quickly, a tumor needs a good supply of blood. If the blood supply is inadequate, cancer cells will secrete a special enzyme to encourage blood vessels to begin growing toward the tumor."

A hand went up in the back row.

"Yes, Josh?"

"Does this mean a tumor is an intelligent biomass?"

"Gosh, I never thought of that." Julia's eyes stayed fixed on the back wall of the classroom.

The class became quiet with anticipation.

Julia's mind's eye transported her deep inside her own body, into her breast, to the site of the lump. There she saw a pulsating mass of thousands of eyeless creatures, feverishly stuffing themselves and reproducing with abandon. The throbbing mass grew while she watched, like the sun moving toward the horizon. A shard of panic shot through her. *Is this a Trojan horse inside me?* she wondered. *Is this lump smart enough to think for itself?* Julia gasped. "I must stop it!" she shouted.

Raised eyebrows quietly filled the classroom.

Julia looked as though she'd seen a dead body lying in the street.

"Mrs. Peters?"

"I'm so sorry. I was just remembering something."

A wave of fear washed over the classroom. Jessica and Susan looked at each other in alarm.

Julia pulled her emotions up by the bootstraps, but her face still carried the weight of someone leaving a funeral. She looked at the students in front of her. "To all of you who know someone with cancer, please remember that cancer is not contagious. You can't catch it from anyone. There is nothing to worry about. Please remember that."

The bell rang, and the students streamed out the door. Julia stepped into the hallway, still caught in her dark tornado.

"Julia?" Marsha called.

Julia turned toward the friendly voice.

"Julia, are you okay?"

Julia looked at Marsha, but her eyes seemed focused elsewhere. "I saw my cancer. I actually saw it."

"You got your results back?"

"No. They haven't called yet."

"Then how do you know?" Marsha asked.

"I just know."

FIVE

JAMIE PUT HIS BOOKS in his locker and slammed it shut. He made his way down the hall, ignoring everyone around him, his eyes fixed on some theoretical point a mile away. Students slid past, ignoring him as he went by. In the distance, Murphy approached. He was alone, his tough-guy swagger in full tilt.

"Mr. Murphy," a teacher called.

Murphy stopped.

"I hope we're going to see a better effort on your homework tomorrow."

Murphy responded with a reluctant nod.

"You don't have much leeway, Mr. Murphy. You're one test away from flunking civics."

Jamie gained momentum.

"Is that it?" Murphy asked the teacher.

"You're going to be in for a rude awakening, Mr. Murphy, if we don't see—"

Bang. Jamie's fist connected with Murphy's jaw like a battering ram. Murphy flew off his feet and landed a few yards away. The teacher tackled Jamie to the floor. Students scattered.

Jamie sat up and rubbed his hand, trying to make sense of what had happened. "That wasn't me. That wasn't me."

"It certainly was you, Mr. Peters," the teacher said. "I saw the whole thing. We're going straight to Principal Skinner's office. Murphy, you report to the school nurse."

Murphy wobbled to his feet, looking as though he'd seen a ghost.

— — —

Julia ambled down the high school hallway, still dazed from her cancer presentation. A loudspeaker in the hallway squawked. "Attention. Mrs. Peters, please come to the office."

Julia made her way to the principal's office. The secretary greeted her. "Julia, you're needed over at the middle school office. Something to do with your son."

Julia's mind flashed to the dinner scene and Jamie's dinner knife stuck in the table. "Oh my God," she whispered.

The middle school building was right next door. Julia sprinted down the corridor, her heart pounding. The secretary waved her into the principal's office. Principal Skinner sat behind his desk and Jamie on a metal folding chair by the wall. Jamie glanced at Julia and then fixed his eyes on the floor.

Skinner leaned on his elbows, hands folded in front of him. "Mrs. Peters, your son has been involved in a serious incident. With no provocation whatsoever, he attacked another student in the hallway."

"It wasn't me, Mom," Jamie pleaded.

"A teacher was speaking to the student when Jamie struck him."

"Jamie?"

"I might have hit him, but I didn't mean to do it. Something made me do it. Something just took control of me."

Skinner leaned forward. "Jamie, we are each responsible for our own actions. Even if we are provoked, we are still responsible for what we do."

"I didn't even want to do it. I'd have to be crazy to do something like that to Murphy. He'll kill me."

Julia looked alarmed.

"I don't think you need to worry about Mr. Murphy," Skinner said. "I've had a word with him already. But how do we know you won't do something like this again, Jamie?"

Jamie sat silently and stared at the floor.

"It's just not like him," Julia said. "Is Murphy one of the bullies you were talking about, Jamie?"

"I guess."

"I think we're only seeing part of the picture here, Mr. Skinner. My husband and I have been concerned about this bullying for some time. Jamie is not the sort of kid to make trouble on his own."

"Nevertheless, I will have to put Jamie on probation for the next month. He will be permitted to attend school, but his conduct will be closely monitored. If there is even the slightest infraction, he will be suspended for the remainder of the semester. Do you understand, Jamie?"

"Yes, sir."

"Okay, Jamie, you can return to class. Mrs. Peters, I'd like to have a word with you alone."

Jamie stood up, glanced at Julia, and left the office.

Skinner sat back in his chair. "Mrs. Peters, is there anything that you think might have brought this on, something going on at home perhaps?"

"Mr. Skinner, I really do believe bullying is at the root of this."

"I'm just thinking that perhaps there is another contributing factor. These bullying episodes often have roots at home for both the bully and the victim."

Julia closed the office door. "Yes, we do have some problems. My husband has been out of work for a number of months. Things have been stressful."

"Have you noticed any unusual changes in Jamie?"

Julia thought for a moment. "Well, now that you mention it, he has recently expressed an interest in joining the army."

"And this struck you as unusual?"

"It was just out of left field, not like him at all."

"Well, let's keep an eye on him. Hopefully, this was a one-time incident."

"Thank you, Mr. Skinner."

"Thank you for coming by, Mrs. Peters."

Once outside the building, Julia pulled her cell phone from her purse and called David. The home telephone rang and rang. Finally, the answering machine picked up. Julia left a message. "David, I don't know where you are right now, but there has been an incident at school involving Jamie. He's okay, but we need to have a talk with him. Something's going on. Call me when you get this. Where in God's name are you anyway?"

— — —

Wilson handed David an eagle feather. "Wovoka would have wanted you to have this. You must keep it away from the white man's eyes. It is illegal for non-Indians to possess them. The eagle's feather will protect you."

"Cool." David stroked the feather with his finger, but realized he didn't have a way to conceal the feather. He slid it down the collar of his T-shirt and patted his chest. "Safe and sound."

Wilson's telephone rang. "Excuse me for a moment." Wilson lifted the receiver. "Yes? What is it, Numa? You know what I've told you about that. It's not right. It's not our way. You must not forget where you came from. We will continue this later. I can't talk right now. Tonight then. Bye."

David tried to remain disinterested in the telephone conversation, but couldn't hide his curiosity.

"That was my twenty-year-old son. Sometimes he forgets who he is. Now where were we?"

"The satellite video. Do you really think it could be connected to the ghost dance?"

"David, I am a man of science, but I am also a man of spirit. The Paiute make no clear distinction between these two worlds. When I saw your video, I knew right away there was a connection to Wovoka's ghost dance—the circular clockwise movement, the speed of it, the way the circle rotates in short bursts, like a pulse. This is exactly the way Wovoka taught the tribes to dance. I saw this in your video right away."

"So you think there's something spiritual going on here?"

"I will answer your question with another question: do you think there was something tangible going on in Wovoka's ghost dances?"

"Well, the government certainly didn't have mind control back then," David said.

"Mind control?"

"Making people do things without their knowing it."

"You're talking about psyops. The government, and the military in particular, has been dabbling in behavior modification for years, though civilian applications in the United States have been pretty limited. You can witness some of this stuff in action around election time."

"The national elections?"

"Right. The Republican National Committee uses psyops protocols to herd the working class into their camp."

"With some kind of space laser, right?"

"No, there's nothing particularly covert about it. The protocols rely on simple cause-and-effect relationships that can be used to affect people's opinions. For example, if you put government pressure on meat producers—causing meat prices to rise—gun owners will become more sensitive to antigun legislation."

"Give me my gun and my Bible, and you've got my vote."

"Exactly. Republicans know they can't win on economic policy alone, so they use the protocols to win over the huddled masses."

"Perfect. They've got the haves, and the too-dumb-to-know-they-don't-haves."

"The liberals play a similar game when they play the money card—making people despise anyone with wealth. For years, the tribes bought into that thinking, but now they see the other side of it because the Native American casinos have made millionaires out of many Indians."

"Does the media know about the protocols?"

"Even if you were to inform the public of the use of the protocols, few people would change their behavior. It's human nature. Look at how many people still think driving is safer than flying, in spite of overwhelming statistical evidence."

"So you don't think the protocols are behind the circle dance in my video?"

"Interesting question. For fifteen years, the government has tried to hire me to do psyops research, but I've refused them. I know they'll use it for some illegitimate purpose. No, I seriously doubt that they're behind this."

"I wonder if they even know about it?"

Wilson gazed out the window. "My instinct says no. The way you did this, with your unusual time synthesis technique, is not something one would easily stumble upon. If the government knew of the dance, they would never have declassified the satellite."

"Then what the heck is it?"

Wilson thought for a moment. "I'm not sure. It appears to be an echo of the ghost dance. I'm just not sure what it means."

David remembered Katie's comment about bee dances. "I wonder if honeybee dances could be related to it."

"The honeybees have a very simple dance that, as you know, is used for communication. Each bee does its own dance, unlike this behavior, where we have thousands of people participating in the same dance."

"And our dancers have no idea they're doing it. Heck, you and I might be part of it."

"Very interesting indeed. You have uncovered an enigma."

Wilson picked up the telephone. "Please cancel my appointments and classes for this afternoon. We'll reschedule for next week. Thank you."

"I don't wanna mess up your day, Dr. Wilson."

"On the contrary, this could turn out to be a very important day for both of us. And please, call me Jack." Wilson extended his hand and gave David a traditional Paiute handshake. "We have work to do."

David smiled. "Okay, Jack. Where do we begin?"

"I suggest we start by taking a closer look at your video. With the remote control, we can inch through frame by frame if necessary."

David started the video, and the mysterious dance filled the television screen again. Wilson leaned toward the screen. "If you look closely, you can see that the circle is constantly picking up new people and losing others. There is constant turnover, but the overall circular movement stays intact."

"The circle seems to be staying in place," David said. "Do you think geography could have anything to do with it?"

"Well, certainly not the physical geography of the city. It doesn't seem to be following any of the city's street patterns."

"How did the Indians choose a location for their ghost dances?"

"The site was usually chosen by the medicine man, a natural place, unencumbered by human-made things. The size of the circle would depend on the number of dancers, but the center was always considered sacred."

"The center?"

"Yes, Wovoka believed the energy became focused at the center of the circle. Stepping into the center of a ghost dance could be like stepping into a lightning storm. Only the most experienced dancers were allowed to do it."

David placed the tip of his index finger against the television screen, right in the center of the big circle. "Are you thinking what I'm thinking?"

For the first time, fear showed on Wilson's face. "I am a man of science, but I am still an Indian. We must tread carefully."

David looked closely at the television. "It looks to me as if the center is in Theodore Wirth Park."

Wilson crossed his arms in front of his chest. His brow tightened. He paced to and fro in front of the television. "Okay, we will go; we will look."

"I'm with ya all the way, Jack."

David's Honda belched its way down East River Road. Wilson rode shotgun, his black braids blowing in the wind. *What would Julia think if she passed us now?* David thought. *What a strange turn of events to have an Indian riding in the passenger seat, an Indian who appears to have just stepped out of a time machine.*

Wilson gazed out the window and studied the clouds. "You know, there are messages in those clouds."

"What are they saying to you, Jack?"

"That there is a natural balance to things. If we make changes in our world, we must expect consequences."

"Well sure, just look at global warming."

"Recognizing change on that scale is a very difficult task for humans. Our time reference is very limited. Most people won't accept change that happens that slowly, even though science supports it."

"Sounds like the same problem Darwin is having these days."

"Darwin asked the right questions, but we must be careful not to assume that science is linear—that everything must be built on top of the knowledge we already have."

"You think we might have missed something?" David asked.

"I have a hunch that science, as we know it, may turn out to be a dead-end street."

"How's that?"

"With science, we have limited ourselves to things we can prove to be true. But because of our limited perception, we may be missing a great deal. Computers and microscopes have allowed us to magnify our perception, which is fine. But perhaps there are more than just five senses."

"Interesting thought."

David turned on the car radio. The announcer was in midsentence: "… she was really something—made me wish I had more than just five senses."

David's jaw dropped, and he turned toward Wilson. "What the hell?"

Wilson just smiled out the window.

"Now how the heck did you do that?" David hollered.

"Time does not always move in the same direction. I must have heard the radio before I spoke those words."

"In the future?"

"You see there is much that science cannot explain."

David took Glenwood Avenue to Wirth Parkway, past Birch Pond to Theodore Wirth Park. The park was expansive, the largest in Minneapolis. Beautiful wildflower beds stretched across the green acreage, everything in full spring bloom. In the center of the park, standing alone, was an enormous oak. David and Wilson stood at the park's edge and gazed out at the huge tree.

"That's quite a tree," David said.

"Judging from its age, I would not be surprised if it was planted by the Sioux."

"Let's take a look." David walked toward the oak.

Wilson didn't move.

"Funny, there's no people out here," David said. Then he realized Wilson wasn't with him. "Is something wrong, Jack?"

Wilson had fear in his eyes. "I'm not sure."

"You can wait there if you want."

Wilson took a few tentative steps toward David.

"It's just a tree," David said.

Wilson followed David, staying a few paces behind him. The massive trunk loomed before them.

"Well, this seems like the only thing of significance out here," David said. "Sure is a beauty."

Wilson motioned toward the limbs just above the trunk. "We are not alone." A large swarm of bees clung to one of the fat limbs.

"They must be looking for a new home. Not a bad location, given all the flowers out here."

Wilson remained perfectly still, his eyes fixed on the bees. He held his hands out in front of him, palms up, as if to divine any stray spirits that might be lurking.

David took a step backward.

The fear left Wilson's eyes, and he sighed. "Perhaps this tree is not important. We can go."

As they walked back to the car, David looked over his shoulder at the tree. "Yes, it is quite a tree."

— — —

Dinner was in the oven. It was 7:00 p.m. and still no sign of David.

"Where's Dad?" Katie asked.

"I don't know," Julia said. "He must be talking to someone about a job."

"I'm getting hungry," Jamie said.

Julia pulled a casserole from the oven. "Well, we're going to go ahead and eat."

Katie leaned against the kitchen counter. "Mom, do you think Dad could have a girlfriend?"

Startled, Julia accidentally touched the hot casserole dish. "Ouch!"

"Katie!" Jamie shouted.

"Honey, what on earth would make you think something like that?"

"Lucy Carter told me her dad was late for dinner a few times, and it turned out he had a girlfriend."

"Well, that's not the sort of thing to spread around, and Lucy should not be telling her friends about it."

Katie drummed her fingers on the counter.

Julia scooped out the casserole. "I'm sure your dad does not have a girlfriend." The word *girlfriend* fluttered around Julia's mind like a caged bird. As bad as things had been, it was a scenario she still couldn't imagine. *How could anyone find David attractive in his current state?* she thought. It seemed beyond reason.

"I guess Dad wouldn't buy you things if he had a girlfriend," Katie continued.

Julia didn't respond.

"Unless he was trying to fool you."

"Katie, I think you've taken this line of reasoning far enough. Your dad does not have a girlfriend."

"Why don't you talk about something else," Jamie growled.

"Well, at least I didn't get in a fight."

Jamie lowered his eyebrows. "You don't know anything about it. Just mind your own business."

— — —

The kitchen door opened, and David stepped inside. "Sorry I'm late. Had a meeting that ran over."

"Where on earth were you?" Julia asked.

"At the university, talking to someone about a project."

"What sort of project?"

"I can't really talk about it, because it might involve the government."

"The state government?"

"No, federal."

Julia put down her fork. "While you were having your secret meeting, I was summoned to the principal's office at the middle school."

Jamie kept his eyes on his dinner.

Julia's words floated right past David. He was still thinking about Jack Wilson—the great-grandson of Wovoka—the psyops protocols, and the mysterious oak tree.

"Hello … Earth to David."

"Sorry, I was distracted."

"Without provocation, your son punched another student right in front of one of the teachers."

"Jamie? What was this about?"

Jamie said nothing.

"Apparently, it had something to do with a bully."

David sat down next to Jamie. "Was it someone who was picking on you?"

"Yeah, I guess. But I didn't even want to hit him. Something made me do it."

"That's what you said at Mr. Skinner's office," Julia said.

"What do you mean, something made you do it?"

"I put my books in my locker and started walking down the hall. I never even saw him. Then I guess I slugged him, but I don't remember any of it. It was like something was controlling me."

Julia looked perplexed.

David believed him. "I believe you, Jamie. I don't know what it was that made you do this, but I do believe you."

"Thanks, Dad."

"Whoever this guy is, I don't imagine you'll have any trouble with him again."

Julia scowled. "Regardless of the outcome, hitting is not a solution to any problem."

When Julia wasn't looking, David winked at Jamie.

— — —

It was 10:00 p.m. Julia and David brushed their teeth at their respective sinks, speaking to each other's reflections. "I'm worried about Jamie," Julia said.

"He'll get over it."

"Get over it? What about all that talk about guns and bombs and killing?"

"Boys all go through a stage like that."

"And they stick knives in the dinner table?"

"He was just acting out."

"I think we should talk to his doctor about getting some help. Marsha Reeves knows a very good shrink. I think we should get him into therapy."

"Can we really afford that?"

"What we can't afford is for you to be out of work much longer."

"I'm working on it. I'm working on something very important."

"That's what you keep saying, but when are we going to see a paycheck?"

"Money is not the only goal. Sometimes, there are more important things."

"There you go again. I just don't get it when you talk like that— like you're living in Tibet."

David looked at his reflection in the mirror. It was a different reflection than the one he'd seen recently. At that very moment, he knew. He knew his legacy lay in front of him, that he was on the right track. "You'll see. Things are happening for a reason."

Julia left the bathroom and climbed into bed. David pulled off his T-shirt and the eagle feather floated to the floor.

"What in God's name is that?" Julia asked.

"Oh that." David bent over and picked up the feather.

"That thing's got to be carrying germs."

"It's an eagle feather."

"Aren't those illegal?"

"I've been deputized to carry it."

"Oh, God," Julia moaned, "by some street character, I imagine."

David was tempted to spill the beans about Wilson, but he resisted. "I've got some work to do downstairs," he said. "I'll be up in a little while."

"I won't hold my breath."

Julia turned off the bedroom light. She stared into the darkness of the bedroom.

— — —

David placed the eagle feather on top of his computer. His mind churned. So much had happened in the past two days. Nothing looked the same to him anymore. Something as simple as a group of children crossing the street had taken on new meaning and relevance. Something extraordinary was going on, and David hoped he and Wilson would get to the bottom of it.

The image of Jack Wilson standing by the huge oak with his hands held out was fixed in David's mind. The undulating mass of bees had captured Wilson's attention. *What if Jack really did sense something about the tree but pretended he didn't?* David thought.

Could there be something he didn't want me to know about? Could the bees have something to do with the dance?

David searched the Internet for videos of honeybees. He found one video of honeybees taken through the side of a glass observation hive. He downloaded the video and opened it up. The computer screen filled with bees, thousands of them, pushing up against one another. It reminded David of a crowd at a rock concert, shoulder to shoulder, the kind of group situation he had learned to avoid. He recalled the idiot at the rock concert who threw a beer bottle and, the next thing David knew, hundreds of bottles were flying. He spent that night in the emergency room. The only thing those people needed was one idiot to make them think it was okay to throw beer bottles—the idiot president.

David studied the mass of honeybees in front of him. Looking closely, he could see a few bees doing their circular dances, but otherwise, the bees' movements appeared to be random. "I wonder what would happen if …?" David leaned back in his chair. He had an idea. It was time to get out his time synthesis tools and see if there was anything hidden in the honeybee world.

David scanned the honeybee videos for a segment long enough to use for his experiment. The longest segment he could find was only thirty seconds. To get the compression he required, he would need something on the order of thirty minutes of video. The only option was for David to shoot it himself.

David typed the words "bee research Minneapolis" and clicked search. A web link for the State of Minnesota Entomology Laboratory appeared. He clicked on the link, and a website appeared, featuring the sign in front of the laboratory. Displayed below it were the hours of operation.

David's agenda for the next morning was clear to him: he needed to learn a few things about honeybees.

SIX

JULIA AWOKE TO THE sound of the shower. She squinted at the clock: 6:30 a.m. David showered like a man on a mission—soap and shampoo applied with deft precision, not a second wasted. It was a welcome sign, Julia conceded, even though she hadn't the faintest idea what he was up to.

"Something going on?" Julia asked.

"Meeting with some researchers this morning."

"Okay."

David put on a clean shirt.

"More of your top secret work?"

"Ah—yeah."

Julia shook her head and walked toward the bathroom. "Don't forget to ask them about benefits."

David finished getting dressed and went downstairs, where Katie was fixing herself a bowl of cereal. "Wow, you're up early, Dad."

"I have a meeting this morning."

"Is it with a lady?"

"Well, gee, honey, I guess it might be with a lady. But then she could be a man."

Katie looked confused.

"I'm working on a secret project. But because it's secret, I can't talk about it."

"That's okay, Dad. I think you told me enough already."

Jamie walked into the kitchen.

"Good morning, Jamie," David said.

"Hi, Dad."

"Did you sleep okay?"

"I had another one of those dreams."

"What dreams?"

"Like I was on a battlefield. Some bombs went off around me, but I was okay. I shot all sorts of people. It was really cool."

"Well, the real thing might not be nearly as much fun. Real war is much scarier than dream war."

The telephone rang. Julia answered the telephone in the bedroom, and David picked up the kitchen phone at the same instant.

"Julia, it's Ted Austin calling. Your results came back early, so I thought I would relay them to you right away. I'm sorry, Julia; your biopsy was positive for breast cancer."

Julia shuddered at the word *cancer.*

"We'll want to get you back in as soon as possible to discuss your options."

David's face froze.

"Thank you," Julia whispered and hung up the phone.

David held the phone for a moment and then hung it up.

"Everything okay, Dad?" Katie asked.

"Ah—yeah, everything's fine."

Julia stood in the bedroom like a still photograph—a moment in time that would define her life henceforth. The news was not entirely a surprise, but at the same time, she felt as though her life had just changed forever. Her issues with David suddenly seemed trivial but, at the same time, critical. She wondered how she could rely on his support in his current state. And how would she tell him?

— — —

The words *breast cancer* sat in David's mind like a broken-down truck in the middle of the road. He tried his best to make them go away, but there they were. *At least Julia doesn't know that I know,* he thought. *I'll let her bring it up when she feels ready. She still doesn't know how serious it is yet.*

Julia walked into the kitchen. She avoided eye contact with David and began making the kids' lunches.

David watched intently as Julia put the sandwiches together. "Anything special going on for you today?" he asked.

"Just going to work as usual."

"Well, I hope your day gets better. Better than yesterday."

Julia looked at David as if he was speaking Chinese.

"I guess I'll be on my way," David said. "I hope everybody has a really good day." He picked up his briefcase, the video camera, and tripod, and he went out the door.

"Dad's meeting with a secret lady," Katie announced.

Julia stared out the window as David's car rolled down the street.

— — —

After the kids got on the school bus, Julia called her friend Marsha.

"Hi, this is Marsha Reeves. Sorry I missed your call. Please leave me a message."

"Marsha, it's Julia. The doctor called this morning. Looks like I was right. I still don't know how serious it is, though. Don't worry; I'm okay. Maybe we can meet for lunch. See you at school."

— — —

"Hey there, good lookin'," Sue said, adding a little nod to acknowledge David's improved appearance.

David sidled up to the counter where his coffee awaited. He still reeled over Julia's breast cancer and struggled to get his head around it. It just didn't make sense. Julia had always been such a nut about taking care of herself, eating healthy foods, exercising.

Sue breezed over. "You seem a little off today. Everything okay?"

"Well, actually, I just found out someone I know has cancer—a friend of mine."

"Gosh. I'm sorry, honey."

"Thanks."

Sue shook her head. "Well, I'll be. You're the third person in the past two days to tell me that."

"About somebody getting cancer?"

"Yup."

David sipped his coffee. "Probably just a coincidence."

Sue wiped down the counter as she spoke. "Well, if it isn't a coincidence, I wonder what it could be? Somethin' in the water?"

David's mind jumped to the protocols ... the government ... the military. *Could there be something going on here?* he wondered. *But why would they want to give people cancer? What would be the point? Unless it's the result of something that went out of control, some kind of experiment. And, if that's the case, wouldn't they be warning people? Of course they would. They'd never be able to keep something like that a secret. No way.*

Sue backed off. "Sorry, I guess you've got a lot on your mind."

"That's okay, Sue. It's definitely just a coincidence—like knowing a bunch of people who like the color red. A coincidence, that's all it is."

"I guess you're right, honey. I hope your friend gets better."

"Thanks."

David left Max's and drove toward the state entomology lab. Along the way, he passed a florist shop and thought of Julia. She always liked daffodils, David recalled—yellow daffodils. It seemed like another lifetime when he last bought her daffodils. *Things were so different then*, he thought. He was a big shot, working on big projects with big people. He worked hard and played hard. Julia's teaching career was a nice added benefit but certainly not the main course. Her job was the icing on the cake. Now everything was turned around. Life had played a cruel trick on both of them—David losing his job and Julia getting cancer. Yes, indeed, David decided, he would definitely buy daffodils for Julia. *The entomology lab can wait*, he thought. He turned the car around and returned to the florist shop.

David rolled into the parking lot and stopped dead when he saw the scene ahead of him. A line of customers extended out of the florist shop and down the sidewalk. "Well, that's weird. They must be having a sale or something." The Honda coughed a generous blue cloud toward the waiting customers. David climbed out and apologized. "Sorry, it's going in for a tune-up tomorrow. Nice day for buying flowers," he announced to no one in particular.

A mother and young daughter nearest to David glanced in his direction and then turned away.

"Seems like everybody has flowers on the brain today," David continued.

A few others in the line responded to David with blank stares.

"Excuse me," David said to the mother standing near him, "is this Mother's Day or Secretary's Day or something like that?"

The woman reluctantly turned toward David. "No, it's not."

"I just wondered why so many people would be buying flowers at the same time."

"Why are you buying flowers?" the little girl asked.

"For my wife, Julia. She's always liked daffodils."

"We're buying flowers for my aunt. She's sick."

"I'm sorry."

"That's enough, honey," the mother said, turning her daughter away from David.

David gradually made his way inside the florist shop. A slight, bespectacled man with sympathetic eyes stood behind the counter. "And what can I get for you, sir?"

"It's for my wife."

"I'm so sorry," the florist replied, somehow knowing that David's purchase was not simply a token of affection.

David was startled by the man's intuition. He turned and looked at the others in line behind him, wondering if they might be buying flowers for the same reason.

"Sir?"

"She's always liked yellow daffodils," David said. "I get them for her all the time," he added, trying to dispel the notion that this was a sympathy purchase.

"Let me show you what we have," the florist whispered. David followed him to the back of the shop and into the walk-in cooler. The heavy door closed behind them with a clunk.

"We have some beautiful yellow daffodils, just in yesterday."

"Those will be fine," David said. "I'll take a dozen."

The florist gently lifted the flowers from the plastic bucket. "I wish you all the best of luck," he said. "I lost my wife a few months ago."

"I'm sorry," David replied, still curious about how the florist could have known about Julia.

"There are so many," the florist said, shaking his head, "so very many."

— — —

The state entomology laboratory resided in a low-slung gray building on the edge of an industrial park. A sign outside read,

State of Minnesota
Entomology Laboratory
"We know what's bugging you."

David entered through the windowless front door, into what appeared to be a storeroom. All four walls brimmed with books, manuals, and cardboard boxes. A man with a flat-top buzz cut in a khaki jumpsuit sat behind a massive army surplus desk. He looked up from his paperwork and noticed David was carrying a video camera and a tripod. His eyes bulged. "You with the media?"

"Ah—no. I wanted to see your honeybees."

"Federal inspector?"

"No, I just want to shoot some video."

Jumpsuit's brow furrowed. "Who did you say you were with?"

"I'm not really with anybody. I'm just interested in honeybees."

The furrows deepened. "Got to have written authorization."

"Where would I get that?"

"From the state." Jumpsuit resumed writing on something in front of him. "Come back with authorization, and I can help you."

David headed toward the door. Then he stopped. "Actually, it's a federal project."

"What project is that?"

David looked around, as if to check if anyone else was within earshot. "What's your name, sir?"

"Hadley," jumpsuit said, "Homer Hadley."

"Well, Mr. Hadley, I'm sure you can appreciate that what I'm about to tell you must be kept in the strictest confidence."

Hadley acknowledged this with a perplexed nod.

"And any breech of this confidence would involve the FBI and other agencies that I am not at liberty to name."

Hadley nodded again.

"In particular, mentioning my visit to any other employee of this facility or anyone connected with the state of Minnesota would constitute a breech of this confidence."

Hadley swallowed hard. "Okay."

"Actually, I work for the military—advanced weapon systems.

We're studying honeybees as a possible weapon delivery system. It's still in a very early stage of development. We have our own bee lab in Virginia, but we're gathering video from other labs before we asseverate our findings."

"Asseverate," Hadley echoed.

"So, if you would be kind enough to show me where your observation hives are located, I'll get under way."

Hadley stumbled out from behind the massive metal desk. "Right this way," he said, and he led David down a hallway to the lab. "Weapon delivery systems, huh? You should have mentioned that right off." Three glass-sided observation hives were set up along an outside wall. A white countertop ran the length of the opposite wall, crowded with microscopes and other pieces of equipment for examining bees.

David began unfolding his tripod. "Are you the only person working here today?"

"We've got two entomologists here part time. They're both out teaching today."

"I need to capture about thirty minutes of video, viewing straight on at one of the observation hives."

"This one down here has the most bees in it." Hadley pointed.

"That should do," David said, "and the window light is good there too." David attached the video camera to the tripod and aligned it with the side of the observation hive.

"What is it you're lookin' for?"

"We don't like to talk about this work unless it's absolutely necessary. I'm sure you can appreciate that."

Hadley's brow furrowed again.

"Group dynamics. We need bees with good teamwork—better for military applications." David pressed the record button.

"I can see that," Hadley nodded. "What are the bees going to be delivering?"

"I'm not at liberty to discuss that."

Hadley's eyes bulged.

"Are you familiar with nanotechnology?"

"Yeah, I've heard of that."

"Well, it's got something to do with that. That's all I can tell you."

Hadley's eyebrows climbed up his forehead. He stood back and watched, while David watched the bees. A hum could be heard through the plate glass. "Busy little critters, aren't they?" Hadley beamed.

David responded with a polite grin and continued watching the bees.

"You'd never know they were in trouble."

David looked up. "Trouble?"

"CCD. You federal guys must know about colony collapse disorder."

"Oh yeah, we wrote the report on that back in Virginia," David said, though he had no idea what Hadley was talking about.

"Poor little buggers are getting wiped out. And meanwhile, we're making them work their little tails off on the industrial farms. There'll be hell to pay if we wipe them out altogether. The public has no idea how important they are. Most people think they're only good for honey and bee stings."

"How much longer do you figure they have?"

"Well, let's put it this way. We have half as many hives around the state as we did ten years ago. Not long, I'd say."

David gazed through the plate glass at the wall of bees. "How many bees are in there, would you say?"

"A healthy hive is around fifty thousand. But lately, they've been getting smaller. We thought it had something to do with Asian mites. Then we realized the bees were doing themselves in."

"Killing each other?"

"No, committing suicide. They've got a built-in poison pill—a cancer gene."

"Really."

"We don't know exactly what triggers it. Our guys discovered it here at the university recently."

"A poison pill. The boys back in Virginia will be interested in that." David sat down on a nearby chair. "If you've got some other things to do, I can just hang here until this is done."

"I'll be right out front if you need anything," Hadley said.

"Thanks, Mr. Hadley."

A few minutes later Hadley returned. "You know, there's something else I think you might be interested in."

"What's that?"

Hadley led David to another part of the lab where an observation hive stood by itself. The hive had plywood covers on each side, and Hadley removed one of them. The hive buzzed with activity. "We're not supposed to have this in here. One of the entomologists got it started by accident, so we just let it continue."

"What is it?"

"Those are Africanized killer bees. We've got this hive set up on a closed loop with its own food supply, so the bees can't get outside."

David stared wide-eyed through the plate glass.

"We'd be in some big trouble if the federal inspectors found out about this. You have to have a special license to keep killer bees."

"I've heard about them, but I've never actually seen them before."

"Talk about a weapon system. These guys will attack without being provoked. If you could figure out how to control killer bees, now *that* would be a weapon system."

"Mr. Hadley, you might be onto something here. I might have to shoot some video of this hive as well."

Hadley's brow furrowed again.

"But I will disavow any knowledge as to its location. And, of course, you'd be helping your country."

"Well—okay, but we never talked."

— — —

Wilson leaned back in his chair. "Your satellite video still perplexes me. I have watched it many times. I still sense a connection to the ghost dances of Wovoka, but I am not sure what it means."

"Well, things just got a bit more complicated," David said. "I tried another experiment."

"Tell me about it."

"After we saw bees in Wirth Park clinging to the oak tree, I got thinking that maybe honeybees are somehow connected to this."

"Yes?"

"So I went down to the state entomology lab and shot some video of their observation hives."

"Honeybee behavior is already well documented."

"Not exactly. I took the tape home and tried the same time synthesis trick I used on the satellite video. Take a look." David pulled a disc from an envelope and put it into the DVD player.

A mass of bees filled the television screen. "This is what honeybees look like to the naked eye when viewed through the side of the observation hive," David explained. The bees moved about randomly, every individual appearing to have its own agenda. "Now let me show you the time synthesized version." David pressed a button on the DVD player, and the image changed. While the bees in the center of the screen stayed in place, those near the perimeter began moving in a large clockwise pattern, just like the humans in the satellite video. The honeybees were doing their own version of the dance.

Wilson's eyes grew wide.

"I guess this means the bees in Wirth Park might be important after all," David said.

"This is unbelievable," Wilson stammered.

"You know, Jack, I think we might have to go take a closer look at that oak tree."

Wilson nodded in agreement, but his enthusiasm was bridled with caution.

"We'll take my car," David suggested.

"Okay, you drive."

The pair left the office and walked toward the visitors' parking lot. "Hey, Dad," a voice called out. Wilson stopped and squinted across the parking lot.

"It's my son, Numa," Wilson said.

Numa's Indian features were less obvious than Wilson's. Were it not for the resemblance between father and son, David never would have pegged Numa for a Native American. He had a clean, Princeton-style haircut, short-sleeved polo shirt, and tan slacks.

"This is David Peters," Wilson said. "We'll be reading about him some day."

Numa extended his hand and gave David a non-Indian handshake. "You can call me Ned," Numa said as if to apologize for his eccentric father.

"Numa has avoided all things Indian, including his name," Wilson pointed out.

"I think you could have done worse," David said. "Nice to meet you, Ned."

Numa looked Wilson in the eye. "Dad, I need to talk to you."

"Can't this wait until tonight?"

"They made me an offer, and I have to respond to them today or someone else might get in front of me."

Wilson stood with his arms folded in front of him, his face resigned to compromise. "You already know what my feelings are on the subject." Wilson paused for effect. "But you must do what you must do."

"Thanks, Dad." Numa gave Wilson a hug. "Nice to meet you, Mr. Peters."

"Good luck, Ned," David replied.

"Well, something sure killed a hell of a lot of bees," David

"If this tree is truly in the center of the dance, it might ac[count] for these forces. Wovoka taught the medicine men to be wary o[f] energy at the center of a ghost dance. Many spirits converge the[re]. Only the most experienced dancers were allowed to dance in th[e] center."

"What would happen to them?"

"Wovoka described it as having your emotions in a vortex. Dancers spoke in unfamiliar tongues and had visions of the future. They delivered messages from the Earth Mother."

"Maybe the bees were delivering a message," David said.

"True. The bees might be telling us something—like a herd of beached whales."

"You mean like a suicide note?"

"Perhaps. Humans have been pushing against nature, and nature is pushing back. The white man lives under the illusion that this battle can be won, that humans can harness nature like a farm animal. The Indians and the Aztecs knew better. They lived in balance with nature and respected it."

David shook his head. "I don't know. With global warming and the world population doubling every fifty years, it seems as if nature doesn't have a chance."

"Nature may lose a few battles, but in the end, it will win the war. After humankind is gone, nature will reclaim what is hers. These forces are stronger than any bomb or bulldozer."

"But if we get rid of disease—"

"Nature will adapt and come up with more lethal ones."

David thought of Julia. "Do you think nature cares who gets sick?"

"No, nature does not discriminate. I know two professors who were just diagnosed with cancer. They are both ardent naturalists. Where's the justice in that?"

David and Wilson climbed into the Honda. "Nice boy," David said.

"A boy who has completely lost touch with his roots."

"Maybe he'll figure out different ways to express his heritage, different from yours."

Wilson stared out the windshield. "He wants to do an internship at the FBI."

"That's—quite an opportunity for a twenty-year-old."

"David, the FBI and the Native American community have not had the warmest of relationships over the years. I fear that Numa will become isolated from his Indian friends when they learn of this. The parents and grandparents of his friends will remember. They still don't trust the federal government."

"You know what, Jack? The FBI could probably use some new blood. Look at it this way. Numa might be able to help them understand Indian culture. That would be good for everybody."

Wilson frowned at the car in front of them. "I guess you're right."

— — —

The wildflowers at Theodore Wirth Park glowed in the afternoon sun. David and Wilson climbed out of the Honda and surveyed the scene. There was no one in sight. The huge oak towered over the flat landscape, its leaves gently shimmering. Wilson stood steadfastly by the car.

"It still looks like a plain old oak," David said.

Wilson said nothing. His face became austere, like the face of a warrior preparing for battle.

"Hey, Jack, lighten up a little. It's just a tree, for Christ's sake."

Wilson forced a half smile, but his fear was palpable.

"You're starting to freak me out here, Jack. Is there something you're not telling me about this place? Is this an Indian burial ground or something?"

Wilson kept his eyes fixed on the distant tree. "I don't think so. You go. I'll wait here."

"What is it you're not telling me, Jack?"

"It is not easily put into words."

"Try me."

"When I was very young, my brother and I spent many hours in the woods. We pretended to be great warriors, stalking our enemy. It was make-believe, of course, but I became fearful that something was going to happen to my brother. The wind began to pick up, and we hid behind some rocks. My fear became stronger, but I ignored it. Then, without warning, a nearby tree fell down and killed my brother."

"Oh my God. That's terrible."

"It was long ago, another lifetime."

"I can see why you have a thing about trees."

"Trees are not a problem. The native cultures had a gift, and some Indians still have it—though most have forgotten how to use it. It is like a sixth sense."

"What is it?"

"The ability to sense impending danger. You see, I knew my brother was going to die. The feelings I had were very strong, but I didn't trust them. Wovoka's generation would have known better."

"Did the Indians use this sense to avoid death?"

"It is a survival instinct found in nature. Modern humans still have these premonitions, but they don't understand them."

David gazed out at the oak. "So, what is this tree telling you?"

"There are powerful forces, dark forces."

"It just looks like an oak tree to me. Wait here. I'm gonna go take another look." David walked gingerly toward the tree and stopped about halfway. "Jack, am I in any sort of danger?"

Wilson held his palms out toward the tree and "No, I don't think so."

David continued walking. As he approached the that the bee swarm had disappeared. "Looks like the he shouted.

Moving closer, David felt an odd sensation under soft bog. He noticed a dark ring around the base of th ten feet out from the trunk, a couple of feet in width. to get a closer look. Under his feet lay a carpet of dead hundreds of thousands of them arranged in a perfect r the base of the tree.

"Wait!" Wilson shouted.

David quickly stepped back from the tree. He touched expecting to feel the spine of the eagle feather, but he'd forg

"We should leave this place," Wilson said.

David felt a chill and walked quickly back to Wilson. " more bees, way more than before. And they're all dead."

Wilson listened but said nothing.

— — —

The drive back to Wilson's office was spent mostly in silence. W looked shaken. David tried to imagine why someone would wa kill the honeybees in Wirth Park. With all the wildflowers the seemed a natural place for them. The perfect circular arrangen around the tree seemed odd too. It certainly didn't look like a nat phenomenon. *On the other hand*, David wondered, *could there connection to the dance?*

Finally, David broke the silence. "What do you think, Jack? D somebody do this, or is something else at work here?"

"The forces of life and death are very strong around that tree That much I know."

"You know two people with cancer?"

"Actually, I know four people with cancer. Amazing, isn't it? It defies our sense of logic. Humans think they can control their destiny, but it's an illusion."

"But this cancer thing—have you noticed? There seems to be a lot of people getting it lately."

"It's probably just that more people are talking about it. Often, we think we see trends, when it's only our perception that's changed. Look at teenage pregnancy. The public thinks more teens are getting pregnant, when in fact just the opposite is true. What has changed is that more of them are being reported."

"I know someone with cancer too," David said. "Not sure how serious it is yet."

"Well, if there was some sort of cancer epidemic, I'm sure we would know about it by now."

"You're probably right."

— — —

It was 3:00 p.m. when David reached the house. Julia and the kids wouldn't be there for another hour. David thought of Julia and wondered how he could broach the subject of cancer with her. It seemed like such a big step, given the state of their marriage. *And what about all this cancer?* David thought. It just seemed hard to believe that there wasn't an epidemic going on. So many people seemed to be getting it.

David got an idea. He pulled out the telephone book and looked up the number for the Minneapolis Department of Health and dialed the number. A receptionist answered.

"Department of health."

"Yes, I wanted to get some information about a possible cancer epidemic."

"Are you a doctor or a patient?"

"Neither."

"Please hold. I'll connect you with information services."

David waited.

"Information services. May I help you?"

"Yes, I have a question. Is there any sort of cancer epidemic going on in Minneapolis?"

"Nothing of this nature has been reported."

"I just wondered, because I keep running into people who know people with cancer."

"Well, nothing of this nature has been reported."

"Okay then, thank you."

"Have a nice day."

Might be somebody who's outside the loop, David thought. He looked up the number for Abbott Northwestern Hospital and dialed it.

"Abbott Northwestern. May I help you?"

"Administration, please."

"Please hold while I try that extension."

"Administrative offices. May I help you?"

"I was just curious. Has your facility noticed an increase in new cancer patients in the past few months?"

"Nothing of this nature has been reported."

"I see." David noticed that the woman used the same wording as the woman at the health department: *nothing of this nature ...* "So you must be seeing just the typical number of cancer patients."

"Was there anything else, then?"

"That should do it. Thanks."

David dialed the number for Methodist Hospital.

"Good afternoon, Methodist Hospital."

"I'd like the oncology department, please."

"Let me connect you."

A nurse answered, "Oncology."

"I wondered if you could give me some information."

"What can I help you with?"

"Can you tell me if you've seen an increase in new cancer cases in the past few months?"

"Nothing of this nature has been reported."

David's jaw dropped. "Well, let me rephrase that. If I was to make an appointment today, how soon would you be able to get me in?"

"Appointments have to be set up by your primary physician."

"Sounds like you're pretty busy down there."

"I can't really comment on that."

"I'll take that as a yes. Thank you very much for your help."

David raced out the door and jumped into his car. Methodist Hospital was only a few minutes away. He walked into the front entrance, checked the directory and took the elevator to the fourth floor. The elevator doors opened to reveal a line of patients stretching down a long hallway. The line went all the way to the oncology waiting area, where another twenty patients waited to see doctors. There were few smiles and little talking.

Something caught David's eye: a beautiful head of hair, a young woman sitting with her back to him. The hair had a familiarity to it. She turned her head slightly to the side, and her cheekbone came into view. It was Julia. She still hadn't seen him. David started to move toward her, and then he stopped. He slid quietly back onto the elevator. On the way to the ground, he thought about Julia, about how she'd become ensnared in this cruel net with so many others. At least she wasn't alone. That made it slightly less terrible. But there were so many of them. *Clearly, something is going on*, he thought. *This is not normal.*

— — —

In Room 99, at the Centers for Disease Control and Prevention in Atlanta, Dr. Charles Miller continued his presentation. Jerome

Roberts sat quietly in the men's room stall, wishing he hadn't needed to use the toilet when he did. Jerome tried to doze off, but Miller's voice boomed through the tiled men's room—thanks to the loudspeaker in the ceiling. Jerome didn't much care what went on at the CDC, as long as his paycheck came through. They made him sign all sorts of things saying he wouldn't talk about his work at the CDC, which he thought was pretty silly. After all, he figured, he was only a janitor.

A map of the central United States filled one of Room 99's large plasma displays. Another display revealed the president and his senior staff listening intently from the White House Situation Room. Dr. Miller spoke in no uncertain terms.

"In the past six months, we have received data indicating a dramatic rise in newly reported cancers in several metropolitan areas of the midwestern United States. Data from medical centers in Minneapolis, Denver, and Kansas City indicate an increase on the order of 500 percent over the same period one year ago. These cancers are of various types, though the increase seems primarily the result of internal cancers, not cancers of the skin. As of yesterday, these three cities have been officially designated as cancer clusters under CDC protocol 339. In the interest of national security, we have contacted all medical centers in the region and implemented a priority 4 data lockdown. Medical administrators have been contacted and priority 4 protocols initiated to avert public suspicion. I need not tell you what a mess we'd have if the media got a hold of this.

"The CDC has completed a preliminary study, a copy of which is in front of you. We have reviewed several possible causes for these cancers, including carcinogenic and radiological factors. To date, we have not been able to account for any specific source that could be responsible for this increase over such a wide geographic area. The CDC has contacted state departments of health in the region and reviewed air and water quality data from the past five years. Air and water have consistently met federal standards and are not considered a factor. The CDC is not aware of any military or intelligence activity that could pose a health risk, but of course, certain projects are beyond our purview. Would representatives of the military care to enlighten us on their activities in this region?"

Frantic whispering erupted among the military brass. Several spoke cryptically into their cell phones.

Miller eyed the commotion. "Gentlemen?"

"Please bear with us, Doctor. We're getting clearances from Washington."

"Tell them we have the president on the line. We don't want to keep the president waiting, now do we?"

The scrambling continued among the military brass. "The Pentagon is doing a quick assessment based on your geographic data."

"It's very simple, gentlemen. I want to know about any and all activity in the region, anything that could even remotely be related to these cancer clusters."

SEVEN

"SOMEONE OTHER THAN ME must have noticed this," David said to himself. He sat down at his computer and typed *cancer* into his web browser. A list of cancer-related websites appeared. He clicked on the first one, Cancer Blog, and a cancer discussion page opened in front of him. There, he found discussions about prostate cancer, colon cancer, lung cancer, breast cancer, but nothing about a cancer epidemic in Minneapolis. "Well, I'll just start my own discussion." He clicked on *New Discussion* and began typing.

"Is anyone familiar with the cancer situation in Minneapolis? There seems to be a cancer epidemic, although the authorities are denying it." He signed the entry with the nom de plume "BirdsEyeView." David heard the kitchen door open, and he signed off the cancer website.

Julia entered the kitchen to the sight of yellow daffodils. A wellspring of emotion rose up inside of her. Yellow daffodils. She recalled the time David left a trail of yellow daffodil petals from the kitchen door to the upstairs bedroom, where the bed was completely covered with them. Then there was the time David rented a cherry picker and appeared outside her second-story classroom window with yellow daffodils in hand. And finally, there was the time David had daffodils delivered to her in the middle of a staff meeting by a violinist, bringing all the female teachers to tears. The wellspring began to take hold of Julia, but she pushed it back. *Things are not right,* she thought. *There are problems, problems that won't be solved with daffodils—unless David* knows. *Could David have spoken to my doctor behind my back?* she wondered. *Not likely. David is just being David. But I have to stand firm. Daffodils don't change the fact that David has completely lost touch with reality,* Julia thought. *No, daffodils don't change anything.*

From the den window, David could see Katie and Jamie walking toward the house. "Wow, Mom," Katie exclaimed, as she entered the kitchen. "Did Dad get you yellow daffodils?"

"Yes, honey, it looks like he did."

"I guess that means you don't have to worry about the secret lady."

Julia didn't reply, but she thought of something Katie said that morning—that it could be a diversion. *Come to think of it,* Julia mulled, *why on earth would David be buying flowers anyway? He can't possibly think daffodils are going to make up for his shortcomings. Maybe there is someone else,* she thought.

David stepped into the kitchen. "I hope everybody had a good day."

Julia ignored him and emptied the dishwasher, while the yellow daffodils beamed like the proverbial elephant in the kitchen.

"Nice daffodils, Dad," Katie said. She and Jamie grabbed their backpacks and went upstairs.

Julia continued to busy herself, keeping her eyes away from David's.

"So, how was your day?" David asked.

"Not as good as yours, I'm sure," Julia replied.

"Well, I've had better days. But then you can't expect every day to be a great day, can you?"

"No, I guess you can't."

"In fact, maybe it's the bad days that make the good days feel like good days," David said.

"The bad days are just bad. There's no point trying to make them into something they're not."

"Well, I guess what I'm trying to say is that you can't appreciate a really good day unless you've had some really bad days."

"If you say so."

"And, if you're having a bad day, you can always look forward to having a good day in the future, because fortunately, not every day is important."

And thus, David inched along in an attempt to comfort Julia, without letting on that he knew about her cancer. Julia, for her part, thought David was talking about himself—that his top-secret job opportunity hadn't panned out, and this was his way of rationalizing his failure. "The flowers were a nice thought," Julia said, "but we shouldn't be wasting the money."

— — —

"We have just received clearance from the Pentagon," one of the military brass announced.

"Please enlighten us then," Dr. Miller said.

"Doctor, General Gerber will present an overview of our activities in the region."

The general made a contemptuous scan of the audience. "Dr. Miller, first let me say, this is not normal military protocol—to discuss top secret military activities among civilians."

"This is not an exercise, General. People are dying, and we intend to get to the bottom of it."

"I understand your concern, Doctor, but it is my duty to inform our audience of the highly confidential nature of this information. National security is at stake. Anything discussed henceforth shall be considered top secret."

"General, we get your drift."

Jerome's daydream came to an abrupt halt at the words *top secret*. "Man, this is real shit goin' on here." Jerome took a new interest in the words emanating from the men's room loudspeaker.

General Gerber continued, "The military currently has no active bases in the state of Minnesota. However, during the past several years, the air force has conducted training exercises throughout the midwestern sector from Grand Forks, Ellsworth, and Peterson Air Force Bases."

"And what has been the nature of those exercises, General?"

"For the most part, combat readiness training—mock battles, refueling, countermeasures."

"And what would the *other* part be?" Miller asked.

"Eighteen months ago, the air force participated in Project Blue Rain, a CIA-directed operation to test dispersal rates for VX nerve agent distributed from aircraft. For the sake of the test, a deactivated version of VX was used. We received assurances from weapons development that this version of VX posed no health risks and could only be detected by our ground-based sensors."

"And where, may I ask, was the test conducted, General?"

General Gerber hesitated. "Minneapolis, Denver, and Kansas City."

"General Gerber, I'm not one to jump to conclusions, but doesn't it strike you as interesting that these are the same three cities where we are experiencing a cancer crisis?"

"'Coincidence' is the word I prefer, Doctor, until all the facts are in."

"I suggest we assign a task group to oversee some tests on this deactivated VX," Miller ordered. "It appears that Minneapolis was the first of these areas to exhibit the cancer cluster, so we will concentrate our investigative efforts there first."

A CDC researcher approached Miller and whispered something to him.

"I understand that we now have correlated address data on the Minneapolis cancer patients," Miller announced. "These are patients who have been diagnosed within the past six months."

Miller motioned to the display technicians. "Could we bring up a map of Minneapolis, please, and overlay the patient addresses? Thank you."

A detailed map of the city of Minneapolis appeared on one of the plasma displays. Clusters of red dots began to appear across the map, indicating the home addresses of the cancer patients. Gradually, they filled in, thousands of them, forming a red mass that spread across the city. When the last dots appeared, there was silence in Room 99. The doctors, researchers, military, and intelligence officials all stared at the big screen in the same state of bewilderment. The cancer cluster formed a giant ring around the city of Minneapolis.

— — —

Jerome finally extricated himself from the stall in the men's room without being noticed. He waited until the meeting was over to make his exit. His legs were sore from holding them up against the toilet stall door for so long. He opened his locker and hung up his blue coveralls. A photo of Jerome's new friend Catherine, and one of his mother, hung on the back of the locker door. He changed into his street clothes, passed through security, and boarded city bus 313 to Southside.

Jerome lived with his mother and sister in Atlanta's Southside neighborhood. His mother Coretta worked as a cashier at Walgreens. "A job brings you joy," she said. "No job is too low to make you happy."

"But I'm just pushin' a broom," Jerome replied.

"You're working for the Centers for Disease Control, Jerome! You're working for the US federal government. You got yourself a job that makes a difference for people!"

But Jerome knew it was the doctors, the researchers, the folks with the education who really made a difference at the CDC. His was the kind of work that wasn't even noticed—unless it wasn't done right. Then he'd catch hell from the supervisor.

"Don't you play yourself down, Jerome," Coretta said. "You got a good head on your shoulders, and what's more, you got a good heart."

Jerome sat at the computer in the living room while his mother cooked dinner. "Your sister's gonna be home soon, so don't get too busy there."

"Yes, Ma," Jerome sighed.

Jerome's mind flashed back to Room 99. There was some serious shit going on there, he thought, something about a cancer epidemic. Jerome opened up his web browser, typed the words *cancer epidemic*, and clicked search. A list of websites appeared in front of him. The very first one was from a site called Cancer Blog. Jerome clicked on it, and a recent message posted to the site appeared in front of him:

BirdsEyeView: Is anyone familiar with the cancer situation in Minneapolis? There seems to be a cancer epidemic, although the authorities are denying it.

Jerome froze in his chair. This had to be the same thing he heard about over the men's room loudspeaker, he thought. The apartment door opened, and his sister Felicia came inside. Jerome quickly closed the browser window and got up off the chair.

"Hey, bro," Felicia said. "Whatever you just stopped doing, you probably shouldn't be doing."

"I wasn't doing anything."

"You're not a very good liar, Jerome."

"Well, it ain't none of your business, anyway."

Spicy fragrances wafted from the kitchen. "Welcome home, Felicia. Now y'all get your hands washed for dinner," Coretta hollered.

The three of them sat around a small kitchen table. Coretta closed her eyes. "Bless this bounty you have brought us, oh Lord, and make us thankful. Amen."

Jerome quietly ate his dinner and thought about the person who asked about the cancer epidemic in Minneapolis. Cancer is no picnic, he knew. His dad had died from it.

"You must have something on your mind, Jerome," Coretta said. "You're quiet as a mouse."

"He's been sending love notes," Felicia said.

"No, I ain't!"

"Jerome's a grown boy. He can have his privacy."

Jerome put down his fork. "Ma, if you knew somebody who was sick, and you knew stuff that could help, would you help them even if it was against the law?"

Coretta looked up from her dinner, her eyes speaking like the inscription on a great monument. "If you can help someone, you *always* help, no matter what. Just think of all those Jewish families during the holocaust. There were laws that said you couldn't help them, and millions died. You always help your neighbor, no matter who it is, no matter what the law says. That is God's way."

— — —

While Julia cooked dinner, David went to the den and sat down at the computer. He couldn't believe that the Minneapolis cancer epidemic, if it really existed, had escaped the notice of the press. *Maybe Wilson is right*, he thought. *Maybe it just has the appearance of an epidemic because more people are talking about it.* David scanned the news headlines on his web browser. One particular headline caught his attention: "Remember Raves? Now It's Swarms."

David began reading ...

Remember "raves," those drug-induced gatherings out on the desert? Well, say welcome to the super-rave, also known as a "swarm." Swarms tend to happen closer to town. The leader, always a female, selects a time and location, and the word quickly spreads—thanks to cell phones and texting. Swarmers pack themselves together, using as little real estate as possible. Physical contact is what it's all about. Three hundred swarmers recently occupied a street corner in Minneapolis. "It's a chance to touch and smell other human beings without getting anybody mad at you," said one swarmer. "It opens up new possibilities."

A new window popped up on David's screen—an invitation to receive an instant message. It was from someone using the screen name "MisterClean." David wondered who that could be. He clicked connect to begin the conversation.

MisterClean: saw your message on cancer site

David typed a quick response.

BirdsEyeView: have you heard of this?
MisterClean: you're on the right track. something is going on for sure

"This guy sounds as though he knows something." David typed another message.

BirdsEyeView: are you a doctor?
MisterClean: no, but I know people at cdc

"Holy shlt," David whispered. "The CDC is involved in this?" David frantically typed another message.

BirdsEyeView: any idea what the cause is?
MisterClean: could be military, not sure. denver and kc got it too
BirdsEyeView: why are hospitals playing dumb?
MisterClean: govt rules
BirdsEyeView: anything else you know?
MisterClean: yeah. sick people live in a big ring around the city. strange.

David's jaw dropped. *This can only mean one thing,* he thought. *The cancer is related to the circle dance. And if the circle dance is connected to honeybees, there might be a connection between honeybees and the cancer.* David sent off another message.

BirdsEyeView: i've seen the big ring too. tell cdc to look at honeybees.
MisterClean: will do

Julia screamed from the stairs, "You must come to your son's room immediately." Her voice had an urgency reserved for emergencies. David sprang up the stairs.

Jamie sat on his bed, holding a 22-caliber pistol. Pictures of political figures, famous athletes, and celebrities graced his bedroom walls—with bull's-eyes taped to each of them. Julia cowered in the hallway.

"Jamie," David gently inquired, "can I take a look at your gun? It looks like a real nice one."

Jamie threw a vacant smile in David's direction and took a two-handed aim at a picture of the president. "Bang!" he said, pretending to pull the trigger.

"It's my turn. Let me try it, Jamie," David coaxed.

"Die, Mr. President, die!"

"My turn, Jamie."

Jamie gazed at David again, trying to get a fix on his intentions. David smiled at him.

"Okay, your turn," Jamie said in a child's voice and handed the pistol to David.

David deftly slid the gun into his pants pocket. "We'll have to continue our game later because dinner is almost ready. Time to wash our hands."

Jamie walked to the bathroom.

"Where in God's name did he get *that*?" Julia whispered.

"Who knows? Probably from school."

"What is going on with our son? Why is he so focused on violence?"

"I don't know," David said.

"This is not like Jamie. He's always had a gentle soul. Something is changing him into—"

"—a killer bee," David said, flashing back to Hadley.

"A what?"

"A killer bee. It's just a figure of speech. Killer bees will attack without being provoked."

"Tomorrow we are getting that boy into therapy."

— — —

It was still dark outside when Jerome got off the bus at the CDC. He passed through security, donned his blue coveralls, and took the elevator up to the eighth floor where his floor-polishing machine awaited. Jerome had honed his floor-polishing skills to perfection under the watchful eye of Abraham Brown, the maintenance supervisor. Controlling the polishing machine was like playing a musical instrument—"Only certain people have the feel for it," Abraham had told him—and Jerome was a prodigy. A slight push downward on the handle and the polisher glided to the right. An upward lift and the polisher moved to the left. Working backward down the hallway, Jerome buffed the white tile floor to a spit shine gloss. "Very nice," Abraham said as he did his morning rounds.

Jerome watched Abraham get onto the elevator, and the elevator doors closed. Jerome polished a few more yards of hallway and paused next to an office door. A sign on the door read, "Dr. Charles Miller, Executive Director." Jerome pulled a small white envelope from his pocket and slid it under the door.

Outside, Dr. Miller navigated his silver Mercedes-Benz sedan through the CDC main entrance. He paused at the security booth and held up his ID. The gate opened, and Miller drove into the executive parking garage.

Miller emerged from the elevator at the eighth floor, accompanied by two assistants. They walked purposefully down the gleaming white hallway. "Please tell Dr. Sanchez I want to see him right away," Miller instructed. "And we want to get that VX sample into testing as soon as possible."

Miller entered his office and sat down at his desk, but didn't notice the small white envelope on the floor right away. Dr. Sanchez appeared in the doorway. "Good morning, Bob," Miller said. "Please come in."

Sanchez already had the sleeves of his blue button-down rolled up, and his shirt pocket carried an arsenal of pens and mechanical pencils. "What do you make of it, Doctor?"

Miller leaned back in his high-back chair. "It's the strangest thing I've ever seen. I asked the guys in statistics to recheck their data. There were no errors. That big cancer ring around Minneapolis really exists."

"Reminds me of the Hocksburg case," Sanchez said.

"Hocksburg?"

"Delvin Hocksburg, the serial killer whose victims lived in a geographic pattern that formed his initials."

"Oh yes, I remember. It turned into a virtual board game between him and the FBI. But it's hard to imagine cancer could be induced in such a precise way. My money is still on the military. I've ordered cancer patient address data for Denver and Kansas City, on the outside chance we might see something similar there too."

Sanchez opened a folder on his lap. "Last night, I did a bit of research into naturally occurring ring-like infections."

"Interesting idea," Miller said.

"Of course, we're talking about a very different scale. First, there's the red-ring nematode that infects palm trees. Then we have necrotic ring spot that occurs in turf grass. And finally, ringworm fungal infection in the human population. They all occur in a ring pattern, generally leaving the central region unaffected."

"There is no precedent for a cancer cluster of this kind," Miller said, tapping a pencil against his note pad.

"Perhaps the cancer is a secondary response to something else. What all these ring infections have in common is that they begin in a specific location and quickly move outward to create a defensive perimeter. I suggest we take a look at the center of that cancer ring."

"I want you to fly out there this afternoon and take a look around. I'll get you the map coordinates on the center of that ring."

"I've already got them. Looks like it's a park—Theodore Wirth Park."

"Not a word of this leaves this office, Bob. We're going to stay completely under the radar. I want to get to the bottom of it before the Pentagon boys go in and sanitize things."

"Yes, sir."

"Report directly to me when you get out there."

— — —

A black Ford Expedition with a Midwest Power & Light logo on the door pulled up in front of Max's Diner. The driver pressed a speed dial button on his cell phone. The line rang a couple of times, and a voice answered, "Authenticate."

"Preston four-two-two-seven," the driver replied.

"Target is fourth from left."

"Got it." The driver put the cell phone in his pocket and climbed out of the SUV. His bright yellow coveralls caught Sue's attention when he opened the door.

Sue turned to show off her best angle. "Hey there, good lookin'."

The man in yellow nodded in her direction and took a seat at the counter.

"I gotta find my sunglasses," Sue said, as she poured his coffee. "There's no missin' you, that's for sure."

"That's power company issue," the man said. "They got us all lookin' like rubber duckies up there on the big towers."

"You work up on those things?"

"Yeah, but I make a point of not lookin' down."

"I'm Sue," she said.

"Sam Preston," he replied, extending a hand. "Nice place ya got here."

The door opened, and David walked in.

"Hey there, good lookin'," Sue said.

"Hey, Sue." David took his usual stool, fourth from the left, right next to Sam Preston.

"David, meet Sam Preston," Sue said. "He's with the electric company, works on the big towers."

"Pleasure," David said.

Preston gave him a nod.

"Live around here?" David asked.

"No. Midwest Power brought me in from back east to do some line maintenance."

"Really? All the way from back east?"

"Not too many guys out here are certified to do the airborne work."

"Airborne work?"

"Choppers. We do most of the line maintenance from choppers."

"Really?"

"They hang me outside the chopper in a harness, and I do my thing. After a while, it just becomes routine."

"I'd be worried about the chopper hitting one of those wires."

"We got the best pilots around, ex-marines."

David shook his head in amazement.

"What do *you* do?" Preston asked.

"I worked for a marketing company until a few months ago. Since then, I've been lookin'."

"I'm sure somethin' will break for ya."

"Well, in a way, it already has."

"How's that?"

"I've invented something," David said.

"Anything you can talk about?"

"It has to do with altering people's perception. That's the short version."

"Hope I get to hear the long version someday." Preston took his last sip of coffee and dropped two dollars on the counter. "Well, I got a date with a helicopter. See ya next time."

"Yeah, take care," David said.

"You come back now," Sue said.

Preston smiled. "You can count on it."

David reached into his pocket for some change and realized that Jamie's pistol was still there from the night before.

"You wouldn't catch me up on those towers," Sue said.

"That makes two of us," David said. He gulped his coffee and headed for the door. "Have a good one, Sue."

"You too, honey."

David slid out the door and climbed into his car. He checked to make sure the coast was clear and then pulled the gun from his pocket and slid it inside the glove compartment.

— — —

The door to office 109 opened, and Jack Wilson's haggard face hung in the doorway. "Jack, are you okay?" David asked.

"Just a little tired," Wilson replied.

"I need to talk to you. There has been a development."

"Come in."

"After we talked about the possibility of a cancer epidemic, I made a few calls."

Wilson stroked a magpie feather. "Go on."

"I called the health department to see if they knew anything. They gave me a blanket answer, something like 'nothing of this nature has been reported.' That's all they said. It was like they didn't really want to talk about it."

"You probably just caught someone when they were busy."

"Well, then I called one of the hospitals, and would you believe it, they gave me the exact same answer—'Nothing of this nature has been reported.'"

Wilson's face began to tighten.

"After that, I called another hospital and got connected to oncology. Guess what? They gave me the same line—'nothing of this nature has been reported.'"

"Protocols," Wilson muttered.

"The nurse was very careful about not telling me anything, so I just got in my car and drove down there. The oncology department looked like an airport terminal."

"The state must be sandbagging," Wilson said.

"Oh, it's much bigger than that. I went on the Internet last night and put a posting on a cancer blog, just to see if anyone had heard about an epidemic in Minneapolis. Within an hour, I got a message from an insider at the CDC. They know about a cancer cluster out here."

Wilson froze.

"And here's the weirdest part: the CDC has mapped the addresses of the cancer patients. The addresses form a giant ring around Minneapolis. Sounds familiar, doesn't it?"

"The dance," Wilson whispered. "The Earth Mother is trying to tell us something."

"They think it might be related to something the military has been up to, but they're not sure."

Wilson closed his eyes. Something came to him that he had forgotten. "Wovoka visited me the other night, in a dream. It was as real as our conversation is right now. He told me a story about how the soul of the buffalo became part of the soul of humankind when the buffalo were killed off by the white man. Wovoka said this was nature's way of making humankind remember their mistakes."

"I had a dream too," David recalled. "I spoke to my grandfather, Albert. He died twenty years ago. He knew I had made a discovery. He told me to remember that everything is connected. As he was leaving, he said, 'Remember the buffalo.' I had no idea what he meant by that."

"We are both part of the dance," Wilson said.

"Really?"

"The Indians often had conversations with dead relatives while performing the ghost dance. There are probably many people having similar dreams in Minneapolis. We are all part of the dance."

— — —

Julia sat alone in the examination room. The floor felt cool against her bare feet. There was a knock on the door, and Dr. Austin entered. "Good morning, Julia." "How are you feeling?"

"Still a little shell-shocked."

"That's completely understandable. It takes time to adjust. How is David taking it?"

"Well, actually, he doesn't know yet."

Dr. Austin took off his glasses.

"I just haven't been able to tell him. He's had so much bad news lately. He'd be crushed."

"You're going to need his support, Julia."

"There are just so many things going on right now. We found Jamie in his room last night with a gun. We have no idea where he got it. Jamie's been moving in a very strange direction. He's gone from being a thoughtful, gentle kid to a kid obsessed with violence and killing."

"Some of that could be developmental. Most boys play army in the backyard at some point."

"Yes, I know—with toy guns. This was a real one. Fortunately, it wasn't loaded. He was taking aim at pictures of famous people on his wall."

"That might be a cause for concern. You should get him in to see someone."

"Yes, we're working on it."

"But back to your health, Julia." Dr. Austin opened a file folder on his lap. "I've received a recommendation from oncology. The news is not all bad."

Julia held her breath.

"They are recommending a lumpectomy followed by chemotherapy. The perimeter biopsies all came up negative, so it appears that we may have caught this at a very early stage."

Julia felt a wave of fresh air fall over her. "Thank God."

"It looks as if you'll be able to keep your breast. Of course, chemotherapy is no picnic. You have some work ahead of you. You're going to need David's support."

"Yes, I know," Julia said, wondering how she would break the news to him.

— — —

David drove toward his house, thinking about what Wilson had said—that he and David were part of the dance, that the dreams they had were no coincidence. He turned on the car radio. A local talk show was under way:

"We're opening things up today, folks. The lines are open for anything you'd like to talk about. Call us at 666-7979 and let us know what's on your mind. Hey, that's kinda catchy, isn't it?"

David pulled out his cell phone and dialed the number.

"Welcome to *Talk Line*. You're on the air. What's on your mind?"

"My name is David. I spoke with my grandfather in a dream the other night. He died twenty years ago. The thing about this dream was we were really talking to each other. He knew things about me, things that have happened recently. I'm curious if anyone else out there has had a similar experience."

"That's an interesting one, David. So, how about it, folks? Anyone else out there been visiting with deceased relatives?"

The radio host's telephone lit up like a Christmas tree.

"Wow. We seem to have hit a nerve with that one. Let's hear from Tammy in Minneapolis. Go ahead, Tammy."

"I had a dream like that just the other night. I had a long conversation with a woman named Charlotte Thomas. I had no idea who she was, but she seemed to know a lot about me. I mentioned

EIGHT

A SMALL WHITE ENVELOPE on the floor caught Charles Miller's attention. Inside, he found a piece of paper with a message scrawled across it:

Check honeybees in Minneapolis.

Could this have something to do with the cancer cluster? he wondered. *And who could have left it?* His thoughts were interrupted by the voice of his secretary on the intercom.

"Dr. Miller, it's Dr. Sanchez on your private line."

"Thank you." Miller lifted the receiver. "Bob, what have you got?"

"I headed straight to Wirth Park when I got out here. Interesting spot. The park is pretty much wide open, except for one huge oak tree in the middle. I walked around a little, and when I got near the tree, I noticed the ground was covered with dead bees—honeybees, I believe. Never seen anything like it."

"You don't say."

"Tens of thousands of them."

"That's very interesting," Miller said.

"And here's the weird part," Sanchez continued. "The bees were arranged in a large ring around the base of the tree. Looks like somebody put them there."

Miller picked up the little note on his desk. "Something is going on here, Bob. No question about it."

"I'll bring back some dead bees for testing," Sanchez said.

"Good idea. The state of Minnesota has an entomology lab in Minneapolis. I want you to go and pay them a visit. See what you can find out."

"Will do. I'll check in with you later."

"Thanks, Bob."

Dead honeybees, Miller thought. *Maybe this is related to the VX testing. But even if it is, how could it have anything to do with cancer in humans?* Miller gazed at the little message in front of him. *Yes, indeed*, he thought. *I think we may want to look into the honeybee situation in Minneapolis.*

— — —

Hadley bit into his sandwich just as Bob Sanchez entered the entomology lab. "And what can I do for you?" Hadley sputtered.

"My name is Dr. Sanchez. I'm with the federal government."

"You guys are back again?"

"Again?"

"Yeah, there was a guy here just a couple days ago. Don't remember his name."

"Did he mention who he was with?"

"Advanced weapon systems, I think he said. Very hush-hush."

"I see. What exactly was he here for?"

Hadley hesitated until Sanchez pulled out his CDC credential. "The guy just wanted to shoot some video of the observation hives. That's all."

"What do you make of the situation at Wirth Park?"

"There's a situation? What situation?" Hadley stammered.

"They've got a lot of dead honeybees out there."

"What's a lot?"

"Enough to cover a quarter-acre," Sanchez said.

Hadley dropped his sandwich. "Something must have set off their cancer gene," he muttered.

"Cancer gene?"

"Yeah, our guys discovered it recently. It's like a built-in poison pill. We think they use it to control overpopulation."

"How come we haven't heard about this at the CDC?"

"I guess they haven't published the paper yet."

— — —

Julia arrived home unexpectedly.

"What are you doing home?" David asked.

"We need to talk."

"You're right about that."

The telephone rang, interrupting Julia. "Hello. Yes, I plan to be back by fourth period."

Julia placed a pile of mail on the counter.

David made a quick scan of the mail. It was mostly bills and credit card come-ons. At the bottom of the pile lay a pamphlet called *Cancer and You* from the doctor's office.

"See you later, then. Good-bye." Julia hung up.

David placed the cancer pamphlet onto the top of the mail pile. "You have cancer, don't you?" he said.

"You knew?"

"I just thought you might, because so many other people do."

"What are you talking about?"

"The city-wide epidemic—the cancer epidemic."

"There's no epidemic. What are you talking about?"

"Actually, there is an epidemic. I got it confirmed by an insider at the CDC."

"And this is no doubt a source to be trusted. What is this person's name?"

"Well, I only know his online name, which is 'MisterClean.'"

Julia rolled her eyes. "I rest my case. Look, David, you have got to get back to reality. There is no epidemic. It is your wife, Julia, who has breast cancer. That's what is really happening."

"How serious is it?"

"It could be worse. They don't think it's spread yet. They're going to do a lumpectomy and then chemo."

"Thank God."

"At this point, I'm more worried about Jamie than the cancer."

"I'm working on Jamie's problem—on the cause of it. He may be more like a killer bee than I had imagined."

"What's that supposed to mean?"

"I don't completely understand it yet, so I can't explain it."

"There you go again, off in space. Let me know when you're back on Earth. I have to get back to school."

"I'm sorry. Let me know if I can do anything."

"Thank you." Julia drifted out the door.

Thank God she isn't worse, David thought. "There are so many things going on right now. I have to stay on track. There are questions that need to be answered. I have to figure out what's going on with Jamie."

To David, Jamie's behavior seemed way out of character; he had always been a gentle kid. David knew that this had to be more than just developmental. Something was affecting Jamie—something beyond Jamie's control.

David went up to Jamie's bedroom to see if he might find any clues. The tidiness of the room startled him. Jamie's books, clothes, and belongings were organized with military precision—a far cry from the way the room usually looked. The bull's-eyes had been removed from the celebrity photos. A folded note lay on the bed with "Jamie" written on it. David unfolded the note and read it:

Jamie,

I know you're going through a lot these days. We've all had a difficult time with Dad being out of work. I just want to let you know that no matter what happens, we love you.

Love,
Mom

"Julia must have cleaned up the room," David surmised. "She probably did it to make Jamie feel better about things."

A spiral notebook lay on Jamie's desk. David opened the cover, and the first page brimmed with math equations, as did the next several pages. But midway into the notebook, David found something altogether different: the pages were completely filled with carefully drawn interlocking hexagons—at least twenty pages of them. David flipped through page after page. The drawings were strangely reminiscent of the observation hives at the state entomology lab. Jamie had been drawing honeycombs.

Could it be, David wondered, *or is this just an interesting coincidence?* He thought of the story of the buffalo, and how the buffalo's soul was passed onto humans. Is it possible that honeybee behavior somehow got transferred to humans? It was time to talk to Wilson again.

— — —

Technicians prepared to go live in the CDC teleconference room. Dr. Miller sat in front of the television camera and arranged his notes on the table in front of him. "Dr. Miller, we'll be live with the White House in five seconds ... four, three, two ..."

"Good afternoon, Mr. President."

"What's the latest, Charles?"

"There have been some developments in Minneapolis. The data is not all in, but it appears that we are dealing with a superinfection."

"Now, what do we mean by that?" the president asked.

"Imagine a small infection on your skin. Now magnify that infection, so each skin cell is a human being, and the infection covers five hundred square miles. That's the kind of thing we have here."

"This sounds like science fiction, Charles. What about that big ring around the city? How the hell do I explain *that* to the American people?"

"Ring-like infections are not uncommon in nature. We've just never seen one take the form of a human superinfection."

"Charles, if I go to the American people with this, we are going to have mass hysteria on our hands. Minneapolis will be a ghost town, not to mention Denver and Kansas City."

"Mr. President, my recommendation is to keep everything on the QT until we know exactly what we're dealing with here. I have full cooperation from the Minneapolis medical community."

"The boys at the CIA are sleeping kinda light over this. Do you think the VX could be involved?"

"Probably not directly, but we might be looking at some sort of chain reaction. Too early to tell."

"Charles, I want you to update me as soon as you know more."

"Will do, Mr. President."

— — —

David knocked on Wilson's office door. He faintly heard Wilson's voice on the telephone. A door across the hall from Wilson's opened, and a man wearing a suit and glasses emerged and headed down the hall. David noticed that the man had an unusual gait. Something about him seemed familiar. Finally, Wilson's door opened. "Do you know that guy?" David asked.

"That's Dr. Schwab, a visiting professor from NYU," Wilson replied. "Just arrived a few days ago."

"I thought I knew him from somewhere. Probably just a coincidence."

"Come in," Wilson said.

"I was thinking about what you said about the buffalo."

"What about them?"

"Do you think the same thing could be happening with honeybees?"

"How do you mean?" Wilson asked.

"Could the soul of the honeybee be passed over to humans, in the same way as soul of the buffalo?"

Wilson stroked his eagle feather. "It's an interesting idea but unlikely. For one thing, the honeybee is not native to North America. The white man brought the honeybee here from Europe. The Indians called it the white man's fly."

"I was just wondering if it is possible that honeybee behavior could be passed over to humans."

Wilson smiled sympathetically. "David, there is no question that honeybees are somehow connected to the dance. Either they caused it, or they are part of it. But I think we need a lot more evidence to conclude that bee behavior is being passed to humans. It is a beautiful theory but probably impossible to prove."

"It was just an idea," David said.

— — —

Charles Miller dialed a number on his desk telephone, and a woman answered. "Laboratory. Michelle speaking."

"Michelle, this is Dr. Miller. I need to speak to Dr. Murray."

"Right away, Dr. Miller. I'll get him for you."

"Dr. Murray here."

"Dr. Murray, this is Dr. Miller."

"Yes, sir."

"Have you started the tests on the deactivated VX?" Miller asked.

"The samples just arrived this afternoon. We'll begin testing tomorrow morning."

"Good. I'd like you to do something else for me."

"What's that?"

"I'd like you to run a deactivated VX exposure test with live honeybees."

"Honeybees?" Murray asked.

"That's correct. Try a concentration similar to the ground concentrations in the CIA tests. Let me know if you see anything at all, mortality rates, anything."

"We should be able to secure some bees by tomorrow afternoon. We'll get right on it."

"And Dr. Murray, one more thing. No one but you and me knows about this test. Disguise it as something else if you need to."

"Yes, sir, Dr. Miller. I'll contact you directly as soon as I have results."

"Thank you."

— — —

The idea of Jamie's behavior being derived from killer bees was intriguing, but David needed more proof. He sat down at his computer and opened up the satellite video. The dance gracefully rotated in front of him. David located his neighborhood in the image and clicked on it. The image magnified. He clicked several more times, until his block filled the screen. He clicked on his house, and four yellow dots became visible inside it. Three of the yellow dots floated serenely, but the fourth one moved in a unique way—with a peculiar oscillation. David knew from Its location in the house that it had to be Jamie. *Could this be a sign?* he wondered.

David recalled that he hadn't yet experimented with the killer bee video he shot at the state entomology lab. So he went to work on it. He processed the video the same way he had processed the regular honeybee video, using the same time synthesis technique. But when he played it, the magic wasn't there. The killer bees weren't doing a circle dance. There were no hidden patterns at all.

David studied the killer bee video more closely. He zoomed in on individual bees, looking for anything that might distinguish them from ordinary honeybees. That's when he saw it: the same peculiar oscillation he'd seen in Jamie. "There it is," he said. "My God, all of the killer bees are doing it." David had found the killer bee signature.

While the pieces seemed to fit together, there were still unanswered questions. Why Jamie? And who else was singled out to receive this killer bee behavior, he wondered? David scanned the satellite video, looking for other signs of the killer bee signature. He scanned the houses on the streets around his, but only Jamie's heat signature oscillated in that particular way.

Then, three streets away, at the corner of Oak and Second Avenue, David found what he was looking for. The house on that corner had two people inside, and one of them moved the same unique way that Jamie did.

"I'll be out for a few minutes," David said as he passed Julia in the kitchen.

David walked over to Second Avenue and proceeded to the corner of Oak. The house on the corner—number 201 Oak—was a small 1950s ranch, set back from the sidewalk and bordered by a cedar hedge. A break in the hedge allowed a limited view of the front door and porch. The rest of the house was well hidden. David paused on the sidewalk and tried to get a good look at the house through the narrow opening.

The front door flew open and a hulk of a man jumped out onto the porch. "You got business here?"

David stepped back. "Sorry, I must have the wrong house."

"You sure as hell do," the man thundered. "If I see you around here again, I'll break your arm."

"Sorry, my mistake," David said, retreating up the sidewalk.

The man went back inside and slammed the door.

No question about it, David thought. *There is a killer bee living at* that *address.* He hustled straight home to his computer.

David knew there was someone else living at that house on Oak Street. He could see someone else in the satellite image. "I wonder who lives there?" he said. David typed "201 Oak Street, Minneapolis MN" into his web browser and clicked search. A name, address, and telephone number appeared on the screen:

Anne Hoepner
201 Oak Street
Minneapolis, MN 55450
612-588-3307

"That guy must be her boyfriend," David theorized. *But what if she doesn't know about his tendencies*, David thought, *his real potential for violence? She could be in serious trouble.* David stared at Anne Hoepner's telephone number. "I'll try calling her later, when hopefully the boyfriend isn't around." He jotted her number on a scrap of paper.

— — —

Julia wiped down the counter, even though she'd already wiped it down once—anything to keep herself busy. "I go into surgery the day after tomorrow."

"I can take you," David said.

"That's okay. Marsha has already volunteered. She's got the day off. They said the operation would last less than an hour. Then I come right home."

"What about the kids?"

"I'd rather tell them afterward. I don't want them to worry."

"I think I know what's wrong with Jamie," David said.

"Really."

"It's actually related to the cancer epidemic."

"David, for the last time, there is no cancer epidemic."

"We're picking up bee behaviors, all of us. The cancer is part of it."

"David, my cancer has nothing to do with bees. It's probably the result of some kind of industrial pollution. I'm making amends for our modern lifestyle."

"Don't you see? People are acting more and more like bees, losing their individuality."

"What I see, David, is that you are spending way too much time inside your head. You need to join the real world again."

"The real world doesn't see it yet," David said.

The doorbell rang. David thought it might be the UPS man or the Jehovah's Witnesses. He'd seen them canvassing the neighborhood. He opened the front door to a very different sight. Tony Marchetti, a well-known mob figure around Minneapolis, a guy who looked right out of central casting for *The Godfather*, stood on David's doorstep clutching Jamie's upper arm. "Did you lose this?" he asked.

Jamie looked like a helpless kid standing next to Mr. Marchetti. Marchetti's son sat alone in the back of the car with a black eye.

"Jamie, what's going on here?"

"Yes, what is going on here?" Julia butted in. She grabbed Jamie's arm and pulled him inside.

"I went to pick up my kid at school, and I found Rocky Marciano, here, pounding my kid right in front of everybody."

"I'm sure something must have provoked him," Julia said.

"Or not," David said, thinking out loud.

"Well, whatever it was, your son made a bad choice."

"Did he apologize to your son?" Julia asked.

"Oh yeah, we took care of that, but I can't be responsible for repercussions."

"Repercussions?" David said.

"Do you know who I am, Mr. Peters?"

"Yes, you're a well-known figure in these parts, Mr. Marchetti."

"I have many friends in the area. There are people who might not like the idea that a Marchetti was pounded in the schoolyard. This is really out of my control."

Katie trotted up to the front porch, just home from school. She looked up at Mr. Marchetti. "Hey, you're Tony Marchetti, the Mafia guy, aren't you? I've seen your picture in the paper. You look better in real life."

Marchetti's jaw dropped.

"You'll have to excuse my daughter, Mr. Marchetti. She hasn't learned the concept of restraint." David yanked Katie inside.

"You're right, young lady," Marchetti said, "except for the Mafia part. That part's fiction."

"Well, thank you for bringing Jamie home, Mr. Marchetti. No disrespect was meant to you or your family, I'm sure." David extended his hand, but Marchetti pretended not to notice it.

Julia pushed Jamie toward the doorway. "I'm sorry, sir," Jamie said.

Marchetti scowled at Jamie, turned, and walked back to his car. David closed the front door.

"Why was Tony Marchetti here?" Katie asked.

"None of your business," Jamie said.

Julia trembled. "Oh my God, Jamie. What has gotten into you?"

"Do you believe me now?" David said.

"Is that all you can think about, your silly theories? This is not about you, David. It's about our son!"

"What's going on?" Katie asked.

"I know just what he needs," David said. "Just hang on." David went into the kitchen and rummaged through the drawers until he found an old box of incense. He placed a piece of incense on a coffee saucer and lit it. A swirl of fragrant smoke rose toward the ceiling. "It's an old beekeepers' trick," David said. "Smoke calms them right down."

Julia rolled her eyes.

"What's Dad doing?" Katie asked.

David pulled the cabinet doors open. "How's our honey supply? Jamie needs to be on a daily dose of honey. Bees become less agitated when they have plenty of honey."

"What is Dad talking about?" Jamie asked.

"Your dad thinks you're turning into a bee," Julia said.

"Well, not exactly turning into one, but picking up some bee behaviors."

Jamie's brow wrinkled. "I'm acting like a bee?"

"It's a long and complicated story," David said. "Right now, we need to do whatever we can to suppress your instincts."

"Whatever," Jamie said.

"Jamie starts his therapy tomorrow," Julia said. "We are not going to waste time with smoke and honey."

Katie ran around the house flapping her arms, "Buzz, buzz, buzz …"

— — —

After dinner, David returned to the den. Anne Hoepner's telephone number lay next to the telephone. David lifted the receiver. *What if the boyfriend answers?* he thought. *I'll just hang up and pretend it's a wrong number. Even if he's got caller ID, there's no way he'll know I'm the guy he saw on the sidewalk.* David dialed the number. After several rings, a woman's voice answered.

"Hi, this is Anne. Sorry I missed your call. Please leave a message, and I'll call you back."

"Hi, Anne. You don't know me, but I wanted to warn you that you might be in danger. Please be careful." David tried to think of something else to say. "Be especially careful around your—" *Beep.* The machine cut David off. "Damn. Well, I guess she'll get the idea."

— — —

Miller's Mercedes-Benz rolled down Interstate 285 under the pink glow of the sodium-vapor highway lights. His cell phone rang.

"Doctor, it's Sanchez here."

"What else have you got, Bob?"

"I went to the state entomology lab. Seems the Pentagon had someone there two days ago—from weapons development."

"But that would have been before our briefing," Miller said.

"Yes, it was."

"I thought DARPA gave up on bees years ago."

"I didn't know they had a bee program, Doctor."

"Honeybees were being trained to sniff out explosives in Afghanistan," Miller said, "but the program got canceled after 9/11."

"There is something even more interesting though."

"What's that?"

"The Minneapolis lab recently uncovered a cancer gene in honeybees. They say it works like a suicide pill, to prevent overpopulation."

"This is news to me," Miller said.

"They said the findings haven't been published yet."

"We will definitely want to run tests on those dead bees you found. The sooner you get back here, the better."

"I also visited two of the larger medical centers here, just to see what things look like. The oncology wards are already running over capacity. I don't know if the protocols will hold up for much longer."

"I want you out of there as soon as possible, Bob."

"Yes, sir. I'll catch the next plane out."

"See you in the morning."

— — —

The morning bustle outside Max's Diner made it seem peaceful inside.

"Hey there, good lookin'," Sue chirped.

"Hi, Sue." David joined his coffee at the counter.

"Got the world figured out yet?"

"The pieces are falling into place," David said. A splash of yellow filled David's peripheral vision.

"Well, if it isn't our high-wire artist," Sue bubbled.

"Hi there, honey," the man in yellow said.

Sue poured his cup. "Always good to see the handsome ones come back again," she said.

"It's Sam Preston, right?" David said.

"And you're the marketing man. I have to admit, though, you're better with names than me."

"It's David Peters," he said, extending a handshake. "How are things going up on the big towers?"

"The weather's been good to us. My chopper pilot doesn't like to be up there if it's blowing more than five knots."

"I can see that," David said.

"How's the job search going?"

"Actually, I've been sidetracked with more important things."

"Oh yeah, you said you'd been working on an invention," Preston said.

"It's more like a discovery."

Preston took a sip of coffee. "Sounds interesting. Can you share any hints? I love this kinda stuff."

"It has to do with seeing things in a new way. You know how time-lapse movies allow us to see plants grow?"

"Yeah."

"Well, this is the next generation of that idea. It allows us to see patterns where we never knew they existed," David said.

"And that led to your discovery?"

"Several discoveries, actually."

"We just made a weird discovery at work," Preston said.

"What's that?"

"Three guys on our crew have come down with cancer in the past few months. I mean, what are the odds of that? They think it might have something to do with exposure to the high-tension lines, but one of them doesn't even work the lines."

David leaned in close. "It's not the high-tension lines. There's a cancer epidemic."

"An epidemic?"

"The health department and the hospitals will deny it if you call them. The government has orchestrated a huge cover-up."

"This is what you discovered?"

"I uncovered it by accident. Someone at the CDC confirmed it."

"So what's causing it?" Preston asked.

"I think it's got something to do with honeybees."

"Honeybees? How did you come up with that?"

"I can't go into the details. There are still questions to be answered, but it looks like bees are involved."

"Wow. The guys on my crew will want to hear about this. They were getting worried about the high-tension lines."

"You might want to keep that under your hard hat," David said. "I wouldn't want you to get in trouble."

"It stays right here," Preston said, tapping his helmet. "Hey, I better get off to the site, or my pilot will be wondering. Good talking to you, David."

"Yeah, see ya 'round," David said, lifting his cup. Preston stood up and lumbered toward the door. He had an unusual gait, favoring his left side. *Probably an old injury*, David thought.

— — —

"You can go in now," the receptionist said to Jamie.

Jamie stood up and approached the open office door. An engraved sign on it read, "Daniel Goldberg, PhD."

"Please come right in, Jamie. I'm Dr. Goldberg. Make yourself comfortable." Dr. Goldberg closed the door and sat on a leather chair near his desk. "How about that one right there," he said, pointing to a large stuffed chair nearby.

Jamie took a quick inventory of the room while Dr. Goldberg made a few preparatory notes on his yellow pad. The office was very quiet. Jamie could hear Goldberg's pencil moving across the yellow paper. Dr. Goldberg had a degree of imperfection about him that appealed to Jamie. His neatly trimmed beard didn't quite hide the acne scars of his youth. He was dressed more like a college student than a doctor. His eyes were dark but friendly.

"Is this your first time to a therapist, Jamie?"

"Yeah."

"Why do you think you're here?"

"I guess I hit a couple of guys."

"Why do you suppose you did that?"

"I don't know. Something just made me do it."

"Do you think you're an angry person?"

"Not really."

"How do you get along with your family?"

"Okay. I get along fine with my mom and dad. My younger sister is a pain sometimes."

"I think we all know someone like that. Do you have some close friends?"

"Sure, I've got a few friends, guys I went to grade school with. They couldn't believe it when I punched Murphy. They thought I lost it."

"Why would they think that?"

"Because messing with Murphy would be like suicide, unless you're a lot bigger than him. He's bigger than most kids in middle school, including me. He likes to mess with people."

"Have you ever thought about suicide?"

"Only once, when Tina Parker dumped me. I dreamed about her coming to my funeral, how cool that would be."

"Yes, Jamie, I think we've all had that dream before. What were you thinking right before you hit Murphy?"

"I wasn't thinking anything. It was like something took over my body and made me run over and hit him. I wasn't even near him before that."

"Who else did you hit?"

"Tony Marchetti Jr. I don't even know the kid. His dad's some kind of Mafia guy. He wasn't too happy about it."

"I think any father wouldn't be too happy about it. Did you have an audience when you hit Tony Marchetti Jr.?"

"An audience?"

"Was there anybody you hoped would see you do it?"

"Not really. I don't even remember doing it. The first thing I remember is riding in the back of Mr. Marchetti's car. He took me home. Before that, I can't remember anything."

"Do you remember Tony Marchetti Jr. looking at you before you hit him?"

"Nope."

Goldberg paused to write on his yellow pad.

"My dad thinks I'm acting like a bee."

"A bee?"

"A honeybee. He thinks smoke and honey will calm me down."

"What kind of smoke?"

"Incense."

"Why do you suppose your dad thinks you're acting like a honeybee?"

"Beats me. It's some kind of theory he's been working on. He thinks I'm picking up bee behavior. My mother thinks he's nuts, though."

"Bee behavior," Goldberg said, as he scrawled the words onto his yellow pad.

NINE

Julia's cell phone rang.

"Julia Peters."

"Mrs. Peters, this is Dr. Goldberg. I met with your son, Jamie, this morning."

"Yes, Dr. Goldberg."

"I'm calling to give you a quick evaluation on Jamie. Is this a good time?"

"Certainly. Go right ahead."

"Jamie appears to be in denial about his aggression and believes that something outside of him is causing his aggressive behavior. He uses a kind of self-induced amnesia to support his story. Usually in cases like this, there is a systemic basis for the aggression, such as an abusive parent. But Jamie says that this is not the case. Is there any reason to think that he might be trying to protect someone at home, someone who might have abused him?"

The air left Julia's lungs. Her mind spun. *David has been acting strangely,* she thought. *What if David's weirdness is a front for something much worse?*

"Mrs. Peters?"

"Sorry, something distracted me here at work. I'm sure Jamie must be telling you the truth. That's just the kind of kid he is."

"He mentioned something about incense and honey."

"That would be his father."

"And adopting the behavior of a honeybee?"

"A killer bee, actually. His father's been developing some kind of crazy theory about humans turning into bees. He's been out of work for a while, so he has a lot of time on his hands."

"I see. Your husband's pursuits aside, I don't think it is particularly beneficial for Jamie to buy into this theory. It only serves to support his belief that something outside of him is responsible for his aggressive behavior."

Julia's mind drifted away again. *David could have come up with this killer bee story to help explain away Jamie's behavior,* she thought, *when he knew damn well it was caused by something else.*

"Are you still there, Mrs. Peters?"

"Yes, I am. From the sounds of it, Dr. Goldberg, perhaps my husband should be the one seeing you."

"I was going to suggest that. If nothing else, it will give me a clearer insight into Jamie's behavior. I suggest that we proceed on that basis."

"If the purpose is to talk about Jamie, I think I can get him to go."

"Have your husband call my secretary to set up an appointment."

"Thank you, Doctor."

— — —

Dr. Miller's secretary adjusted her headset. "Dr. Miller at the CDC calling for General Gerber. Yes, I'll hold."

Miller picked up his telephone. "General, it's Charles Miller."

"What's the latest on our situation?" Gerber asked.

"Things have taken another turn. We have reason to believe that honeybees are involved in this."

"You're pulling my leg."

"No, I'm quite serious, General."

"What could honeybees possibly have to do with it?"

"I was hoping you might be able to tell me something about that," Miller said.

"Me?"

"One of your DARPA guys was sniffing around a state bee lab in Minneapolis prior to our meeting."

"This is news to me," Gerber said. "DARPA gave up on bees right after 9/11. I'm going to make a few calls, and I'll get back to you."

"I'll look forward to that, General."

— — —

Marsha Reeves knocked on Julia's open office door.

"Marsha, come on in. I'm glad you stopped by."

Marsha closed the door behind her. "Are you all set for tomorrow?"

Julia's face dropped. "God, it is tomorrow, isn't it. I've been a preoccupied with Jamie and David."

"What's going on with Jamie?" Marsha asked.

"He's been acting very strangely lately, getting into fights."

"That doesn't sound like Jamie."

"He gave Tony Marchetti Jr. a black eye. Mr. Marchetti delivered Jamie to our front door yesterday."

"Ooo … that's not good. There's bound to be some fallout from that," Marsha said.

"I know. We tried to calm down Mr. Marchetti, but I'm worried for Jamie. It's a matter of honor for the Marchetti clan."

"But Jamie must have been provoked."

"They said he wasn't. Even Jamie says he wasn't."

"You mean he just hit the kid out of the blue?"

"That's what it looks like."

"What about counseling?" Marsha said.

"Jamie went to see Dr. Goldberg this morning."

"Have you heard anything?"

"Yeah. Goldberg wants to meet with David next. He thinks David could be playing a role in this."

"Really."

"I swear, I'm beginning to think I don't even know the person I'm married to," Julia said.

"The secret life of David Peters," Marsha mused. "I'd sure like to be a fly on the wall at that session."

"Not a word of this to anybody," Julia said.

"You know you can count on me, Julia."

— — —

Dr. Goldberg placed a gold pocket watch on the arm of his leather chair. "Do you mind if I call you David?"

"Sure, no problem."

"David, as you know, I have met with your son, Jamie."

"Yes, I know."

"Can you tell me about Jamie? What sort of boy is he, from your point of view?"

"Well, he's a good kid—not a jock or the president of his class or anything like that. He's just an all-around good kid."

"But he's had some trouble lately."

"Yes, he's become aggressive—out of the blue, really."

"Getting into fights?"

"I don't know if I would even call them fights. His actions seem completely unprovoked."

"David, how would you describe *your* relationship with Jamie?"

"Me? Oh, we get along great."

"Have you ever hit your son?"

David winced at the question. "Of course not."

Goldberg made a notation on his yellow pad. "David, describe for me, if you will, your relationship with *your* father."

"My father?"

Goldberg nodded.

"Well, I've never completely connected with my father. He's always had low expectations of me."

"I see you've been out of work for a while."

"I haven't been paid in a while, but I'm working on something fairly important."

"This thing you're working on, do you think it will change your relationship with your father if you're successful?"

"I hadn't really thought of it that way. I guess he would find it interesting, but I'm not doing it for him."

"Who are you doing it for?"

"For humankind, for our future."

"Does the idea of being famous appeal to you?"

"Not if it means being pestered by people for interviews and handouts."

"And taxes," Goldberg added.

"Don't get me started on the government. For all I know, they're listening to our conversation right now."

Goldberg made another notation. "Why would the government be interested in *our* conversation?"

"They'd love to get their hands on my discovery, because of what it will expose."

"I see. Let's get back to Jamie. What do you think is causing *his* problem?"

"I don't completely understand it yet, but I believe he has adopted some killer bee behaviors. He's not alone. There are others."

"How did you arrive at this theory?"

"It's a long story. I may have to write a book."

"Do you often come up with theories about things?"

"I'm a generally curious person. I think there are many things yet to be discovered. You just need to be open to the possibilities."

"But don't you need specialized training to make new discoveries?"

"Science has been chasing its own tail for years. It's time for some fresh ideas."

"I see." Goldberg made a final notation. "I believe you've answered my questions, David. I'll be getting back to your wife with my recommendations for Jamie. Thank you for coming in."

"No problem."

Goldberg placed the gold watch in his pocket.

David left Goldberg's office and climbed into the Honda. Across the street, a man in a black Ford Expedition removed his headphones and started his engine.

— — —

"Hi, Mrs. Peters, it's Dr. Goldberg."

"Did my husband make it in?"

"Yes, he did. I'm going to give you my professional opinion, and then it will be up to you and your husband to decide what to do."

"I understand."

"While it is not entirely clear that your husband is at the root of Jamie's behavior, I am not ready to rule it out. Your husband is exhibiting a mixture of delusional fantasy and mild paranoia. He suffers from delusions of grandeur. He has a grandiose sense of his own capabilities and importance."

Julia stared out the widow at the overgrown lawn.

"These symptoms would be consistent with someone who has been out of work for an extended period. The longer these situations drag on, the more likely it is for the delusions to manifest themselves. Eventually, the delusions can become self-sustaining—a situation where the delusional behavior prevents someone from getting reemployed. In some cases, this can be a point of no return."

"What about Jamie?"

"The root of Jamie's aggression could be due to your husband's suppressed anger over his lack of success. While your husband does not exhibit this anger outwardly, I believe he is deeply concerned about disappointing his own father."

"*His* father?"

"Yes. It is not unusual to have these patterns passed on to the next generation. Jamie may be acting out because he is worried about disappointing David. But at the same time, he may worry that he is destined to repeat David's legacy. Jamie is caught in a catch-22."

"Well, what can we do for him?" Julia asked.

"To be honest, I think it's your husband who needs therapy. If he begins to recognize his limitations, I think his employment prospects will improve, and everything will get back to normal. With these changes, I would not be surprised if Jamie's aggression disappeared altogether."

Julia heard the belching Honda pull into the driveway. "Thank you, Dr. Goldberg. You've been very helpful. I will speak to my husband and get back to you."

— — —

"Dr. Miller, Sanchez here."

"What have you got for me, Bob?"

"When I got back this morning, I dropped the bees from Wirth Park at the lab for postmortems. I asked them to put it on the fast track. The results just came in."

"Find anything?"

"They died of cancer, all right. And it appears that the Minnesota bee lab is right. The cancer was triggered by an internal gene, something the bees have had all along."

"We still don't have a direct connection to the cancer cluster out there, do we?" Miller said. "Do you think these two things could be related?"

"It's really the only thing we've got to go on," Sanchez replied.

Miller tapped his pencil on the desk. "I want you to pursue the superinfection theory, with honeybees as the initial source."

"There is no other path that makes sense," Sanchez said.

"I expect to get patient data from Denver and Kansas City soon. If we find the same situation in those cities—a ring cluster with a million dead honeybees at the center—then we'll have something."

— — —

David turned on the radio in the kitchen. Neil Young was singing, but the DJ cut the song off before the last verse…

"Hey there, music fans. Here's a quick note from the Minneapolis Department of Health. The city will be getting sprayed for mosquitoes tonight, thanks to our Air National Guard. Why do we hate mosquitoes? It's the West Nile virus thing. You've heard of it, and believe me, you don't want to catch it. So keep those windows shut tonight. They swear the stuff is harmless to humans and animals, but shut those windows anyway. And now it's back to more music …"

West Nile, David thought. *Seems like it's a little early in the season for that.* "Did you catch that?"

"Catch what?" Julia replied.

"The Air National Guard is going to spray the city for mosquitoes tonight. We're supposed to keep the windows shut."

"Whatever."

"I haven't even seen any mosquitoes yet," David said.

"I'm sure they have their reasons."

Julia pulled a few ingredients from the cupboard. "David, it looks like we're almost out of honey. I wish you wouldn't give so much of it to Jamie. His teeth are going to rot."

"He needed that honey."

"I know, I know, to keep him from going postal," Julia said.

"Do you have a better solution?"

Julia put down the honey jar and folded her arms in front of her. "Well, actually, I do. I spoke to Dr. Goldberg right after your meeting with him. He believes that you, not Jamie, should be in therapy. He believes Jamie's problems are related to your problems, and that your problems are related to your father."

"My father! Good God."

"I know it must be hard to hear this, David, but you really need to think about Jamie and how this will help him."

David shook his head. "Everyone has it so wrong. Here I am on the verge of something really important, something that will explain Jamie's behavior and a million other things. Sure, I'd love to be working a regular job, but something much bigger than a job has come along, something that could change the world."

"Dr. Goldberg said you suffer from delusions of grandeur. Does that sound familiar?"

"He doesn't see it."

"See what?"

"What I see." David knew it was a hopeless, pointless discussion. "I'm going to go buy some honey."

— — —

David found a spot in the supermarket parking lot and climbed out of his car. He heard a commotion in a small park across the street and walked over to get a closer look. A large group of people had gathered there, several hundred at least. They were all packed together like sardines. The group undulated like a giant sea creature, moving a few feet this way and that. Oohs and ahs erupted each time it changed direction.

David crossed the street and approached the group. When he got close, a girl reached out and pulled him into the mayhem. "You're swarmin', man!" she shouted. Other swarmers quickly enveloped David, pushing him further into the melee. A busty teen pressed her chest against his. She spun him around and was replaced by another girl. He could feel breath on his face, in his ears. The swarm veered a few feet to the left, then to the right. David didn't need to move his legs—they were moving by themselves, as if controlled by the group. He thought of the blackbirds, the way they moved as one giant organism.

David felt himself being drawn toward the middle. The smell of sweat and flesh became stronger. He felt his rock concert panic beginning to set in. Approaching the nucleus, the voices became louder, the sighs more urgent. Finally, he saw her: the queen, her blonde head towering over those around her. A dozen hands flowed over her naked body. Those closest to her tore off their clothes and rubbed themselves against her generous breasts. Slowly, she rotated, sharing her bounty with as many as possible.

David felt his jacket sliding down his back. A relentless current pushed him toward the queen. Her intoxicating scent enveloped him. She slid her hands up his waist and pulled his shirt up over his head. Her body pressed against his. "I want you to do me," she whispered in his ear. David looked into her vacant eyes. She peered right through him, and then slowly turned and offered herself to someone else.

David groped around for his shirt and jacket. "I just came down to buy some honey," he shouted to a guy pressed up against him.

"Good luck," the guy replied.

David pushed his way to the edge of the swarm and pulled free from the last of the groping hands. "I love you," a girl shouted toward him. David turned away and crossed the street.

— — —

David couldn't remember which part of the supermarket had the honey display. *They all seem to have a different place for it,* he recalled. Some put it in the baking aisle, others with the peanut butter. "You'll find it in the natural foods aisle," an employee informed him.

He made his way to the natural foods aisle, but the honey shelves were empty. A small sign apologized for the inconvenience and indicated that the product had been recalled. "Well, that's odd," David said. "I've never heard of honey being recalled before. Guess I'll try another supermarket."

There was another supermarket a few blocks away. This time, David decided to save himself the searching and went directly to the customer service counter. "Can you tell me where the honey is located?"

"Well, it's normally in the baking aisle," the manager explained, "but I'm afraid we're out."

"Really?"

"There's an industry-wide recall."

"You mean, not just one brand?" David asked.

"Right. I guess they're worried the bees might be carrying something. The order came down today, right from the FDA. We don't get those very often."

David gazed at the supermarket manager. *Something is definitely going on here,* he thought. *This is no accident. The feds are on the move.*

"Was there something else?" the manager asked.

"No, that's all I needed." He turned and walked toward the exit.

Holy shit, David thought. *I guess this means MisterClean got my message to someone at the CDC about the bees. They must think honey is carrying the cancer trigger. But how could that be possible when the cancer cluster is shaped like a big ring? Something doesn't add up.*

David drove straight home. The kids had just arrived.

"There's no honey," David announced as he walked into the kitchen.

"What do you mean, no honey," Julia replied.

"There's been a recall by the FDA. Industry wide."

Julia wrinkled her face in disbelief.

A scowl came over Jamie. "No more honey?"

"They're making a big mistake," David said. "They think it's going to stop the epidemic, but they're wrong."

"What epidemic?" Katie asked.

"It's nothing, honey," Julia said. "There is no epidemic."

Katie scratched her head. "Does this have to do with the bees on your computer, Dad?"

"Well, sort of …"

Julia butted in. "I'm sure the honey situation has nothing to do with your dad. You're just going to have to get used to jelly on your sandwiches."

"And your secret meeting?" Katie added.

"Yes, that too," David said.

"Okay, I've heard enough of this," Julia said. "It's time for you kids to go up and get some homework done. Oh, and by the way, you need to keep your windows shut tonight. They're spraying for mosquitoes."

— — —

The next morning, David left the house early. While climbing into his car, he noticed a couple of dead honeybees on the driveway. He didn't give it much thought until he stopped for gas. He noticed a familiar figure at the gas station wearing a khaki jumpsuit—Homer Hadley, the guy from the state entomology lab. "Good morning, Mr. Hadley," David called.

Hadley gave David a blank stare. He turned away long enough to tighten his gas cap and hang up the hose. Then he approached David. Hadley looked as if he hadn't slept. "They're all dead," he muttered.

"Who's dead?" David replied.

"I don't need to tell you. You guys were responsible. You killed them all."

"I have no idea what you're talking about."

"There's not a honeybee left in the county. They shut us down, wiped out everything."

"Holy shit."

"Those weren't mosquitoes they were spraying for last night. I know the smell of that stuff like I know my wife's cooking. They were going after the honeybees."

"I swear I didn't know anything about this," David said.

Hadley turned and climbed into his truck. "There'll be hell to pay. You'll see." And he drove off.

— — —

"Hey there, good lookin'." Sue poured David's coffee and slid the morning paper in front of him. "Did you see this?" she said, pointing to a headline on the front page. "Isn't that your neighborhood?"

Minneapolis Woman Murdered

An Oak Street resident was found murdered in her home yesterday. No motive has yet been established, but Minneapolis police are searching the residence for clues. The murder is believed to have occurred around 4:00 p.m. The identity of the victim is being withheld in the interest of the investigation. Anyone with possible information is requested to contact the Minneapolis Police Department.

"Yes, that's not too far from my house," David said. "Probably some sort of domestic thing."

"That nice man from the electric company stopped in again."

"Sam Preston?"

"Yeah, Mister Mellow Yellow. He was asking some questions about you. Nothin' personal."

"Really. Like what?"

"He just wondered who you used to work for, stuff like that."

"He probably just wondered if I was for real."

"Was that okay?" Sue asked.

"Yeah. No problem."

"I was thinking about callin' him," Sue said.

"You mean for a date?"

"Well, yeah, somethin' like that." Sue tugged on the sides of her uniform to get rid of the wrinkles around her chest.

"He seems pretty harmless. I'd go for it."

Sue smiled.

"Hell, if I had the likes of you dialing me up, I'd be making a run to the wine store!"

"Go on."

"Why don't you call him right now," David said, "right while I'm sitting here."

Sue drummed her fingers on the counter. "What the hell." She grabbed the cordless phone. "I didn't get his cell number."

"Then you'll need to call Midwest Power and ask for line maintenance."

Sue pulled a telephone book from under the counter and looked up the number. "Well, here goes." She dialed the number.

"Hello, Midwest Power."

"Line maintenance, please."

"One moment, I'll connect you."

"They're connecting me," Sue said to David.

"Line maintenance," a woman answered.

"I'm trying to reach Sam Preston."

"Sam Preston. One moment. I'm sorry, we don't have anyone working here by that name."

Sue put her hand over the phone. "They've never heard of him."

"Tell them he's a temp line worker," David said, "from back east."

Sue got back on the phone. "He's a temp line worker, from back east—up on the big towers."

"I'm checking our directory again. There's no Sam Preston, including the temps."

"Thank you," Sue said, and she hung up the phone. "Well, isn't that the damnedest thing. He doesn't exist."

David put down his coffee. "I think Mr. Preston might be somebody other than who he says he is."

Sue folded her arms in front of her. "What's this project you've been working on, anyway?"

— — —

Charles Miller waited through several rings for Bob Sanchez to answer.

"Sanchez here."

"Bob, it's Charles Miller. I just got the results on the VX exposure test with the honeybees. After twenty-four hours, there was absolutely no effect. Not a single dead bee."

"Really," Sanchez replied. "I assumed that you had received a positive result on that test."

"Why would you assume that?"

"Didn't you order the fogging in Minneapolis?"

"Fogging? What fogging?"

"The air guard fogged the city last night," Sanchez said, "and apparently they shut down the state bee lab as well. There's probably not a live honeybee within a hundred miles."

"My God," Miller murmured.

"The public thought the spraying was for mosquitoes—you know, for West Nile. That's how it was packaged for the media."

"That order did not come from the CDC. Someone has hijacked this thing."

— — —

Julia placed a few items of clothing in a tote bag.

"Are you sure you don't want me to come to the hospital?" David asked.

"Marsha will be here any minute. Besides, you'll have to be here when the kids get home, especially with a murderer in the neighborhood."

David followed Julia down the stairs. "What if they have to keep you overnight?"

"Well, then I guess you'll have to tell them something."

"I'll tell them you did a sleepover."

"Whatever."

The doorbell rang. "That must be Marsha," Julia said. She opened the front door to find two Minneapolis city police officers. "Can I help you?" Julia said.

"We're looking for David Peters," the officer replied, referring to his notepad. Three patrol cars sat in the street with their blue strobes flashing.

The blood left Julia's face. "Are you sure you have the right David Peters?"

"Yeah, we're sure." The officer nodded.

Julia winced. "David, somebody wants to see you."

David came to the door. "Yes?"

"Are you David Peters?"

"Yes, I'm David Peters."

"Do you know a Miss Anne Hoepner?" the officer asked.

"Well, I don't really *know* her," David said. "I know where she lives."

Julia clutched the front door.

"Did you leave a telephone message for Miss Hoepner recently?" the officer continued.

"Yes, I did."

"What was the purpose of your message?"

"To warn her that she might be in danger."

The officer turned to his partner. "I think we better bring him in."

The other officer nodded.

"Mr. Peters, we'd like you to come downtown to answer some more questions for us."

"Am I under arrest for something?" David asked.

"No, you're not under arrest," the officer said. "We're just asking for your cooperation."

David quickly pondered his options, while the officers watched for any sort of incriminating reaction. "Okay, I'll come with you," David replied.

"Are you Julia Peters?" the officer asked.

"Yes, I am," Julia stammered.

"We'll be in touch with you."

David turned and gave Julia a half smile and then followed the officers to the patrol car. As the three of them marched across the shaggy front lawn, Marsha Reeves pulled into the driveway, her eyes as wide as saucers.

Nearby, David noticed a man sitting in a black Ford Expedition. David recognized the man immediately. It was Sam Preston, but he wasn't wearing yellow.

TEN

DAVID SAT ALONE AT a table in a small, windowless room. A large mirror covered one wall—*No doubt a one-way mirror*, David thought. Acoustic tile covered the rest of the walls and the ceiling. He heard the faint shuffle of feet outside in the hall.

The door opened, and two casually dressed men came in. One of them carried a telephone answering machine. "Hello, Mr. Peters."

"Hi," David replied.

"I'm Officer Carlson, and this is Officer DePinto."

David started to extend a handshake but changed his mind. He didn't want to raise suspicion by being too friendly.

"We just want to ask you a few questions," Carlson continued. "We'll have you out of here in no time."

Officer DePinto plugged in the answering machine and set it on the table. He pressed the play button. A voice came from the machine—David's voice:

"Hi, Anne. You don't know me, but I wanted to warn you that you might be in danger. Please be careful. Be especially careful around your—" *Beep.*

"Is that your voice, Mr. Peters?"

"Yes, it is."

"According to the telephone company, you called Miss Anne Hoepner on Friday at four thirty-six p.m."

"I don't remember exactly, but that's probably right."

"Why did you think Miss Hoepner was in danger?" DePinto asked.

"It's a long story," David replied.

Carlson smiled. "We've got all day."

— — —

Wilson's office telephone rang.

"Hello."

"Dad, it's Numa."

Wilson smiled. "Numa, how are things going at your new job?"

"Fine, so far. But something has come up that I thought you should know about."

"What could that be?"

"Your friend, David Peters. I just came across his name on an FBI watch list."

"Really? Are you sure it's the same David Peters?"

"Yes, they have his picture on the file."

Wilson froze. "Thank you for telling me about this, Numa. You are a good boy."

"I'll let you know if I learn anything more."

"Don't get yourself in trouble," Wilson said.

"I'm always careful, Dad. I'm an Indian. I use my sixth sense."

"You are a wise warrior, Numa."

"See you soon, Dad."

— — —

"Now let me see if I understand you," Officer Carlson said. "Your son started acting like a killer bee, and through your satellite view on your computer, you found another guy who reminded you of your son, so you went and paid him a visit."

"Well, that's sort of the idea," David said.

"So you walked over to 201 Oak Street," Carlson continued.

"Was that before or after you called Anne Hoepner?" Officer DePinto asked.

"Before."

"And what happened when you got over there?"

"I was just standing in front of the place when the front door flew open and this body-builder type with a lot of attitude came outside and threatened me."

"So what did you do?"

"I went home and looked up the address on the Internet. That's how I got the phone number and Anne Hoepner's name. I didn't call the house right away because I figured he might answer."

"So your idea in calling her was to warn her about the guy on the porch?"

"Right."

"You don't have any idea who that guy is?"

"No idea."

Carlson and DePinto looked at each other.

"Let's get back to the killer bee part of this," Carlson said. "Could you explain for me again why you think your son is acting like a killer bee? I'm still a little fuzzy on that part."

"There's a behavioral transfer going on between bees and humans. It has something to do with dwindling bee populations."

"Is that your profession, Mr. Peters, working with bees?" DePinto asked.

"Actually, I'm in marketing."

"That was before you lost your job, right?"

"Well, yeah. If you call Dr. Jack Wilson at the university, he'll confirm all of this stuff about the bees."

Carlson took a seat at the table, at a right angle to David. "Mr. Peters, I understand your wife has cancer."

David wondered how they could possibly know about Julia.

"She's one of the many," David pointed out.

"What exactly do you mean by that?" Carlson asked.

"She's part of the epidemic, the cancer cluster."

"There's a cancer epidemic, huh?"

"If you call the department of health, they'll deny it up and down," David said, "but I heard it from someone at the CDC."

Carlson gave DePinto the go-check-on-that nod, and DePinto left the room.

"So you have a friend working at the CDC in Atlanta?" Carlson continued.

"I don't actually know his name, but he has connections there."

"I see. And through this ... friend, you found out about the cancer cluster."

"Actually, I suspected it before that because I was hearing about so many people around Minneapolis with cancer."

DePinto came back into the room and closed the door. He handed Carlson a small slip of paper and a large envelope.

Carlson looked straight at David. "Officer DePinto just checked with Dr. Wilson. He's never heard of you. And there is no cancer epidemic." He reached into the envelope and pulled out a 22-caliber pistol. "And we just found this in your car."

David felt numb.

"Mr. Peters, why did you murder Anne Hoepner?"

— — —

Charles Miller's secretary came over the intercom, "Dr. Miller, General Gerber is on the line."

Miller grabbed the telephone. "General, what have you got for me?"

"DARPA swears they didn't have anyone out there at the Minnesota bee lab. That bee program's been dead for years."

"What can you tell me about the Minneapolis fogging last night?" Miller asked.

"Well, those guard boys did a hell of job, just as you ordered."

"I ordered?"

"Come on, Doctor, I saw your signature on the authorization."

"Just checking you, General," Miller joked.

"That is some weird thing with the bees giving folks cancer," Gerber said.

"Hopefully, the fogging will correct the situation."

"If we can do anything more for you, you know where to find us," Gerber added.

"Thank you, General." Miller put his telephone back on the cradle and tried to imagine who could have forged an authorization to fog Minneapolis.

— — —

David studied the walls and ceiling. He had never given much thought as to how one would construct a jail cell. Obviously, it necessitates sturdy materials—cinderblock walls, concrete floor and ceiling. No doubt, they ran rebar through the cinderblocks, and they must have filled them with concrete too. The sink and toilet were made from heavy-gauge stainless steel, stamped in such a way so as to prevent any sharp edges. A metal cantilevered bed hung from the wall, leaving the space under it free of supports. The tile floor had a gentle slope toward the center, where a chrome drain marked dead center. That bit of chrome was the most welcoming part of the place. *Thank God they put that in here*, he thought.

The county jail was a fairly new facility, and David assumed it must have all the latest bells and whistles. That had to include electronic surveillance. He'd already spent hours trying to locate the microchip camera that was undoubtedly trained on him. *They're making those cameras so damn small now,* David griped. *I'll never find the damn thing.* The bars and their related hardware had an industrial feel to them—built heavier than anything you'd find in the average home. *There's probably enough steel in those bars to make a dozen Maytag washers,* he thought.

In the distance, David heard the tinny resonance of a small radio. Music was coming from it, but from his cell, he couldn't make it out. The acoustics of the place were terrible, thanks to all the hard surfaces. It was perhaps the one part of jail that was most unlike home. Even with his eyes closed, David couldn't escape the perpetual reverberation. It reminded him of a carnival nightmare.

— — —

Sue got off the bus and walked the last two blocks to the Peterses' home. She knew she had the right address when she saw the overgrown lawn. Sue had dressed up for the trip—a bright red skirt, heels, and a knit top that was a little snugger than her diner uniform. Her platinum hair was in the country and western mode.

Julia was recuperating on the couch when the doorbell rang. She made her way to the front door, unlatched the lock, and cracked it open. "Yes?"

"I'm here about David," Sue said.

"Who are you?"

"I'm Sue. I'm a friend of his. I work at the diner."

Oh God, Julia thought, *one of David's street urchins.* Julia's imagination quickly divined a naked image of this woman. "What do you want?"

"I think I can help David."

Julia's face wrinkled up.

"I know about his project," Sue continued.

Julia stood in the doorway and said nothing.

"I thought he was crazy too—all this talk about alternative realities and bee behavior and cancer. I see a lot of nut cases in my line of work. To be honest with you, I thought he was another one of them."

"Maybe you were right," Julia said.

"The last time I saw him, he told me the whole story. Before that, I only heard little bits and pieces of it. I don't know how to tell you this so you'll believe it, but your husband is a genius. Plain and simple, a genius."

"My husband is in jail for murder."

Sue looked away for a moment. Then she looked Julia squarely in the eye. "You've got cancer, don't you?"

"Did he tell you about that too?"

"No. He told me it was a friend of his. But I could see it in his eyes. I figured it had to be you. David is innocent, plain and simple. He was working on something that will prove he's innocent."

Julia's face slowly unwrinkled.

"David loves you, you know. He's told everyone at the diner about the lovely Julia. You're very lucky to have a guy like him."

A tear rolled down Julia's cheek.

"I know he's been lookin' a little rough around the edges, but if you'll just let me explain what's been goin' on."

Julia wiped the tear away.

"Would you mind if I come in for a few minutes?"

Julia smiled and opened the door wider. "Of course not. Please come in."

"You've done a beautiful job with your house," Sue said.

"Thank you. The lawn is a bit embarrassing."

"David mentioned the lawn more than once. I think he misses having a full-time job."

"But he hasn't been working very hard to find one," Julia said.

"Oh, he's been working all right. He just hasn't been getting paid. Let me tell you, David is onto something very important. I don't think anyone knows just how important it is yet, including David."

"What do you know about it?" Julia asked.

"It started with a video you asked him to edit."

"The block party?"

"Yes, I think that's what it was," Sue recalled.

"He told me it was unusable."

"Well, that wasn't exactly true. He did some kind of trick on his computer that turned the video into something like ballet, he said. He figured out a way to synthesize time."

"Sounds like David," Julia said.

"Well, there's more. He saw a blurb in the newspaper about a government satellite that can detect humans, even through the roof of your house. He started collecting satellite pictures of Minneapolis and made a movie out of them."

Julia began to hang on Sue's every word.

"When he used his time-synthesis trick on the satellite video, something very weird showed up—a giant circle dance that stretches from one side of the city to the other. Thousands of people in Minneapolis are involved in this huge circle dance, and they don't even know it."

Julia's jaw dropped.

"And here's the best part. Thanks to a tip from a guy at the CDC in Atlanta, it seems that most of the new cancer patients in the city live right in the path of that big circle."

"And you saw this?" Julia said.

"No, I haven't seen any of it yet. But you know what? I believe him. I meet a lot of people in my line of work, and there are very few of them with pure souls. Your husband may look a little worse for the wear lately, but he has a pure soul, plain and simple. I believe him."

Julia shook her head. "I'd really like to believe this story, but I have to see some proof."

"Where's his computer?" Sue asked.

"It's in the den—right this way." Sue followed her.

"Oh my God," Julia cried. "It's gone."

Sue snapped her finger. "You know, there might be another copy of David's computer file."

"Where would that be?" Julia asked.

"He mentioned something about an Indian."

Julia recalled the eagle feather that fell out of David's shirt.

"He's some kind of professor at the university," Sue continued.

"Do you remember his name?"

"David just called him Jack."

"An Indian named Jack. Just a minute." Julia pulled out a telephone directory and looked up the number for the University of Minnesota.

"How many could there be?" Sue said.

Julia dialed the number. "Hello. I'm trying to locate a professor at the university. Unfortunately, I don't know his last name. His first name is Jack, and he's a Native American."

"One moment."

"They're checking," Julia said to Sue.

The receptionist came back on the line. "That would have to be Dr. Jack Wilson. I'll connect you."

"They're connecting me," Julia told Sue.

"Behavioral sciences, may I help you?"

"Dr. Jack Wilson, please."

"I'm sorry, but Dr. Wilson is on leave from the university. I'm afraid he didn't leave any forwarding information."

"Thank you," Julia murmured and hung up the phone. "He's gone, and he didn't leave any forwarding information."

Sue grabbed the telephone directory and quickly thumbed toward the back. "Maybe he's got a home number."

"Good idea."

"Wilson, Wilson, Wilson." Sue's finger ran down the page. "There's no Jack, John, or J. Wilson," she said.

"We'll try directory assistance," Julia suggested and dialed the number. "Hello, I need the number for a Jack or John Wilson in the Minneapolis area, please."

"One moment."

"Come on, come on," Julia fretted.

"I'm sorry; looking in the Twin Cities area, there is no listing for Jack or John Wilson."

Julia felt a twinge of fear. "Thanks anyway."

"Maybe David knows some way to reach him," Sue said.

"Yes, I suppose. I was planning to go see David in the morning."

"You know, there was someone else, a man who came into the diner a few times," Sue said.

"Who was he?"

"The first time I saw him, I said to myself, now *that's* a man I wanna get to know. You know what I mean?"

Julia nodded.

"He was dressed in bright yellow from head to toe. Said he worked for the electric company up on the big towers. Said his name was Sam Preston."

"How does he fit in?"

"Well, he came in a few times and always sat right next to David. He was curious about what David was up to, but not too curious. I tried to call him up for a date, and the electric company said they never heard of him. Can you believe it?"

"Do you think he was casing David?"

"Well, it wasn't totally obvious, but when you put all the pieces together, it sure starts to look fishy."

"Was David suspicious of this guy?"

"He was after I tried calling."

Julia stood up. "Well, I guess that's something else for me to ask him about in the morning."

"I hope you'll stay in touch with me, Julia. I might be able to help."

"Of course. Why don't you jot your number down for me."

Sue smiled and wrote down her number.

"Can I give you a lift back to your place?" Julia asked.

"That's okay; I can take the bus."

"No, I insist. It will do me good to get out of here for a little while. The children are at a friend's house tonight."

"Well, it would be easier than the bus," Sue admitted. "I'm just fifteen minutes away."

The women climbed into Julia's car and ventured across town. Along the way, they passed by a mass of people huddled together on the sidewalk.

"What the heck is going on there?" Sue asked.

"I have no idea."

"Oh, I know!" Sue exclaimed. "It's one of those human swarm things. I read about it in the paper."

"Really. I must have missed that."

"They're happening all over. It starts with a girl, who they call the queen. She sends out text messages to ten people. And those ten people each text ten other people and so on. They all meet somewhere and sardine themselves together. It's an excuse to get physical with some total strangers."

"And they call this a *swarm*?" Julia asked.

"Yeah, a swarm—like a bee swarm."

Julia's mind flashed to Jamie's odd behavior.

"Sometimes they even get naked in the middle of those things," Sue added.

"I wonder what made them think of doing swarms?"

"I hear they're happening all over the city. Kinda weird, isn't it?"

169

"Well, I guess they could be doing something worse."

The swarm let out a collective sigh as Julia's car drove away.

— — —

Bob Sanchez grabbed a telephone in the CDC data center and dialed Charles Miller's extension.

"Dr. Miller, it's Sanchez."

"Yes, Bob."

"We've just received the correlated address data for the clusters in Denver and Kansas City. We've got the same thing going on in both cities—a giant ring."

"I'll be damned," Miller said. "I want you to fly out there immediately and check the center of those rings for honeybees. Call me as soon as you have something."

"Will do, Doctor."

— — —

"That's my place right there," Sue said. Julia pulled up in front of a modest three-story apartment building. "Thanks for the lift. I really appreciate it."

"You're welcome, Sue."

An awkward silence filled the car. Julia wondered if this whole thing was a dead end. *Maybe Dr. Goldberg is right,* she thought. *Maybe this is all a figment of David's crazy imagination.*

"Would you like to come in for some tea?" Sue asked. "I'd really like to return the favor."

Julia hesitated.

"Of course, my apartment is nothing to brag about, not nearly as beautiful as your place."

A sympathetic smile came across Julia's face.

"But I do make a hell of a good cup of tea."

"I'd love to," Julia replied.

The apartment was a time capsule of Sue's life. She had dolls from her childhood, framed artwork she did in high school, even a personalized photo of Elvis, signed by the King himself. "I have trouble throwing things away," she explained.

The depth of Sue's collection fascinated Julia. She was struck by not only the quantity but also the choices that Sue had made about which things to save. There were framed photographs but not the typical posed family shots. Sue's photos chronicled events—a framed photograph of a man changing a tire next to the highway. "That's my dad's car," Sue said. "I borrowed it for a trip to Denver and got a flat tire. A nice man stopped to help me; that's him in the picture. He refused to take any payment or anything. He just wished me well and went on his way. I framed the picture as a kind of tribute to him. I never got his name."

While Sue prepared the tea, Julia perused the living room. A photo album lay open on the coffee table. On each page there were several snapshots and some printed remembrances. "Oh, that's my dating journal," Sue said. Julia quickly backed away from it.

"That's okay," Sue said. "You're welcome to look at it."

Julia gently turned the pages, revealing a long and winding path of men, some young, some older. Each page included notes about the good and the bad.

"My girlfriend calls it my trophy collection, but I think of it as my road map."

Julia looked at Sue with curiosity. This was a foreign concept to her. She'd gotten married right out of college. "What do you use your road map for?"

"It reminds me of how I got to where I am now. It prevents me from having regret and helps me remember who I am."

Julia was startled by Sue's perspicuity.

"Of course, sometimes I think how nice it would be to settle down with Mr. Right and live happily ever after. But my road map makes me realize that I haven't really missed out on anything. Love comes to us in many different ways."

"You're a wise person," Julia said. She turned the page. There, she found a man with striking dark eyes and olive skin. His jet-black hair swooped like an ocean swell, and his Mona Lisa smile spoke volumes. Julia could just imagine the sound of his voice.

"Oh, that's Omar. I never imagined myself dating a Muslim guy. He was coming into the diner like clockwork, and I noticed he couldn't take his eyes off me. He was really a sweet person. He'd bring me flowers from his parents' garden, stuff like that."

"Did you ever get to meet his family?" Julia asked.

"He kept talking about introducing me to them, but it never happened. We got pretty attached to each other, but the fear of bringing me into his family life was always in the background. Finally, it just pulled him away."

"That's too bad. He looks like a nice man."

"I see a lot of different kinds of people in my line of work. The diner is like the United Nations of Minneapolis. We get them all. When everyone is there, they are all on the same page, but when they go home to their neighborhoods and families, they're different. That makes me sad."

"Did David ever mention Raj Nabi, the guy in Pakistan who got his job?"

"Yes, he did," Sue replied. "He said he got a message from him recently. David says Raj Nabi is a good person."

Julia stared at Omar's Mona Lisa smile.

— — —

David lay on his back, watching a fly walk across the ceiling of his cell. *Amazing how they can do that*, he thought. *It's all a matter of mass versus gravity. For a human, walking across the ceiling would require some very powerful adhesive, yet the fly walks as if he didn't have anything sticky on his feet at all.*

The sound of footsteps echoed up the cellblock—more than one person, David surmised. The sound got louder and more succinct. David twisted his head around to get a look. A guard and two other men stopped outside David's cell. One of the men signed a clipboard and handed it back to the guard. "Mr. Peters," the guard smiled, "we're done with you."

David stood up and approached the bars. "Well, if it isn't Sam Preston," David said. "Or is it Dr. Schwab?"

The guard opened the cell door and Preston extended a handshake. "It's Sam Preston, Centers for Disease Control. This is my assistant, Bill Bumford."

"So you really were keeping an eye on me."

"We'll talk about that later," Preston said. "Right now, let's get you out of here."

The guard escorted them through the holding area and out to the lobby.

"How did you swing this?" David asked.

"When it comes to public health, you'd be surprised what's possible," Preston replied. The three of them climbed into a waiting Ford Expedition.

"We know quite a bit about you, Mr. Peters. We've been watching your progress."

David recalled the warnings he had read about the NSA—how it is virtually impossible to keep the contents of your personal computer private.

"Your discovery really threw us for a loop back at the CDC. We've got guys with PhDs and supercomputers who never would have figured that out. And here you did it in your den."

"So you know about the dance?"

"And we know about Jack Wilson too. Quite a character."

The SUV turned onto the highway ramp.

"My house is in the other direction," David said.

"Yes, we know. We have a little favor to ask. We just need your help figuring out a few details. Then you'll be free to go."

"How long will it take?"

"No more than a couple of days, I promise. We're going to make a quick trip back to the home office. Everything has been taken care of."

"What about my wife?" David asked.

Preston smiled. "We've already taken care of it."

The SUV entered the airport access road and peeled off at a security-only entrance. The gate went up, and the driver navigated to the general aviation hangar. The huge hangar door slid open as they approached it, and the SUV pulled inside. A Cessna Citation business jet in US government trim awaited them.

"That's our ride," Preston said. "Climb aboard." A small blue and white CDC logo appeared on the fuselage next to the jet's door.

The Citation had seating for six. The rear third of the cabin had an array of electronic gear installed on one side and a rack full of parachutes on the other. "Anywhere you like," Preston said. He noticed David staring at the parachutes. "Ever done any parachuting?"

"Ah—no," David replied.

David took a seat close to the cockpit and buckled himself in. That's when he noticed the seats had shoulder harnesses in addition to lap belts.

"Hopefully, we won't need those," Preston said, trading grins with Bumford. David also noticed an interesting red telephone on the cabin wall near his seat. The keypad on it had more than the usual number of keys; some of the keys had Arabic characters on them.

The Citation idled out to the east-west runway. Then, without much warning, the jet launched itself off the runway at an angle David had only experienced once before—on a roller coaster.

— — —

It was dark by the time they landed. A similar black SUV greeted the Citation, this one with US government plates.

David and Preston rode in the back. The windows were so darkly tinted that David could barely see out. On the drive to the CDC, he recognized only one thing through the tinted glass: a Virginia state police car, its reflective door sticker just bright enough to make out. "That guy's a little ways from home," David said.

Preston smiled and nodded.

The black SUV passed through an automatic security gate and then down a steep ramp into an underground parking garage. Sodium vapor lights inside the garage cut through the dark window tint. David noticed a number of other cars with US government license plates. The driver descended two more levels and parked near a bank of elevators.

Preston pressed the elevator button. "Prepare to get your mind blown, Mr. Peters."

David wondered what could be so special about the Centers for Disease Control. *Probably just a bunch of researchers in white lab coats,* he imagined. The elevator doors closed. Preston stared into a lens above the floor buttons, and a beam of blue light fluttered across his eyes. "Authenticate," a digital voice said.

"Preston four-two-two-seven," Preston responded.

Instead of moving up or down, the elevator's rear wall slid open, revealing an entry foyer constructed entirely of stainless steel and glass. Two security guards stood near a tinted plate glass door. One of them wore a military police uniform and held a sophisticated-looking weapon. David noticed cameras trained on him from several angles. *They're not messing around at the CDC*, David thought. *Must be more fallout from 9/11.*

Preston placed his hand on a scanning device. "Just place your hand on there, Mr. Peters."

David hesitated.

"Don't worry," Preston said, "we've already got your biometrics."

David put his hand on the machine. A chime sounded, and the glass door slid sideways with a precision whirr.

"Right this way, Mr. Peters."

David followed Preston down a glass hallway, through another security door, and into what appeared to be some sort of command center. It reminded David of the Kennedy Space Center. The terraced floor sloped toward the front, where several large screens displayed data, maps, and images. Technicians sat at consoles and computer terminals with arrays of exotic-looking communication gear surrounding them. David never imagined he'd see so many people in military dress working at the CDC.

Preston nodded to one of the technicians. A few keystrokes later, the image on one of the large screens changed to David's own satellite video, the great dance back in Minneapolis. "Quite a discovery you made there," Preston said. "Had we known something like this was going on, the satellite never would have been declassified."

David gazed at the dance.

"We have no idea what this means," Preston continued. "We were hoping you might be able to help us figure it out."

"I'll do whatever I can," David said, "but I think we might be dealing with something much bigger than anyone imagined."

ELEVEN

JULIA STEPPED OUT OF the shower, toweled herself off, and put on her bathrobe. She hadn't seen David in person since the police came to the door. She thought about their upcoming conversation and what she needed to ask him. The visiting hours began at nine o'clock sharp, and she wanted to get there right on time.

The doorbell rang.

Julia tied her robe and flew down the stairs. She pulled open the front door to find Mike Stewart, the Porsche guy, clutching a bottle of white wine.

"Sorry to hear about David," he said.

"Well … thanks."

"If there's anything I can do," he said, his hand perched high on the door jam and his shoulders squared with Julia's.

Julia felt vulnerable in her bathrobe. "I think right now he just needs a good lawyer."

"Actually, I was thinking more about you, Julia." His eyes undressed her as he spoke. "It could be a long time before he comes home, a very long time."

"I guess I'll have to cross that bridge when I get to it," Julia said.

"Well, if you need somebody—to talk to—you know where to find me."

Julia looked him in the eye. "What happened between us is history. It won't be repeated. I've got to run now."

Mike Stewart looked stupefied. "Okay then," he replied, and turned toward the Porsche. He took the bottle of white wine with him.

— — —

Julia entered the county jail building at 8:55 a.m. and made her way to the visitor check-in. "What can I do for you?" the guard asked.

"I'm Julia Peters. I'm here to see my husband, David Peters."

The guard ran his finger down the list of detainees. "You say you're his wife?"

"Yes, that's right." Julia reached for her wallet and pulled out her driver's license.

"Your husband was released late yesterday afternoon."

"Really? On bail?"

"It appears that he was released into the custody of the federal government."

"The *federal* government? Which branch of the federal government?"

The guard looked at the paperwork again. "He was signed for by a Sam Preston of the CDC."

"You mean the Centers for Disease Control in Atlanta?"

"Yes, I believe that's correct."

"How is this possible?"

"Sorry, that's all the information I have," the guard said.

"Thank you."

What on Earth? Julia thought. *What is going on?* She fumbled for her cell phone and dialed the number Sue had written down.

"Hello, Max's," a voice answered.

"Is Sue there, please?"

"Just a minute."

"Hello, this is Sue."

"Sue, it's Julia. I just went to the jail to talk to David, and he's gone. He was released into the custody of Sam Preston late yesterday. Isn't that the name of the guy who came into the diner?"

"Sure as hell is," Sue replied. "Mister Mellow Yellow."

"Apparently, he's with the CDC in Atlanta."

"So much for the electric company," Sue said.

"This is really weird. It doesn't make any sense that David wouldn't call me. He knew I was coming down this morning."

"Hmmm. I think you might want to give Atlanta a call."

"Yeah, you're right," Julia replied. "Somebody at the CDC must know what's going on. I'll talk to you later."

Julia sat in her car and dialed long distance information. "For Atlanta, please—the Centers for Disease Control." She selected the autodial option, and the number rang.

"CDC. How may I direct your call?"

"Mr. Sam Preston, please."

"One moment."

Julia couldn't imagine what was going on. *David has really gotten himself tangled up in something*, she thought.

The operator came back on the line. "I'm sorry, but we don't have anyone by the name of Sam Preston at the CDC."

"Could he be using a different first name?" Julia asked.

"No, we don't appear to have anyone with the last name Preston on staff. I'm sorry."

"Thank you …"

— — —

"Sue, it's Julia again. I called the CDC, and they've never heard of Sam Preston."

"Why am I not surprised to hear *that*," Sue replied.

"David mentioned something about another guy at the CDC."

"What was his name?"

"That's the problem. All I know is that he went by a screen name—MisterClean."

"That would be a janitor," Sue said.

"How do you know that?"

"I don't know. It just came to me. Hell, if I was a janitor, that's the screen name I'd be using."

"You could be onto something, Sue."

"When are we leaving?" Sue asked.

"Are you sure you can leave the diner?"

"Well, I'm sure as hell not going to sit here while you head to Atlanta alone. They owe me a ton of vacation time anyway. They'll understand."

"Sue, you're a jewel. I'm going to get us tickets for tomorrow."

— — —

"Dr. Miller, it's Bob Sanchez. Can you talk?"

"Yes. Go ahead, Bob."

"We have virtually the same situation in Denver and in Kansas City. I plotted the center of the cluster rings and found the same scenario: a ring of dead honeybees."

"Well," Miller said, "I guess it's safe to conclude that the honeybees are related to this somehow. We're going to hold off on taking any action in those cities until we have more data from Minneapolis. I want you to get yourself to Minneapolis and call me when you arrive."

"Yes, sir. And, Doctor, do you have any guess about what's going on here?"

"I'm leaning toward your original idea: a circular superinfection. It's something we've never seen before. We're really going to have to think outside the box on this one."

"I'll call you from Minneapolis."

— — —

David sat in a small conference room with Sam Preston, Bill Bumford, and two men in uniform. David had spent the night at the underground facility in an attractive hotel-style room. The room had no telephone, and the Minneapolis investigators still had his cell phone, so David had no way of calling Julia. He worried that Julia might wonder where he was. "I'd really like to call my wife," David said.

"We've given her an update on your whereabouts," Preston replied. "She sends her best and said the kids can't wait to see you."

The kids, David thought. *Julia said they were spending the night at Marsha Reeves's house. Funny that Julia would mention the kids when they aren't even there.* David looked around the room. "Quite a place you have here," David said. "I would have expected to see more doctors at the CDC."

Preston traded glances with the military guys. "I guess it's time for us to come clean, Mr. Peters. You're not really at the CDC. In fact you're not really in Georgia."

"Where am I then?"

"You're in a CIA operations bunker in Virginia."

"You're kidding me."

"Nope. We wanted to see what sort of person you were before we spilled the beans," Preston explained. "We wanted to make sure you were really going to be able to help us."

"What about Jack Wilson?"

"The Indian? He vanished into thin air, as Indians sometimes do. But we'll catch up to him sooner or later."

"Well, I've already told you everything I know about the dance. You've got my computer files, my video code, pretty much everything."

Preston sat quietly for a moment. Then a faint smile broke on his face.

"Why does the CIA care about the dance anyway?" David asked.

"It's the part about your son that we're most interested in."

"What about my son? You mean the killer bee thing?"

"That's right. You see, Mr. Peters, you have uncovered something that could revolutionize the US armed forces."

David didn't like the sound of where this was going.

"You have given our recruiters a tool to identify potential soldiers among our civilian population," Preston explained.

"You mean terrorists?"

"That would be a secondary application of the technology. Our primary goal is to harvest the killer bees among us, creating the most fearsome fighting force ever known, a collection of soldiers who know no limits, who will fight without being provoked."

Oh my God, David thought. *This has nothing to do with the cancer cluster, nothing at all.*

— — —

Julia handed the money to the cab driver, and she and Sue approached the glass doors at the CDC main entrance. "Wow, this place is big," Sue said. "I hope we don't catch anything while we're here."

They approached the reception desk.

"May I help you ladies?" the receptionist crooned in a thick Atlanta drawl.

"I have an unusual request," Julia began.

The receptionist smiled. "Try me."

"I'm looking for an employee who goes by the name, Mr. Clean."

"I don't think I'm going to be able to help you with that, honey."

"Just a minute," Sue said. Sue marched across the lobby to a janitor pushing a broom. "Excuse me. I'm looking for a guy called Mr. Clean."

The janitor gave Sue the once-over and then replied, "That would be Jerome."

"Is he around somewhere?"

"It's his day off."

"Do you know where I might find him? It's kind of important."

The janitor gave Sue the once-over again.

"He's not in any sort of trouble, nothing like that. My girlfriend and I just flew all the way from Minneapolis. He'd be pretty bummed if he missed us."

"Just a minute," he said. He parked his dust mop and disappeared down a stairwell.

Sue gave Julia a thumbs-up.

The janitor returned with a piece of paper. "That's his home address right there. Lives with his mother in Southside."

"Thank you, mister," Sue said, shaking his hand. "If you're ever in Minneapolis, you come by Max's Diner, and there's a free lunch waiting for ya."

The janitor smiled and waved her off.

— — —

The cab driver gazed at Julia and Sue in the rearview mirror. "You know that's kind of a tough neighborhood, Southside. I'd be getting your tails outta there by night time, if I was you."

Julia and Sue looked at each other. "Don't you worry about us," Sue said. "You just drive the cab."

The driver pulled up in front of Jerome's apartment building. Trash adorned the sidewalk and street. The remains of a bicycle lay padlocked to a fire hydrant.

"Can you wait for a few minutes, just in case there's no one home?" Julia asked.

"I'll give you three minutes. If I don't see you by then, I'm gone."

Julia and Sue entered the old building and found the apartment door on the second floor. Sue knocked.

Jerome's sister Felicia opened the door. She was startled to see two white ladies standing there. "Yes?"

"Is Jerome here?" Sue asked.

"Who are you?"

"We're friends of his," Julia said.

"He's downtown."

"Well, is your mother here?"

Felicia hesitated and then called her mother. "Mom, looks like two of Jerome's Internet honeys is at the door."

Coretta put down what she was doing and came over. She pushed Felicia aside. "What can I do for you ladies?"

"We need to talk to Jerome. Any idea where we can find him?"

Coretta winced. "Is he in some kind of trouble?"

"No. Nothing like that," Sue said. "We just need to talk to him."

Coretta stood in the doorway with her hands on her hips like the Rock of Gibraltar. She trusted her intuition about these two. "He'll be home soon. You might as well come in, ladies. Make yourself at home."

"Thank you so much," Julia said. "You're very kind."

"I can tell from your accent that you aren't from around here," Coretta said.

"We're from Minneapolis," Sue said. "Minnesota."

"How on Earth do you know my Jerome then?"

"It's a long story," Julia said.

"Your son is a hero," Sue added. "A hero, plain and simple."

Coretta's eyes grew as big as pears. "I'd like to hear that story. I got all day. Let's put on some coffee."

— — —

The next morning, Jerome glided his floor polisher across the CDC lobby. He glanced up just as Julia and Sue entered the building, but he pretended not to notice them.

"Could you please direct us to Dr. Charles Miller's office?" Julia asked the receptionist.

"Take the elevator to the eighth floor. The executive receptionist will assist you."

"Thank you."

Julia and Sue got off the elevator and approached the executive reception desk.

"May I help you?"

"We'd like to see Dr. Miller. It's quite urgent."

"Do you have an appointment?"

"I'm afraid we don't," Julia said. "Could you buzz him and tell him there is someone here who knows about honeybees. He'll know what you're talking about."

The woman looked perplexed.

"It's very important," Sue added, "life and death stuff."

The receptionist reluctantly lifted the receiver and dialed Miller's extension. "Dr. Miller, there is a lady here who says she knows about honeybees. Does that mean anything to you?"

Miller sat bolt upright in his chair. "Why, yes, it does," he said. "Send her right in."

"You can go right in."

"Thank you."

"Thank you," Sue echoed. "This will definitely save some lives."

— — —

David struggled to get perspective on the situation. His fictions were becoming realities, and his realities were becoming fictions. *My God*, he thought, *I'm in a secret CIA bunker in Virginia. Not only is the killer bee behavior trait a reality, but it seems the US government wants to harness it like a hydroelectric dam.*

Preston slid a piece of paper across the table with a block diagram on it.

"What's this?" David asked.

"A family tree—your family tree, actually. You see, Mr. Peters, we know more about you than you do yourself."

David scanned his way up the page. His name appeared near the bottom, his parents above his, his four grandparents above his parents—including his mother's father, Albert—and so on.

Preston pointed at a name near the top of the page. "Does the name Nelson A. Miles mean anything to you, Mr. Peters?"

Indeed, the name was there, just above Albert's: Nelson Appleton Miles. *The family never mentioned Albert's father*, David thought. "The name is vaguely familiar, but I can't place it," David replied.

"General Nelson A. Miles is the father of the US Army. Over one hundred years ago, he laid the foundation for what would become the greatest fighting force in the world. He carried us from the traditional European model of warfare seen during the Civil War to modern intrabattle strategies still utilized today. Your great-grandfather is a pillar of our military legacy."

David searched his memory. The name Nelson A. Miles was there, but he still couldn't quite connect it.

"Your great-grandfather was a great American."

Then David remembered. The word *American* triggered it. The first Americans were the Indians. Nelson A. Miles was the general who brought them down. "He was the US Army commander at Wounded Knee," David murmured.

Preston dropped another piece of paper in front of David like a gauntlet. At the top was printed the name of Dr. Jack Wilson. "Sometimes, things just aren't what they appear," Preston said.

David scanned down the page:

June, 1977—Weapons Violation
February, 1981—Forgery
April, 1988—Illegal Gambling
January, 1990—Conspiracy
December, 1997—Child Endangerment
April, 2000—Striking a Police Officer
August, 2002—Resisting Arrest
March, 2003—Tax Evasion

The list went on and on. David could barely believe this was the same Jack Wilson he knew, the one with the PhD in collective behavior. Apparently, there was more to Wilson than he realized. *I guess this would explain his reticence about the FBI and Numa working for them,* he thought. David tried to piece together the events of the past few weeks. Suddenly, everything looked different.

"We need your help, David. You've shown us what's possible. Now we want to take it to the next level. You'll have some of our best minds working with you. All of our latest technology will be at your disposal."

David thought of Julia and how she'd been nagging him to get a job.

"How does two hundred fifty thousand a year sound to you, Mr. Peters?"

"I guess I could work with that," David replied.

Preston extended a handshake. "Welcome aboard, Mr. Peters."

— — —

Charles Miller lifted his telephone. "Would you please get me the CIA director."

"One moment, Doctor."

"Hello, Bruce? It's Charles Miller. I'm fine, thanks. I thought you would be interested to know that we have not been able to draw any connection between the cancer clusters and the deactivated VX. Of course, we're continuing to keep an eye on the situation. Say, my sources tell me that you guys have a package over there by the name of David Peters. He's from Minneapolis. I believe your man Sam Preston has been handling it, right? We would love to get Peters over to the CDC for a day. We think he might be able to help us untangle the cancer situation in Minneapolis. That would be great. The sooner the better, as far as I'm concerned. Tomorrow morning? Perfect. I'll keep an eye out for you on the golf course. Say hi to that beautiful wife of yours." Miller put the phone back on its cradle. "Tomorrow, nine a.m."

"Thank you, Dr. Miller," Julia said. "I think David can help you."

"I know he can," Sue added, "plain and simple."

— — —

The next morning, David, Preston, and Bumford sat in Dr. Miller's office. "Mr. Peters, I understand you've made quite a discovery," Miller said.

"I was pretty surprised to find it," David replied.

"We're hoping that you'll be able to fill in some missing pieces for us. As you know, there is a serious cancer outbreak in Minneapolis. Here is some of our early data," Miller said, handing David a page brimming with charts and numbers.

David glanced over the information and noticed a small handwritten notation in the margin:

David, ask to go to the men's room.

"This all looks quite interesting," David said. "But before we go any further, I really need to make a visit to the men's room." David handed the page back to Miller.

Preston gave Bumford the nod, and Bumford escorted David down the hall to the men's room. Bumford gave the men's room a quick scan. "I'll be right outside," he said. David entered.

A few moments later, a utility closet door inside the men's room opened, and Jerome stepped out. "Mr. Clean," he whispered and shook David's hand.

Jerome entered one of the toilet stalls, locked the door, and slid out underneath it. "Follow me," he said. He led David into the utility closet, through another door, and into the women's room. The closet doors locked securely behind them.

After a few minutes passed, Bumford pushed open the men's room door and eyed the locked toilet stall. He continued to wait.

Jerome led David to an elevator down the hall. Jerome had locked the elevator doors open earlier. He inserted his pass card and punched in the special code.

When the doors opened again, David couldn't believe his eyes. Standing before him were Julia and Sue. Julia just shook her head, and her eyes welled up. "I am so, so sorry," she said, putting her arms around him. "I haven't been a very good partner lately. I love you so much," she cried.

Tears streamed down Sue's cheeks. "We've been missing you at coffee, too."

"He never called you, did he?" David asked.

"Who?" Julia replied.

"Sam Preston. The CIA."

"We had no idea where you were until Dr. Miller got involved."

"How in the hell?"

"It was Mr. Clean," Sue said.

Jerome smiled at David. "I'm Jerome. Jerome Roberts."

"That Jerome is a hero, plain and simple," Sue said.

"Nice to finally meet you, Jerome."

"So, Sam Preston is really with the CIA?" Julia asked.

"Right. Only yesterday, I realized what's in it for them. The CIA wants to recruit people with the killer bee trait so they can create the ultimate army."

"That means Jamie," Julia said.

"And who knows how many others. They couldn't care less about the cancer epidemic."

The elevator doors opened again, and Charles Miller stepped out. "Security is doing a full building search upstairs at my direction. That should keep them busy. Don't worry. They'll never come down here. Mr. Peters, it looks like you'll be a resident of Room 99 for a while. I think you'll find it quite comfortable."

"Thank you, Doctor." David looked at Julia again. "You know I had nothing to do with that murder. I never even met the woman."

"I know."

"At least they dropped the charges," David said.

"Not exactly," Julia replied. "You're in federal custody."

"Technically, the CIA could put you right back in prison when they're done with you," Miller said. "And my guess is, it wouldn't be a state prison, either."

"Sometimes, people just disappear in those places," David mused.

"I know somebody who's great with makeup and hair," Sue said. "She can make you look like a little old lady from Pasadena."

"I think this is the best place for me right now," David said. "Besides, we've got to figure out what's going on with the cancer and the dance."

Julia opened her purse and pulled out David's eagle feather. "I thought you might be needing this," she said. "Sue and I have to go back home tonight. My chemo starts tomorrow."

"I'm sorry," Miller said.

"Oh, I'm one of the lucky ones," Julia replied.

— — —

Two days later, Charles Miller, Bob Sanchez, and Jerome Roberts were the only people inside the CDC who knew of David's whereabouts. Miller trusted no one, knowing how easy it was for people to talk within the federal bureaucracy.

"I'm curious about this dance you speak of," Miller said.

"The CIA made off with my computer, everything," David said, "but I might be able to reconstruct it here with new satellite images. That is assuming the dance is still going on."

"I think you might find our computer to be a bit more powerful," Miller said. On the other side of the plate glass wall stood a circular six-foot-tall Cray supercomputer. "We call her Gloria."

In front of David lay an ordinary-looking computer keyboard and mouse. Next to it sat a control panel with some additional buttons. Miller reached over and pressed a button labeled *power-up sequence.* The lights in the room dimmed. A faint whine could be heard through the plate glass, like the sound of a jet engine starting up. "Room 99 has its own power source," Miller said. "We like being off the grid. Gloria gets real hungry when we ask her do something difficult." A message appeared on the six-foot plasma display in front of them:

GLORIA WELCOMES YOU

David's jaw dropped. It was like getting out of a single-engine Cessna and climbing into an F16. Indicator lights flickered behind the plate glass.

"I'll put her into PC-emulation mode, so everything will be familiar to you," Miller said.

"Do we have access to the Internet?" David asked.

"You mean for the BIOSAT images?"

"Yeah."

"We won't bother with the Internet," Miller advised. "We'll talk directly to the satellite." He punched a few keystrokes. "And, by the way, we're using a newer satellite, since BIOSAT was declassified. BIOSAT II has a few more capabilities."

An image appeared on the giant screen in front of them: the city of Minneapolis in staggering detail—a real-time, *moving* image. "Oh my God," David said, "it's moving."

"Go ahead; try your mouse."

David grasped the mouse and clicked on a downtown street. The image zoomed in by a factor of ten. He clicked again, and it zoomed in further. Two more clicks and he could see someone sitting on a park bench.

"Care to see what he's reading?" Miller asked.

David clicked once more, and the man's newspaper came into view. The headlines were perfectly legible.

"Go ahead, give it another click."

The text on the newspaper came into view. The article was about Anne Hoepner's murder. David saw his own picture and the story about his escape from federal authorities. There was no mention of the CDC.

— — —

Julia noticed a black Ford Expedition parked on her street when she got home but didn't pay it much attention. She had plenty on her mind already. She hadn't seen the kids for a couple of days and was still trying to decide how much to tell them. David's name was in the news. They couldn't have missed it. Katie was the first to broach the subject.

"Mom, why would Dad want to kill somebody?"

"Your dad would never hurt anybody."

"Well, why was he in jail then?"

"Because somebody made a mistake," Julia said.

"Well, if somebody made a mistake, why did Dad escape from jail? Isn't that the same thing as saying you did it?"

Katie's questions were getting more and more difficult to answer, but Julia knew she had to keep the children in the dark for their own protection. "Sometimes, it's not that simple, honey. Actually, your dad almost saved the life of the lady who was killed. If she had lived, the newspaper would be calling your dad a hero."

Katie's expression changed to a half smile. She liked the idea of her father as a hero. That was much better.

— — —

Jamie walked down the school hallway, a loner. The halls were crowded, but people avoided him, turning away as he passed by.

"I heard his dad is on the lam," Murphy said to his sidekick. "Jamie-boy can kiss Margo good-bye, that's for sure. She'll be history."

"Yeaaah," cackled the sidekick, "totally history."

The story of Jamie's father was all over school.

"Everything okay, Jamie?" Marsha Reeves asked.

"Yeah," though the sound of his voice said, *Everything sucks.*

"You just hang in there, Jamie. In time, everybody will forget about your dad."

Forget about him? Jamie thought. *Why would I want to forget about him?*

"Your dad will probably end up in a jail far away from here. After a year or two, people won't even remember what happened."

Jamie stared at the floor.

"You just have to put this thing out of your mind."

Jamie raised his head and looked Marsha in the eye. "You really think he did it, don't you?"

"I know the truth is sometimes hard to take."

"Well, you're wrong about my father," he said. Then he turned toward the crowded hallway and shouted, "You're *all* wrong!"

— — —

The black Ford Expedition pulled up in front of Max's. Sue noticed a familiar sight approaching the door.

"Hey there, good lookin'."

The man in yellow took his usual seat at the counter. "It's Sue, right?"

"You got it, honey," she said, filling his cup.

"Well, I guess the old brain cells are working today," he said.

Sue folded her arms. "You know, I just can't believe a guy as smart as you would be hanging wires for the electric company, Mr. Sam Preston."

Preston was startled that she remembered his name. "I guess I just love wearing yellow."

"Let's take a poll," Sue said. "Hey, everybody," she shouted to the two dozen customers in the diner. "We're gonna take a vote. Everybody's welcome to join in." Everyone turned their attention to Sue. The kitchen staff peered out from the order window. Even the postman who never said a word looked up.

"Let's see a show of hands," Sue continued. "How many people think Sam Preston here is wasting his time workin' for the electric company when he could be making real money workin' for the government?"

Every hand in the diner went up.

"Well, there you have it, Mr. Preston. You're in the wrong line of work."

TWELVE

"WELCOME TO THE CDC, Mr. Peters." Gloria's voice had a quiet confidence and humility that belied her mind-boggling intelligence. "I'm at your service."

David leaned toward the gooseneck microphone. "Thank you, Gloria. I look forward to working with you too." David felt a little self-conscious, even though Gloria couldn't see him. She wasn't the fictional HAL 9000 from *2001: A Space Odyssey*, but she did have a very clever speech-recognition system that made her seem almost human.

"Tell me a little bit about yourself, Gloria."

"I'd be glad to, Mr. Peters. I'm a Cray XT7 supercomputer utilizing the latest UNICOS 2 architecture. I was constructed in Seattle, Washington, and programmed for medical and health-related applications. For example, I can compile a complete human genome sequence in less than one second."

"That's very impressive."

"Thank you. I hope I will exceed your expectations."

"I hope so too."

"I'm standing by for your command."

David's first priority was to reconstruct the dance video. That was assuming the dance was still going on. The new BIOSAT II satellite offered some potential benefits, provided David could figure out how to utilize them. He scanned a list of the satellite's features and commands.

"Gloria, please bring up the live BIOSAT II image of Minneapolis again."

"How large of an area would you like to look at, Mr. Peters?"

"Five hundred square miles."

"And the epicenter?"

"Theodore Wirth Park."

An aerial image of stunning clarity appeared in front of David. Tiny parades of cars and trucks could be seen crawling across the screen.

"Please switch to infrared imaging."

"Switching to infrared," Gloria confirmed.

The image darkened to a deep bluish purple.

David glanced at the satellite command list. "Turn on heat signature sensing."

"What temperature range would you like, Mr. Peters?"

"We're looking for humans," David replied.

"Activating HSS at 98.6 degrees Fahrenheit—plus or minus 2 degrees."

Instantly, a snowstorm of tiny yellow fireflies dotted the image. They could be seen in moving vehicles, clustered in office buildings, homes, and schools.

"Gloria, what is the frame rate of this video stream?"

"Thirty frames per second, Mr. Peters."

This is a different approach, David thought, *using live video. Perhaps there's a way to process the image in real time, utilizing Gloria's formidable processing power.*

"Gloria, can you manipulate the video stream in real time?"

"Yes, I can, Mr. Peters. The video stream is digital. That is what I'm designed for."

"All right then. Are you familiar with morphing?"

"I don't recognize the term *morphing*," Gloria replied. "It is not in my programming."

Damn, David thought, *there has got to be a way to do this.* "Can I teach you?"

"Yes, I learn very quickly. You may teach me with voice or keyboard commands."

"Let's try voice commands," David said. "Gloria, bring up a picture of a baby's face on the screen."

The satellite image changed to a large image of a baby's face.

"Move that image to the left half of the screen. Now, give me an image of an adult face on the right half of the screen, with the same magnification."

Gloria complied.

"Gloria, compare the two images and define the difference as a formula."

"The task was completed in .01 seconds."

David smiled. "Gloria, use the new formula to define one hundred transitional images, beginning with the baby's face and ending with the adult's face."

One hundred images appeared in a matrix on the screen, with the baby's face at the beginning and the adult face at the end. "Transitional images complete," Gloria acknowledged.

"Transfer images to video."

A video of the baby's face morphing into the adult face played over and over on the big screen.

"Capture the complete formula," David instructed.

"Formula captured," Gloria replied.

"That is the morphing formula," David said.

"I understand."

David paused to consider his strategy. He gazed over at the glowing tower behind the glass wall. "Gloria, bring up the live satellite image of Minneapolis again, with infrared imaging."

The deep blue image reappeared, populated by hundreds of thousands of tiny yellow dots.

"Gloria, compress the video stream by a factor of one hundred to one."

"Compression activated." Everything in the image began moving much more rapidly. The yellow fireflies jittered around in a wild cacophony.

"Add one hundred video frames between each pair of adjacent frames using the morphing formula."

David heard the turbine generator climbing to a higher RPM. Gloria was getting hungry. "Please stand by, Mr. Peters. I'm activating additional processors to handle your request." The whine grew more urgent. The tower twinkled. David kept his eyes fixed on the plasma display. "Real-time processing achieved," Gloria announced. A new image burst onto the screen: the dance. The magnificent dance, as no one had ever seen it before: live.

David grabbed the telephone and dialed Dr. Miller's private extension. "Dr. Miller, I think you better get down here right away."

— — —

A black Ford Expedition sat on the shoulder next to Theodore Wirth Park. "Yes, they're on their way, sir. We'll get them out of here, and no one will be the wiser. I'll report directly to you, sir. Yes, sir." Sam Preston closed his cell phone and checked his watch.

In the distance, a pair of eight-ton tank trucks caravanned toward the park. The trucks were hard to miss with their huge stainless steel cylinders and web of plumbing. Giant vacuum cleaners on wheels, these monsters could inhale five thousand cubic feet per minute through their ten-inch hoses.

Preston saw them approaching and climbed out of the SUV. *Right over there*, he pointed. The trucks drove onto the grass and pulled up near the old oak. When the vacuums started, a deafening roar filled the park. The men maneuvered the big hoses around the base of the tree. In minutes, the ring of dead bees was gone without a trace.

Preston handed each of the men an envelope. "You were never here. We never met. And make sure the trucks' contents are incinerated."

— — —

Julia sat and waited for her first chemotherapy session. Two dozen patients sat in tilt-back chairs with IVs attached to their arms. A doctor entered the room. "Mrs. Peters?"

"Yes."

"I'm Dr. Sanchez. I'd like to have a word with you for a moment."

"Certainly," Julia replied. She followed him into a nearby examination room.

"Please make yourself comfortable." Sanchez closed the door and lowered his voice to a near whisper. "I work for Dr. Miller at the CDC. He sent me out here to check on a few things."

"I see," Julia said.

"Your husband is doing fine. He is perfectly safe staying where he is. It is likely that your home, your telephone, and your Internet connection are being monitored. We don't know for sure, but better to be safe." Sanchez pulled a cell phone from his pocket. "This is a secure cell phone, issued only to government officials. It cannot be traced or bugged. Use this if you need to make calls to me or to Dr. Miller. Otherwise, you should continue to use your regular phone, so you won't arouse suspicion."

"I understand," Julia said.

"For the time being, we think it is too risky for you to speak directly with David. We have established a voice mailbox where you can leave messages for each other. You should use this cell phone for that purpose. The pass code is the year you were married. I've written the telephone numbers down for you."

"This is very kind of you," Julia said.

"Dr. Miller is pleased to have David lending a hand on the cancer mystery. We need all the help we can get on this one."

— — —

Charles Miller stepped off the elevator. "What is it that you—?" He stopped short, his eyes fixed on the plasma screen. "My God. This is the dance, isn't it?"

"Yes, it is," David replied. "We're watching it *live*, thanks to Gloria."

"It is ... *simply beautiful.*" Miller stood behind David, looking like a little boy with his hands in his pockets. "The way it flows like a river is absolutely amazing."

The two men stood and stared at the image for a while without saying anything. The circle rotated in its usual segmented steps, a bit at a time, and then a pause, and then a bit more. Tens of thousands of yellow fireflies joined in. The dance pulsed an oratory on life, never resting, always pushing onward.

"It's changed," David said.

"What do you mean, it's changed?"

"It's much bigger than before. There are many more people now. It looks like it's picked up energy."

"It's fascinating, the way it moves," Miller said. "It has the look of a living organism. Mr. Peters, do you realize this is probably the most important discovery since Aristotle?"

"I'm just a tinkerer," David said. "A week ago, I was an out-of-work marketing guy."

"Have you tried audio synthesis?" Miller asked.

"Audio synthesis?"

"Gloria may be able to synthesize audio from the video data. Sometimes, that gives us a better idea of what we're looking at, even if the sound is abstract." Miller glanced toward the glass wall and raised his voice. "How about it, Gloria?"

"Yes, Dr. Miller. What can I do for you?"

"Can you synthesize audio from the video data stream?"

"My processors are 82 percent occupied with the morphing formula, but I will attempt to synthesize audio. One moment."

The distant whine of the generator became more urgent.

"Attempting to synthesize audio," Gloria advised.

David and Dr. Miller waited patiently.

"Attempting to synthesize ... attempting to synthesize ..."

"Do you think she's running out of memory, Doctor?"

"I don't know." Miller looked back at Gloria. "Are you okay, Gloria?"

"Yes, I am, Doctor. Synthesis complete."

Miller reached down and turned on the audio track. A slow throbbing rhythm filled the room. It was the sound of life and the sound of love. It was the unmistakable sound of a beating heart.

— — —

"Hi, Julia, it's me. Something happened tonight that I just had to share with you. It's a little weird talking to you like this, without being able to hear your voice. I guess we'll just have to put up with it for the time being. Anyway, back to tonight ... I was working on the video, the satellite video, and we asked Gloria—that's the supercomputer—if she could synthesize an audio track from the video data stream. To make a long story short, it appears that the dance is a living thing. It actually has a heartbeat. I know this must sound pretty crazy, especially since you haven't even seen the dance yet. But believe me, Dr. Miller is blown away. I don't think he's going to sleep tonight. The heartbeat made me think of you. I hope you're feeling okay. I'll talk to you soon. Bye."

Julia closed the cell phone. She scanned the bookshelves in the den, searching among her old college textbooks. Finally, she found the book: *Advanced Theories in Collective Behavior,* by J. Wilson, PhD. She flipped to the index in the back and ran her finger down the list. There it was: superorganism—page 232.

— — —

Sue dropped her quarters into the slot and took a seat on the bus, right behind Red, the driver. "Good morning, Red."

"Hi there, Miss Sue."

The bus was the cross-town number forty-two, Sue's usual ride. She'd memorized the route and could recite the exact stops along the way with her eyes closed. But on this particular morning, things were different. The bus took a completely new route. "What's going on, Red? Have we got construction everywhere?"

"Take a look there, Miss Sue," he said, pointing to a line of Army National Guard trucks parked along the street. "They're out in force this morning, got roads blocked off everywhere."

"What do you suppose?"

"I don't know," Red replied. "Never seen anything like it."

Sue stared out the bus window and wondered if this could have anything to do with David. *Could this be part of a manhunt?* she wondered. *If it is, they sure aren't messing around.*

"Maybe it's some kind of terrorist thing," Sue said.

"You could be right about that," Red replied. "Those guys are everywhere now."

"How's your family doing, Red?"

He ignored the question, and then glanced at Sue in the mirror. "Oh, things ain't too good lately."

"I'm sorry to hear that, Red." Sue left the question right there, figuring he'd tell her what was going on if he wanted to.

Red looked in the mirror again. "My wife's got cancer. Just found out."

"Gosh, I'm sorry to hear that, Red, real sorry."

"We're dealing with it," he said, keeping his chin up high.

"Well, she's lucky to have a guy like you."

Red looked out the bus window, and a tear welled up in one eye. He pulled the bus up to Sue's stop, and she hopped off.

"You come in and see me, Red. Coffee's on me."

"I'll do that, Miss Sue. I'll do that." He gave her a smile and closed the bus door.

— — —

Julia studied her old college textbook. She could hear the sound of her professor's voice in her mind as she read the text ...

> Superorganisms are the stuff of fiction. For centuries, theories have been put forth about "distributed intelligence," a magical notion that groups of organisms can somehow combine their brain power into a collective being—a being smarter than any individual within it. Science knows better. Every organized society, from honeybees to human beings, is the by-product of individual instinct. The collective intelligence we think we see is nothing more than the result of our instinctive responses to one another.

It was the same mantra Julia had taught her students for years. The field of collective behavior was built on this foundation. But Julia thought about what David had said about the beating heart, about the dance. Yes, *the dance*: here was a case of people doing something without even knowing they were doing it. It was not simply a case of organisms responding to each other. If the dance really existed, behavioral science would have to be rewritten.

The doorbell rang. Julia opened the door and found a man in a dark suit with a credential hanging around his neck.

"Mrs. Peters?"

"Yes?"

"I'm Detective Thompson with the county prosecutor's office. Do you mind if I come in?"

"Of course not," Julia replied.

The detective scanned the living room and den as he walked in.

"We can talk in the kitchen," Julia suggested. "Would you care for some coffee?"

"No, thanks."

They sat down at the kitchen table, and the detective pulled out a notepad and pen. "Mrs. Peters, do you have any idea why your husband would have escaped from the authorities?"

"Well, it wasn't because he's guilty. I can tell you that much."

"So you don't think he was involved in Anne Hoepner's murder?"

"He never even met the woman."

"But there is evidence of a message he left for her."

"That message was intended to warn her of possible danger."

"But how could he have known about that, if he never met her?"

Julia didn't respond.

"Mrs. Peters, do you understand that harboring a fugitive or withholding information is a crime?"

Julia gazed out the window at the field that was once a backyard.

"Where is your husband, Mrs. Peters?"

The doorbell rang again.

"Excuse me for a moment," Julia said. The detective stood up and parked himself in the kitchen doorway so he could get a look at the visitor. Julia opened the door. "Sue! What are you doing here?"

"There's something weird going on in town. I saw it on the way to work this morning. You've got to come check it out. I think it might be important. I was going to call, but I was worried about the phones."

"I'm a little busy right at the moment," Julia said.

Sue stood on her tiptoes and peered over Julia's shoulder.

"He's a detective with the county prosecutor's office," Julia explained.

"He sure as hell isn't," Sue said, pushing the door open farther. "Well, if isn't Mr. Sam Preston, aka Dr. Schwab."

Julia's jaw dropped.

Sue stepped into the house. "So I guess you took our advice on the career change, Mr. Preston."

Preston backed up into the kitchen.

"County prosecutor's office, eh? I had something a little bit bigger in mind, like maybe a *federal agency*," Sue blared.

Preston grabbed his notepad and scurried out the front door as quickly as his bum leg would carry him.

"That bastard," Julia growled.

"And to think I thought he was cute. What was I thinking?"

Preston climbed into the black Ford Expedition and sped off.

— — —

Julia and Sue drove downtown as far as they could, until army-green vehicles blocked the street. They parked in a nearby lot and headed off on foot. A squadron of city police cars raced by them, and a police helicopter hovered overhead. A colossal mass of people huddled together on the old Stone Arch Bridge. "It's another one of those human swarm things," Sue said. "I think this may be the biggest one yet."

"But why the road blocks?" Julia asked. "What's the point of that?"

"Beats me."

Julia approached a pair of city police officers. "What's going on, Officer?"

"That's what's going on," he said, pointing toward the swarm.

"These kids today," his partner declared.

"Actually, I was referring to the road blocks, the National Guard," Julia said. "What's *that* about?"

"We're not really sure," the officer replied. "The order came down from the governor's office. It's probably an exercise."

"What are you going to do about those kids?" Julia asked.

"We've got to intervene for their own safety. I don't think the bridge can handle many more than that."

Fire engines arrived with their sirens blaring. Hoses were pulled out and hooked up. Then the spraying began. "This should make them think twice in the future," the officer said.

The crowd got soaked but didn't budge. If anything, it had the opposite effect. The swarm just packed itself more tightly together.

The Minneapolis chief of police manned a microphone. "This is the chief of police speaking. For your own safety, you must disperse immediately. Everyone, please go home."

Television news crews caught the entire drama. A TV reporter interviewed the mayor. "Mr. Mayor, is the city actually considering using tear gas on this crowd?"

"These gatherings present a threat to public safety. We will take whatever action is deemed necessary to protect the public."

"Is the city planning to outlaw swarms?"

"Yes, it is. Before we do that, however, we are trying to understand why people want to do this in the first place."

"Any ideas?"

"We think it has something to do with drugs or sex, or perhaps both. Whatever the reason, this is clearly not the kind of behavior we want to see on our streets."

Julia and Sue stood and watched the swarm disburse. The participants quietly filed by, barely speaking to one another. They went their separate ways, looking as though they had already forgotten what happened.

"Is it just me, or does this seem a little weird?" Julia said. "Where's the fun?"

"I'm with you on that," Sue replied. "Something doesn't add up here."

— — —

When Dr. Miller arrived, David looked worried. "There's something going on, Doctor. I had Gloria bring up the satellite view again, just as we had done last night, but it's changed."

Miller's eyes were fixed on the plasma screen. The heartbeat filled the room with its slow, rhythmic pounding.

"Something has happened since last night," David said. "Something is impeding the flow. The dance has slowed considerably."

"Yes, I can hear it in the heartbeat," Miller said. "It sounds weaker, less vital, like the heartbeat of a sick person."

David gazed at the screen. "I wonder what could be causing the dance to slow down?"

"The demise of the bees, perhaps," Miller said. "What is most important to us is how the dance relates to the epidemic. We know it relates geographically. We just don't know if the dance causes cancer or is a response to it. The most important question we must answer is whether the dance is good or evil."

"It is such a beautiful thing," David said. "It's hard to imagine it could be anything but good."

— — —

"Honey, it's Julia. Things are getting crazy here. Don't worry; I'm okay. The National Guard has blocked off streets all over the city. No one seems to know why. And the human swarms are getting bigger. There was a huge one this morning on the Stone Arch Bridge. The police had to come out and break it up. Those swarmers look like they're on drugs or something. They act like zombies. I hope things are going okay there and that you're safe. The kids are fine. They know you're innocent. We miss you. I love you. Bye."

David hung up the telephone. *The National Guard is blocking the streets?* he thought. *What could that be about?* David sat alone in front of the plasma screen. "Unless they're trying to interfere with the dance."

David leaned toward the microphone. "Gloria."

"Yes, Mr. Peters."

"I want you to compare the present movement on the screen with the movement we saw last night at ten p.m."

"How would you like the data displayed, Mr. Peters?"

"I want you to identify the areas of greatest change by shading them in red."

"Analysis complete."

The image of Minneapolis now contained five red-tinted areas, all of them dead in the path of the dance.

"Gloria, turn off infrared imaging."

"Infrared imaging deactivated."

The dance disappeared; the image looked like a normal aerial view—though the red-tinted areas were still visible. David grabbed the mouse and clicked several times on one of the red areas. The image zoomed in, further and further, until one city block filled the entire screen. Right in the center, the road was blocked by a half-dozen dark green vehicles. He saw groups of soldiers blocking sidewalks and nearby side streets. "Holy shit," David whispered. He zoomed the image back out and zoomed in on another red zone. There were more army vehicles. Every one of the red zones marked an Army National Guard roadblock. "They're trying to stop the dance," David said out loud. He picked up the telephone. "Doctor, you've got to get back down here."

— — —

Miller gazed at the dance again. "To understand why someone would want to stop the dance, we must understand what the dance is, why it exists. There is something about this dance that is vaguely familiar." Miller glanced toward the glass wall. "Gloria?"

"Yes, Dr. Miller, what can I do for you?"

"I want you to perform a motion analysis of the video stream and express it as a formula."

"Analysis under way."

A complex formula appeared on the right-hand screen. Gloria modified the formula several times. Then she settled for a definitive version. "Formula complete."

"Gloria, I'd like you to search your database for video data that matches this formula."

"I am searching, Doctor. Please stand by." The turbine picked up steam.

"Five hundred terabytes searched. One match found," Gloria announced.

"Please bring it up on the main screen," Miller instructed.

A new video image appeared, a micrographic video made through an electron microscope. An army of cells moved in a circular pattern around an infection, working together to combat a colony of bacteria.

"That's what I was looking for," Miller said.

"What is it?"

"Those are T-cells. They're fighting an infection. The dance is not causing cancer," Miller said. "The dance is fighting it. I'm sure of it."

"Then why would the National Guard be trying to stop the dance?"

"There must be something in it for them."

— — —

Jamie took a glass from the kitchen cupboard and filled it with water. Then he grabbed the sugar bowl and shoveled spoon after spoon of sugar into it.

"What are you doing, Jamie?" Julia asked.

"Nothing."

"Well, you're certainly doing more than nothing." Julia looked into the empty sugar bowl. "I just filled that bowl this morning. What are you up to?"

"I'm not up to anything."

Julia stared at the glass of water. A half inch of sugar lay in the bottom of it. "This is not good for you, Jamie. This is how kids get diabetes." She poured the glass into the sink and rinsed it out.

Jamie ran up the stairs to his room. He punched his fist into his door and doubled over in pain on his bed.

Julia heard the noise but was distracted by the doorbell. Two US Marines in dress uniform stood on the doorstep.

"Are you Mrs. Peters?"

"Yes, I am."

One of the marines checked his clipboard. "We'd like to talk to Jamie Peters."

"What on Earth for?"

"Oh, he hasn't done anything wrong, nothing like that. We just wanted to speak to him about a career in the US Marines."

"My son is thirteen years old."

The marines looked at each other. "There must have been a mistake. We'll come back in a few years. Sorry to bother you."

Julia closed the door. "That's weird," she said. Then she thought Jamie might be behind it. "Jamie!"

Jamie appeared at the top of the stairs, his hand still smarting. "What?"

"Did you request some information from the marines?"

"Nope. Never did."

— — —

Dr. Miller's secretary initiated the call. "General Gerber's office, please. Yes, I'll hold."

Miller tapped his pencil.

"Go ahead, Dr. Miller."

"General, it's Charles Miller at the CDC."

"What can I do for you, Doctor?"

"There's been some curious National Guard activity going on in Minneapolis. Can you enlighten me?"

"All I can tell you is that Homeland Security initiated that one. Could be an exercise or could be a terrorist net. Those guys don't always give us the full scoop. We just do what we're told."

"Sounds like that order came from pretty high up."

"Don't quote me, Doctor, but this thing has the administration's fingerprints all over it. I don't know what the heck they're up to over there, but this Minneapolis situation has got me losing sleep."

"What exactly was the order, if you don't mind my asking?"

"They've lost their minds. They want us to impede traffic and pedestrian flow in a pattern around the city."

"I agree with you, General. That is sort of odd. Well, I'm sure they have their reasons."

"Those commanders out there will be looking to yours truly for an explanation. I don't know what the hell I'm going to tell them."

"I'm sure you'll think of something. Thank you for your insights, General. And be sure to give my best to that pretty lady of yours."

— — —

"Good afternoon, Mr. President."

"Charles, how are things in Atlanta?"

"Things are fine in Atlanta, Mr. President, but I'm afraid the same can't be said for Minneapolis."

"Have we gotten to the bottom of the cancer situation yet?"

"We've identified a few more pieces to the puzzle," Miller said, "but we still don't know exactly what triggered the epidemic."

"The folks at intel told me that honeybees were involved."

"It's only a theory. There's no scientific proof."

"Well, we shouldn't have any more honeybee problems in Minneapolis from here on out."

"I assume you're referring to the fogging, Mr. President."

"You know I'm not one to sit on these things, Charles, not after New Orleans. We've got an election year coming up, and I am not going to be known as the president who hesitated to take action in Minneapolis. If it has no effect on things out there, so be it. But at least I tried."

"You are a man of action. I'll give you that, Mr. President."

"Now tell me about this recent situation at the CDC, Charles. I heard you had someone in federal custody who escaped from the building."

"Yes, it was a man from Minneapolis who we thought might have some useful information about the cancer cluster out there. Two CIA agents brought him to Atlanta at my request. Unfortunately, he gave them the slip before I was able to talk to him. We searched the building from top to bottom."

"Should we be worried about this guy, Charles?"

"I don't think so. In my brief time with him, he seemed pretty harmless."

"What about the VX gas situation?"

"Every test we've done to date has come back negative. There doesn't seem to be a connection," Miller said.

"Thank God for that. That's the sort of mistake that could cause glaciers to move around Washington. I'm sure you know what I mean."

"We are still working the problem, using all our resources, Mr. President."

"Thank you, Charles. Please keep me posted."

"Will do. Good-bye, Mr. President."

THIRTEEN

"Julia, I have a suggestion."

Julia looked up from her desk. "What's that, Marsha?"

"You've been under a lot of stress, Julia. I mean, it's hard to imagine more bad luck hitting one person all at once." Marsha sat down and leaned closer. "Now, I know you've always had an all-natural attitude about things, but I think it's high time that you made an exception."

"What are you talking about, Marsha?"

"I'm talking about the greatest invention for the female psyche since the vibrator: Pomeen."

"That's an antidepressant, Marsha. I'm not depressed."

"Believe me, if I wasn't your friend, I wouldn't be recommending it. No woman, including *Superwoman*, could go through what you've gone through without taking it on the chin." Marsha lowered her voice to a whisper. "I've been on it myself for *six years*, ever since the creep cheated on me."

"David didn't cheat on me," Julia said.

"They say denial is the first stage of the healing process."

"I love my husband, Marsha."

"But Julia, you may never see him again."

"He's innocent."

Marsha stood up. "Well, think about it."

"Please leave my office, Marsha."

As Marsha walked away, Julia realized something. She realized that Marsha had been using her—using Julia's life to rationalize a life that wasn't working. In her Pomeen world, Marsha didn't feel the real highs or the real lows; she resided in the gray middle. She couldn't learn from her victories or her defeats because she couldn't feel them. Marsha posed as a friend, but her real goal was to find a comrade in defeat. Julia refused to be one.

— — —

Julia placed the scissors on the counter next to the sink. She removed her blouse and hung it on the back of the bathroom door. Her breast was still sore from the operation, but thankfully, it still looked the same in her bra. She pressed her hips against the vanity and studied herself in the mirror. The beauty of her twenties was still there, save for a faint patina of freckles. But inside, she felt older. Her carefree past seemed a million miles away. With her left hand she grabbed a shock of her thick, shoulder-length hair. The sensation reminded her of holding her daughter's hair and brushing it with long, patient strokes. But instead of a brush, Julia grabbed the scissors. The sharp blades cut through the shock in one smooth snip, like cutting through fine linen. She gently laid the six-inch passel on the vanity and prepared to cut another. Tears flowed down her cheeks. Julia knew that losing her hair was inevitable. She could have waited until the chemo took its course, but *she* was going to be in control of her own hair, thank you very much. "Fuck you, cancer," she cried. "You can mess with me, but you can't have my hair."

— — —

Julia sat at the kitchen table and stared out at the backyard. The tall grass shimmered like a wheat field. There was a beauty to it she hadn't noticed before, the way the wind moved across the grass in waves, like an ocean. The house was quiet, but she could imagine the crashing surf, the sound of the gulls. The sky looked bluer than usual too, a deep indigo blue. It was almost the same blue as the turban she wore around her head, tied in the back, the sort of thing Greta Garbo would have worn while going incognito. The turban caressed her head like a pair of warm hands.

The sound of the surf was interrupted by the telephone.

"Hello?"

"Julia, it's Sue. How are you doing?"

"I'm okay."

"One of my regulars just called and invited me to a swarm. Are you game?"

Julia had to think about it for a moment.

"It might be fun," Sue said.

"I'm thinking about it."

"And we might learn something."

"You're right. We should go and see if we can figure out what's behind this."

"Okay, baby! Mission impossible, here we come! Can you pick me up?"

"I'll be right over."

— — —

The swarm had just begun to take shape when Julia and Sue arrived. They parked on the grass nearby and approached the assemblage. There were several hundred people already. They streamed in from all directions. The swarm gathered on a bridge spanning the interstate. There was usually very little traffic on this bridge, so the authorities hadn't taken notice. The highway below them was busy with afternoon traffic.

Julia and Sue quickly became engulfed in the swarm. "We'll meet at the car later!" Julia shouted. Sue acknowledged her with a wave and disappeared into the mayhem.

The swarm perched itself on one side of the bridge, facing the oncoming highway traffic. As vehicles passed underneath, the swarm sang out musical interpretations of each one—similar to Ken Kesey's Merry Pranksters back in the sixties. The swarm didn't sing *words*. Instead, they imitated musical instruments. Julia joined in, imitating a trumpet. A tractor-trailer approached, and the swarm belted out a few bars of "Baby Elephant Walk." A black Corvette, and the swarm broke into the *Batman* theme. As the traffic increased, the music changed more often. In some cases, a group of cars were interpreted with a single melody.

Julia noticed that she always seemed to know what the swarm was going to do next. Every musical tribute felt like it was her idea. The swarm sang melodies she had never heard before, but somehow, she seemed to know them anyway.

All eyes were on the highway. In unison, the swarm began chanting numbers, long strings of numbers. Julia joined in. She knew instinctively what number was next in the sequence. *How strange*, she thought. *How am I doing this? What do these numbers mean?* She had a pen in her pocket, but nothing to write on. She wrote the number sequence on her forearm: 16, 2, 9, 57, 12, 33, 5, 21.

Sue caught a glimpse of the queen, a large woman with enormous, pendulous breasts. The queen pulled anyone near her into the cavernous cleavage. "Come to Mama," she cooed. "Come to Mama."

— — —

"Honey, it's me. Something really strange is going on with these human swarms. Sue and I went and joined one today on the Wirth

Parkway Bridge over the interstate. Rush hour was just starting. There were a few hundred of us there, at least. We watched the traffic approach from the east and go under us. First, we started doing spontaneous musical interpretations of the traffic. Then the whole group chanted a string of numbers over and over. Somehow, we all knew what the next number was going to be. I think I may be losing my mind. Anyway, the sequence was sixteen, two, nine, fifty-seven, twelve, thirty-three, five, twenty-one. I made note of the time too. It was four forty. Maybe you can make sense of it. I love you, and I miss you. Bye."

David scribbled the numbers down. This was certainly an intriguing development. The most interesting thing about Julia's message, though, was the part about knowing what the *next* number was going to be. That, David thought, could only mean one thing: that the people in the swarm had their brains linked together somehow—*a neural network*.

David stared at the numbers. "Well, they're not all prime numbers. Maybe this is some kind of numerical expression, like an array. Gloria?"

"How can I assist you, Mr. Peters?"

"Do you have the BIOSAT II video stream stored in memory?"

"Yes, I do, Mr. Peters. What date and time would you like?"

"Today at four-forty p.m. Central Standard Time."

"Data located."

"Gloria, give me a one-square-mile view of Minneapolis. The epicenter is the intersection of Wirth Parkway and Interstate 394."

The aerial image filled the large plasma screen. David grabbed the mouse and clicked. He could see the dark swarm on the right side of the bridge. The afternoon traffic coursed below them. *She said they were facing east*, David remembered. He clicked on the right side of the image, and the westbound traffic filled the screen. "This is what they were looking at."

David leaned toward the microphone. "Gloria, I would like you to define this traffic movement as a formula."

"Analyzing motion."

The whine of the turbine generator picked up.

"Analyzing. Please stand by."

David stopped breathing.

"Formula acquired."

"Gloria, please display the formula as a number array."

The numbers appeared, one by one, across the right-hand screen. David was transfixed. They were the same numbers he had written down.

— — —

"Julia, it's me. This is absolutely unbelievable. I know what the swarm was doing. I know what the numbers mean. I hope you're sitting down. The swarm was performing a quantitative motion analysis of the westbound traffic in real time. This is not something a human can do. Gloria confirmed it with a satellite view. Do you realize what this means? The swarms are superorganisms. They really exist. I need to call Dr. Miller. I'll call you back later."

Julia slowly returned the telephone to its cradle. The color had left her face.

"What is it?" Sue asked.

"The world as we know it has just changed forever."

— — —

"I've never seen anything like this," Miller said. "It will take me a while to get my head around it. The science of animal behavior may have to be rewritten."

"I think you might want to take a look at honeybees, first,"

David suggested. "There may be more to their behavior than we realized."

"What do you mean?"

"I forgot to mention to you that I made some videos at the Minnesota entomology lab."

Miller smiled. "Oh, you mean the project for *weapons development*."

"It was the only way I could get in there."

"What happened?"

"I used my time synthesis technique on some of my beehive footage, and it revealed a circular pattern in the bees' movement— not unlike what we're seeing in the satellite view of Minneapolis. After that, I got preoccupied with the cancer epidemic."

"Did you show the honeybee video to anyone?"

"Only to Dr. Wilson, a professor at the university. He's Native American, with a specialty in collective behavior."

"And what was his take on it?"

"He didn't know what to make of the circular honeybee pattern. But he suspected honeybees were related to the big dance. The ring of bees in Wirth Park was hard to ignore."

"Yes, we came to the same conclusion," Miller said. "But it's still unclear what the connection is. And now we have these human swarms. Perhaps they're connected to honeybees, as well."

"The behavior transfer theory is looking more and more like a real thing."

"What behavior transfer theory?" Miller asked.

"I thought the CIA told you about it."

"No, they didn't."

"It's my own pet theory," David explained, "that, somehow, Mother Nature has transferred honeybee behavior over to humans."

"How could that happen?" Miller asked.

"The theory is based on Indian folklore from a century ago. The Indians believed the soul of the buffalo was passed to humankind after the buffalo was decimated by the white man. In a similar way, we could be witnessing the consequences of pushing honeybees to the brink of extinction. The bees have been under a great deal of stress due to industrial farming and disease."

"That would be a hard theory to prove scientifically," Miller said.

"Yes, that's exactly what Dr. Wilson said. But since I last spoke to him, I discovered a signature movement in killer bees that matches certain people. My son is one of them. The CIA was hoping to perfect my technique so they could harvest those people as ideal soldiers."

"Oh my God," Miller murmured. "This explains why you warned the woman you were accused of killing."

"That's right."

Miller thought for a moment. "I think it is fair to conclude that the roadblocks in Minneapolis are related to the CIA harvesting project. They must have discovered that the dance is interfering with the bee behavior transfer."

"The roadblocks might also account for the increased swarm activity," David added.

Miller tapped his pencil. "I think we need to get in touch with your friend, Dr. Wilson. He might be able to help us find a way out of this."

"Unfortunately, you might have trouble doing that. He vanished into thin air right before I was put in jail."

"Perhaps we can find him through the CDC's Native American office."

"I have a better idea," David said. "I think I know how we can find him."

— — —

"Julia, it's me again. I met with Dr. Miller. We need your help. We want you to get in touch with one of the swarm queens and organize a swarm at a visible downtown location. Boom Island would work, right along the river. You only need about a hundred people. Once the group is there, try to get them organized into a circle dance, like the Indians used to do. Keep your eye out for an Indian with an eagle feather hanging from one of his braids. That's Jack Wilson. If you see him, tell him who you are. Tell him we need his help. I hope I get out of here soon. I love you. Bye."

"Sue, we've got a project," Julia said. "We've got to find an Indian."

— —— —

The group assembled on Boom Island at 9:00 a.m. The swarm was smaller than usual, and as a result, it was more easily influenced. Sue and Julia coaxed the group into a big circle. The queen stood in the center. "Okay, people," the queen bellowed, "we're doing a circle dance here, just like the Indians." She gazed at the reluctant dancers. "Does anybody know how to do this?"

Sue jumped forward. "I do!" Sue joined the queen in the center. "The first thing is this," Sue hollered. "No need to hold hands. We each dance our own dance, but we keep our place in the circle, and the circle slowly rotates. That's all there is to it!"

"What about music?" someone shouted.

Sue and Julia looked at each other and shrugged. They never thought of music. Sue began clapping her hands in a steady quarter-note time. The queen joined in and then Julia, and finally, the entire circle clapped the beat in unison. Slowly, the circle rotated. The dancers experimented with different foot patterns. Some spun; others swung their hips. Sue and the queen joined the circle. Gradually, they settled into a comfortable tempo, one they could sustain for a while. Traffic on the Plymouth Avenue Bridge slowed to see what was going on. The police watched from a nearby parking lot.

After an hour, Julia felt exhausted, but the dance continued. She scanned the spectators, wondering if Wilson would actually appear. Then one particular spectator caught her eye. He was silhouetted against the morning sun, standing alone with his arms folded in front of him, his feet spread wide. Julia left the circle and walked toward him. She stopped about ten feet away. His black braids swung in the breeze. An eagle feather hung from one of them.

"Hi. I'm Julia."

He didn't respond.

"Are you Jack Wilson?"

Without moving a muscle, his eyes slowly turned toward Julia. "I can help you with that dance," he said.

"We really don't have any idea what we're doing. That would be wonderful if you could help us."

His eyes returned to the dance. "For one thing, you're going the wrong direction. You must go clockwise to be in sync with the Earth Mother."

"I knew something didn't feel right."

"You also need a drum. Clapping will give you blisters after a few hours."

"Would you like to join us?" Julia asked.

His eyes moved to Julia again. "I'll be right back." Wilson returned carrying an old Indian drum.

"You're the reason we're here," Julia said.

"What do you mean?"

"My husband asked me to contact you. He thought the circle dance might bring you here."

"Who is your husband?"

"David. David Peters."

Wilson stopped. He looked away from Julia—at the police cruisers in the parking lot.

"They have nothing to do with this, I assure you. My friend Sue and I put this together."

"Where is your husband?"

"I can't tell you that right now. But I can tell you this: he is innocent. I know he is. He was only trying to do a good deed. He didn't kill her."

Wilson's face remained gray. "Why would he want to contact me?"

"He needs your help," Julia said.

"I am not a lawyer."

"He needs your help with the dance, the dance in the satellite video."

"He has more important problems, doesn't he?"

"Some very important things have been uncovered in the past week. Are you familiar with superorganisms?"

Wilson smiled. "I wrote the book on that."

Julia's jaw dropped. "Oh my God. Of course! You're Dr. J. Wilson who wrote the book on collective behavior. I had your book in college."

Wilson nodded.

"Well, Dr. Wilson, I think your book's going to be due for a revision. We just confirmed that superorganisms do exist. Human superorganisms."

A quizzical look came across Wilson's face.

"Our data was confirmed by a Cray supercomputer," Julia added.

Wilson's jaw dropped.

"Now listen up. There's a cancer cluster in town that's affecting thousands of people. David needs your help to figure out how to shut this thing down."

"Well, of course I can help," Wilson said.

"We're going to arrange a meeting somewhere. I want you to go to Max's Diner on Broadway tomorrow morning for coffee. You'll see a waitress there with beer can earrings. She'll give you the information."

"I want to hear more about your discovery," Wilson said.

"David will fill you in on the details."

Wilson began beating his drum in time with the dance.

— — —

Miller's secretary answered the call. "Dr. Miller's office."

"It's Dr. Murray in the lab. Is Dr. Miller available?"

"One moment, I'll connect you."

"What's up, Dr. Murray?" Miller answered.

"I've been keeping an eye on the honeybees, as you requested. The VX gas in the test chamber depleted some days ago, and the bees appeared to be unaffected by it."

"I see."

"Well, a few minutes ago, I walked past the test chamber and found that all of the bees had died."

"Really."

"Not only that. They arranged themselves in a perfect ring around the base of the chamber. I know the chamber couldn't have been tampered with. I have the only key."

"Dr. Murray, I want you to run postmortems on a dozen of them. Let me know what you find. And it might be a good idea to cover up that chamber. I don't want this to get out."

"I understand, Dr. Miller. I'll call you with the postmortem results."

"Thank you."

— — —

Wilson stopped at the university to check his mailbox. It had been a while, and there was always the possibility that a royalty check from his publisher might be awaiting him. There was only one envelope in the mailbox, a plain white business-size envelope with his name handwritten on it. There was no postage and no return address. He opened the envelope and removed a single sheet of paper. It took a moment for him to realize what he was looking at. The paper had a family tree on it. At the very top of the tree was the name General Nelson Appleton Miles. Wilson knew that name. Nelson Appleton Miles was responsible for laying waste to hundreds of years of Native American culture. He was the US Army commander at Wounded Knee. He was perhaps the single most despised person in Native American history. Wilson scanned further down the family tree. Several generations below, near the very bottom of the tree, was the name David Peters. "Oh no," Wilson whispered. He folded the paper, stuffed it in his pants pocket.

— — —

The next morning, Sue busied herself at the diner and kept an eye out for the Indian. A plan had been hatched, and Sue was the all-important messenger. She had the instructions in her pocket. The morning hours clicked by, with the usual regulars coming and going, but the Indian hadn't shown. Sue called Julia.

"I'll be leaving at two p.m.," Sue said.

"Well, I guess we'll have to come up with a plan B if you don't see him by then," Julia said. "It's very odd. Yesterday, he seemed quite willing to help out."

"I'll give you a call when I get home," Sue said.

"All right. Later then."

— — —

Sue stepped off the curb and onto cross-town bus number forty-two. Her favorite driver was perched behind the wheel. "Hey there, good lookin'," Sue chirped.

"Hi, Miss Sue. Beautiful day, isn't it?" Red replied.

"Damn nice day, except that I got stood up."

"Now what kinda guy would do a thing like that, Miss Sue?"

"An Indian. Not that I have anything against Native Americans. Heck, they were here before we were. But this guy just plain didn't show."

"Not much you can do about that."

"How's your wife doin', Red?"

"Oh, she's hangin' in there. She started her treatments. She's a brave one, she is." Red steered the bus onto the next cross street. "Hey, Miss Sue, lookey there," he said, pointing down the sidewalk. A man with black braids walked down the sidewalk by himself.

Sue craned her neck to get a look. "Pull up past him, so I can get a look at his face."

Red crept the bus down the street.

"That's him," Sue said. "You can drop me right here, Red." Sue hopped off the bus.

The Indian walked slowly away from her.

"Dr. Wilson?"

He paused and turned.

"Jack Wilson, right?"

Wilson nodded.

"You were supposed to come see me this morning."

"There was a change of plans."

"What do you mean? I didn't even give you the plans yet."

"I can't meet with David Peters," he said.

"Why not?"

Wilson reached into his pocket and withdrew a wad of paper. He slowly unfolded it and held it in front of Sue.

"What's this?" she asked.

"A family tree. Do you see this name here?" he said, pointing to Nelson Appleton Miles. "He was responsible for the deaths of more Indians than any other man in history. He is David Peters's great-grandfather."

Sue looked into Wilson's darkened eyes, and she turned away. Then she looked into his eyes again. "Let me ask you something, Jack Wilson. What if the great Wovoka turned out to be a fraud? Do you think it would be fair for the world to hold that against you, his great-grandson?"

Wilson stood speechless.

"People change, Jack. David Peters is a fine person, and he deserves to be judged on his own."

The darkness left Wilson's eyes.

Sue reached into her pocket and removed the slip of paper. "Now you have a date with an airplane, and I sure hope to hell you're on it." She handed him the information.

Wilson nodded, turned, and walked away.

— — —

Bob Sanchez stood by the stairs of the Cessna Citation when the taxi pulled up. Wilson climbed out of the cab and looked at the jet in awe.

"Dr. Wilson, it's a great honor, sir," Sanchez said. "I've been a fan of your work for many years."

"Such beautiful creations these little jets are," Wilson said. "I've never been this close to one."

"Please climb aboard, Doctor. We have a date with a supercomputer."

— — —

Dr. Miller got off the elevator and joined David in Room 99. "David, something new has happened with the bees. It may be relevant."

"What is it?" David asked.

"First, I should give you some background." Miller paused. "What I am about to tell you is top secret classified information. It cannot leave this room."

"I understand."

"A few months ago, the CIA conducted an operation in conjunction with the air force over the cities of Minneapolis, Denver, and Kansas City. It was, for all intents and purposes, a harmless experiment to test the distribution of VX nerve agent over populated areas."

David's eyes widened.

"A deactivated version of VX was used for the test. Ground sensors were placed at various locations in each city to measure concentrations and dispersal rates. The tests went off according to plan, and the data was collected."

"But there was a problem," David guessed.

"A few months later, we began to see the first signs of a cancer cluster in each of these cities, so naturally, our first thought was that the VX gas had caused the cancer. Tests have proven this not to be the case."

"So it's a coincidence?"

"I thought so until today. The ring of bees in Wirth Park was a critical clue, but we just didn't know what it meant. We found similar rings of dead bees in Denver and Kansas City. In each case, the ring was found at the center of a cancer cluster ring like we have in Minneapolis."

"So the VX gas killed the bees?"

"Not directly. When we discovered the first ring of bees, I had our lab conduct a controlled experiment with honeybees and deactivated VX gas. The bees didn't react to it at all, or so we thought. The VX triggered the bees' internal suicide mechanism—their cancer gene. The bees committed suicide."

"Like a herd of beached whales," David recalled.

"While it may be difficult to prove, my best guess is that the bees have triggered a similar suicide mechanism in the human population. We may have a cancer gene similar to the bees, but we haven't discovered it yet."

"Wow."

"If your theory of a bee behavior transfer is credible, this could account for the cancer gene being activated in humans."

"Where does the dance come into the picture?"

"The dance appears to be some kind of immune response to the cancer cluster. I am convinced that the dance is fighting the cancer, not feeding it."

"But we have the National Guard trying to stop the dance."

"I know. They have their agenda, and we have ours. We must figure out a way to shut the cancer down on our own."

— — —

Katie arrived home from school. "Hi, Mom."

"Welcome home, honey."

Katie watched Julia busy herself in the kitchen. Julia could sense that she had something on her mind.

"Mom? When is Dad coming home?"

"I'm not sure, honey."

"If he's innocent, why can't he just come home?"

"It's a little more complicated than that. First, the police have to find the person who really did it."

"But if they think Dad did it, why would they be looking for someone else?"

Katie has a point, Julia thought. "It's not always the police that find the criminals. Sometimes, ordinary people find them too."

Katie tapped her fingers on the kitchen counter.

Julia got an idea. "Would you like to go for a walk?"

"Sure, Mom. Where are we going?"

"Just around the neighborhood."

Julia and Katie walked over to the corner of Second Avenue and Oak. The curtains were drawn at 201 Oak, Anne Hoepner's house, and a for sale sign stood out in front. They went to the house next door—203 Oak—and rang the doorbell.

A woman in her sixties answered the door. "Yes?"

"My name is Julia Peters, and this is my daughter, Katie. Could we speak to you for a few minutes?"

"What are you selling?" the woman snapped.

"We're not selling anything," Julia said. "We just need your help."

The woman looked askance at the two of them. "Are you with a church or something? I already belong to a church."

"We're looking for the person who killed Anne Hoepner," Katie blurted.

A wave of fear came over the woman's face. "Oh, I know who you are," she said. "You're David Peters's wife."

Julia nodded.

"I'm very sorry; I can't get involved."

The woman was about to close the door when Katie said, "My mom's got cancer."

The woman's expression changed. She recognized the blue turban Julia wore, the way it was tied in back. "I had one of those. Why don't you come in for tea."

"That's very kind of you," Julia replied.

The woman opened the door wide to welcome them. Before closing it, she leaned outside and scanned the sidewalk.

"Your home is very lovely," Julia said.

"Most of these things were my mother's," the woman replied.

"My dad is innocent," Katie said.

"You'll have to excuse my daughter," Julia said. "She tends to speak what's on her mind."

The woman looked at Katie and smiled. "You're going to go places, young lady. The world needs more girls like you."

"Katie is right," Julia said. "In spite of appearances, my husband is innocent. He was only trying to warn Miss Hoepner."

"I suspected that your husband might be innocent right from the start. Anne Hoepner had a very volatile boyfriend. I was frightened to death of him."

"Do you remember his name?"

"I never knew his name. But one day after hearing a loud argument over there, I wrote down his license plate number." She slid open a drawer in an antique end table and removed a sheet of stationery.

"Didn't the police come and talk to you afterward?"

"Yes, but I was too scared to give them the license plate number. I didn't want to get involved. When your husband was arrested, I thought maybe I had done the right thing. I'm so sorry."

Julia folded the paper and put it in her purse. "We forgive you," Julia said.

"What kind of tea do you like, young lady?"

"Lemon tea, please, with lots of honey."

FOURTEEN

JEROME PUSHED HIS DUST mop across the CDC lobby. He wondered what was going on down in Room 99. Whatever it was, he knew it was important. He felt differently about his job now. *Yes*, he thought, *even a guy who pushes a mop can make a difference.* As his mother said, the world needs a lot of different people to make it go around. The prospect of telling Catherine the truth about his job seemed less daunting now.

Two men approached the CDC entrance. Jerome couldn't help but notice them. One was an Indian. Jerome hadn't seen an Indian like this before, with long braids and feathers. When they came inside, Jerome recognized the other man—the nice Dr. Sanchez.

"Good morning, Jerome," Sanchez said. "This is Dr. Wilson."

Jerome nodded.

"Dr. Wilson will be with us for a day or two. I want you to take care of anything he requires."

"No problem," Jerome replied.

"Right now, you can take him to Room 99."

Jerome set his dust mop aside. "Right this way, Dr. Wilson."

Wilson scrutinized the cavernous CDC lobby and followed Jerome to the elevator. Jerome entered his code, and the elevator began its long descent. Down, down, down the elevator plunged.

"Not many people are allowed down here," Jerome said. "You must be somebody important."

Wilson nodded but didn't say a word. His face displayed equal parts bewilderment and concern.

Finally, the elevator slowed to a stop. "Anything you need, Dr. Wilson, anything at all, you just ask somebody to page Jerome." The doors opened, and Wilson stepped out. "I think you'll find them right in there," Jerome pointed.

Wilson walked slowly into Room 99. It was like nothing he had ever seen, right out of science fiction. David sat alone, writing on a yellow legal pad.

"We are close to the Earth Mother here," Wilson said.

David sprang out of his seat. "Jack! Am I glad to see you!"

"A lot of water under the bridge." Wilson gave him a Paiute shake.

"I guess you know about my legal problems," David said.

"Not everything in life is what it appears to be."

"It was all just a big misunderstanding."

"I hear you've made more discoveries."

"Dr. Miller and I have put many of the pieces together, but we've reached a dead end with the cancer cluster. We're hoping that you can help us."

"I'll do what I can," Wilson said.

"First, let me introduce you to the brains of the operation. Gloria?"

"What can I do for you, Mr. Peters?"

Wilson's head spun, trying to locate the woman with the lovely voice.

"I'd like to introduce you to Dr. Jack Wilson."

"It's a pleasure to meet you, Dr. Wilson. I've been programmed with all your scientific papers." The titles of Wilson's papers flashed across the plasma display. "It is an honor to be working with you."

"Thank you," Wilson sputtered.

"She's right there," David pointed.

Gloria's lights twinkled.

"Gloria has helped us prove the existence of superorganisms."

"I would like to see that," Wilson said.

"Gloria, please bring up the live BIOSAT II image of Minneapolis."

Gloria complied.

Wilson's eyes grew wide.

"Gloria, turn on infrared imaging and heat signature sensing." The image turned dark blue and became populated with thousands of tiny yellow dots.

Wilson's mouth fell open.

"Now for my own two cents," David said. "Gloria, activate the ghost dance formula."

The turbine generator revved up. The dance began flowing like a great river, and the room throbbed with the sound of a pulsing heart.

"My God," Wilson whispered. "It's the Earth Mother, herself. She's alive." Tears streamed down Wilson's cheeks. "This is what my people have dreamed for centuries."

Miller stepped off the elevator. He watched and listened from the doorway.

"I didn't see it as clearly before," Wilson said. "I thought this was an echo of Wovoka's ghost dance. It is really the other way around. Wovoka must have seen the Earth Mother in a dream and used it as a model for his ghost dance."

"The dance was stronger than this a few days ago," David said. "There are certain people in the government who are trying to slow it down."

"They will not slow it down without paying a price. Nature is a stickler for balance."

"We think the dance may actually be fighting the cancer cluster."

"If that is true, then stopping the dance would seem a bad decision. Why would the government want to do that?" Wilson asked.

"Remember my theory about honeybee behavior being passed over to humans? Well, it looks like it may actually be happening. There have been numerous clues."

Wilson thought for a moment. "This would explain the strange human swarms in Minneapolis, wouldn't it?"

"And it would explain my son's odd behavior," David added. "Certain people have acquired the behavior of killer bees. These are the people the government wants to locate."

"So they can lock them up?"

"No. So they can make soldiers out of them."

"My God," Wilson muttered. "They're mad."

Miller stepped out of the shadows. "We were hoping that you might help us win this battle, Dr. Wilson—help us give the Earth Mother a boost, if you will."

"Jack, this is Dr. Charles Miller, the executive director of the CDC."

Miller extended a hand. "Pleasure to meet you, Dr. Wilson. We are honored to have you here."

"That is an interesting notion, doctor, the idea of giving the Earth Mother a boost. We are so accustomed to working in competition with nature; it is odd to think in terms of helping her do her job."

"Isn't that what the native cultures did," David said, "work *with* rather than *against* nature?"

Wilson sighed. "It is sad that so many Indians have forgotten this—humankind's sacred connection to nature. Our native culture is only a shadow of what it once was."

"Perhaps Wovoka anticipated this," Miller said. "Perhaps he knew the dance would be needed in the future."

Wilson nodded. "You make an interesting point, Doctor. There may have been more to the ghost dance than just speaking to dead people."

David looked at Wilson. "Are you thinking what I'm thinking, Jack?"

"There aren't many Indians around today who know how to do it."

"Well then, we'll just have to teach them."

A broad smile spread across Wilson's face. "I guess I could round up some of the old timers."

"We can use our live image here as a gauge of whether it's working," David added.

"There is absolutely nothing scientific about this," Miller said, "and I love it."

— — —

Wilson watched the clouds glide by from the window of the Citation. He was on his way to find out just how real an Indian he really was. The knowledge and wisdom of his forefathers was going to be put to the test. His reputation was on the line, as was the reputation of his great-grandfather, Wovoka. Wilson knew he had only one chance to get it right. This was his final exam.

Wilson lifted the telephone receiver near his seat and dialed a number. "Hello, Georgie? It's Jack. I'm on an airplane, somewhere east of you, I guess. I need your help. Can you round up the chiefs? We're gonna do a dance, a ghost dance. Yes, you heard me right. I want all the tribes in the region on this. I want to see those boys from the casinos too. It's a matter of life or death. Yes, I'm serious. I need at least a hundred dancers. Three hundred would be better. The day after tomorrow at sunrise. The big oak tree in Wirth Park. I'm counting on you, Georgie."

— — —

The Indians began arriving at 4:00 a.m. Some wanted to get used to the surroundings and showed up hours before sunrise. Wilson wore a ghost dance shirt that Wovoka had worn in 1900. Several eagle feathers hung from his braids. On his feet, Wilson wore soleless deerskin boots tied at the calf, and under his arm, he carried Wovoka's old drum. Cars and pickups filled both sides of Wirth Parkway. Droves of Indians in traditional dress streamed toward the giant oak. As they approached the tree, many could feel the dark energy that Wilson had noticed when he first went there.

Wilson climbed on top of a milk crate to address the crowd. "Thank you all for coming this morning. I know, for many younger Indians, the customs of our forefathers have lost their meaning. The ghost dance is one of those lost customs. One hundred years ago, the US government outlawed the ghost dance. The government claimed that it perpetuated false hopes, that it conflicted with Christian values. I ask you to consider another possibility—that the government recognized the power of the ghost dance and shut it down to prevent it from being used against them. What if the ghost dance had the power to prevent disease and war? That is what we are here to find out today. The Earth Mother is fighting a great battle in our midst. She needs our help. I believe we can help her win this battle. Let's show her what we can do."

Wilson's son, Numa, and two FBI agents sat in a nearby car and watched the proceedings.

The warriors, chiefs, and medicine men and women spread into a great circle around the oak, 380 in all. The circle nearly touched the edges of the park. They stood in silence until the first sliver of sunlight appeared on the horizon. At the moment of daybreak, Wilson raised his drumstick and began to beat Wovoka's drum.

— — —

David and Charles Miller sat at the ready in Room 99. Gloria labored to keep the ghost dance formula functioning. The heartbeat throbbed, and the turbine generator whined.

"The dance looks the way it did yesterday," David said. "The National Guard must still have the streets blocked."

"Yes, Dr. Sanchez confirmed that for me this morning," Miller said.

David looked at his watch. "Sunrise is at five-fifty in Minneapolis. That's right about now. Dr. Wilson should be getting under way."

"Your friend Dr. Wilson is quite an interesting man. We could use more people like him in the field of science, people willing to sail into uncharted waters."

"He's involved in this only for one reason," David said, "to avenge his great-grandfather. It is one thing to be the great-grandson of a hero and quite another to be the great-grandson of a fraud. Wovoka's legacy was trampled on by those who killed the ghost dance."

"It sounds like you have a strong connection with him."

"More of a connection than I realized," David said. "My great-grandfather was General Nelson Appleton Miles, the man who brought down the ghost dance, the archenemy of the American Indian."

Miller was stunned.

"The CIA told me about it. My family had kept it secret all these years."

"So you're here to repay a debt."

"I didn't know that until Dr. Wilson's visit. There is nobody on Earth who would like to see this work more than me."

"Well, this might be your lucky day, Mr. Peters. Take a look at that."

The dance was moving faster, picking up steam like a river after a hard rain. The throbbing heartbeat sounded stronger, more vital.

"Is this really happening?" David wondered. "Gloria?"

"What can I do for you, Mr. Peters?"

"Please calculate a rate of change for the ghost dance video stream."

"The ghost dance video stream is changing at a rate of 10 percent per minute and accelerating."

— — —

The sun was fully off the horizon in Theodore Wirth Park. The Indians spun and bobbed as the circle slowly rotated around the giant oak. A dozen drums provided the rhythm. Wilson could feel the dark energy being pushed back by the dance. He could sense something was happening.

Numa and the FBI agents watched from the car. "This really gives me the creeps," one of the agents said. "I think we should call in the guard."

"On what grounds?" Numa asked. "It's a bunch of people dancing in a park, for Christ's sake."

"Unlawful assembly," the agent replied. "Do you think they have a permit for this?"

"I doubt it," the other agent said.

"Well, we're gonna find out."

They climbed out of the car and began walking toward the Indians.

"I wouldn't get near them if I were you," Numa said. "It's like a force field out there. It can really play with your brain."

The two agents stopped and looked at Numa.

"My relatives invented the ghost dance," Numa said. "Believe me, you don't want to mess with it."

Bob Sanchez drove up and climbed out of his car. "Can I help you gentlemen?"

"Who are you?"

"I'm the organizer. Dr. Bob Sanchez, CDC."

"You got a permit?"

Sanchez reached into his pocket. "Sure, right here."

The agent looked it over and handed it back to him. "We've got the National Guard on standby, Dr. Sanchez. Just remember that."

"I'm sure you do."

The agents turned and left.

Sanchez's cell phone rang.

"Bob, it's Charles Miller. It's working. It is completely and utterly unscientific, but it's working. The dance is back up to full steam and accelerating."

Sanchez walked back to his car. He had two helium balloons inside, one red and one green. He pulled the green balloon out of the car by its string and joined a group of spectators nearby. The balloon floated a few feet above his head.

Wilson danced and shook with fury. Sweat poured from his brow. He pounded the hundred-year-old drum. In the sky above him, a magpie circled the oak tree and landed near the spectators. That's when Wilson saw the green balloon.

— — —

Miller tapped his pencil. "The next question will be whether the dance really has the healing power that we think it does. It will take time to see results."

"If it worked, though," David mused, "imagine the possibilities."

"Well, for starters, we should be thinking about arranging dances in Denver and Kansas City. It stands to reason we'll have the same results there."

David looked at the plasma screen. "From the sounds of what Wilson was saying, I think the power of the dance may go beyond curing disease."

The telephone rang, and Miller picked it up. "Charles Miller. Thank you for passing that on. I'll let him know." Miller looked at

David and smiled. "Indeed, this is your lucky day, Mr. Peters. The police just arrested Anne Hoepner's killer. You're free to go home."

"That's—great." David's elation was tempered by the thought that he'd be leaving Gloria and the top secret Room 99.

"I hope we can keep you on retainer, though, and fly you back here from time to time," Miller suggested.

"I think I might be able to work that into my schedule." David beamed.

"Our Citation is waiting for you at the airport. I'm sure you're looking forward to seeing your family. When you get back to Minneapolis, remember that we are still in a wrestling match with the CIA. You must tread carefully."

David reached down his shirt and withdrew the eagle feather. "I've got this to protect me. Jack Wilson gave it to me."

David turned and looked at Gloria. "Thank you, Gloria."

"It's been a pleasure working with you, Mr. Peters."

Miller scribbled a note to himself on his yellow pad. "I'm going to have our IT people set you up with a secure fiber-optic connection at your house. You'll have direct access to the CDC as if you were in the building, and Gloria will be at your disposal."

"Wow, that's fantastic, Dr. Miller. Gloria and I still have a way to go with our relationship. I might have to get myself a new computer, though. The CIA took my old one."

"Consider it done," Miller said. "Just let me know what you'd like."

— — —

Sue had David's coffee ready before he even reached his seat.

"Hey there, good lookin'."

"Hey, Sue," David smiled.

"Damn, it's good to see you, and not through some metal bars either."

"Likewise, Sue. You and Julia did a heck of a job pulling Jack Wilson out of the woodwork."

"We almost lost him at one point, but I gave him a good talking-to and straightened him out."

"Good thing we had you onboard, Sue."

"Have you seen the paper this morning?" Sue dropped the front section in front of David.

National Guard Breaks Up Indian Rally

"Those bastards," David muttered.

"You mean the Indians?"

"No, the CIA. They're trying to stop the dance. Remember the National Guard roadblocks? That's what they're for."

"I thought I got rid of that Preston guy," Sue said.

"Oh, this starts a lot higher up than him. I wouldn't be surprised if the White House has their fingers in this."

"What can we do about it?"

"Good question." David gazed out the diner window. "First thing I've got to do is find Jack Wilson."

— — —

David could see Native Resorts Casino when he was still a mile away from it. It rose on the horizon like the castle in *The Wizard of Oz*. The parking lots seemed to go on forever. David walked in through the front colonnade, pulled on the gold-plated door handle, and the ten-foot glass door opened by itself without a sound. "Welcome to Native Resorts," a scantily clad squaw chirped. David cruised past her and found the information desk.

"May I help you?" the woman asked.

"I'm looking for a man by the name of Jack Wilson, Dr. Jack Wilson."

"Is he a guest here?"

"Probably not, he lives in the area."

"I'm not sure I'd be able to help you then," she said.

"He's Native American."

"You mean an Indian?"

"Right."

"There are hundreds of Indians employed here, but I don't think we have any who are doctors."

"Maybe I'll just take a look around," David replied. "Thanks."

David meandered into the gaming area. Musical slot machines dominated the atmosphere with a cacophonous symphony of electronic noise. Customers fed tokens into them with abandon. Cocktail waitresses cruised through like jet rangers, and a small army of suited security people kept a close eye on things.

"Excuse me, sir?" David heard a towering voice behind him. He turned around and had to step back to take him all in. The man was Native American, six foot six, at least 250 pounds, and meticulously dressed. He jingled several half-dollars in his pocket as he spoke. "You're looking for Jack Wilson?"

"Yes, that's right."

"Are you a cop?"

"No, nothing like that. I'm just a friend of his."

"You'll find him in the executive poker suite, in the back."

The suite looked like a smokehouse. The air was so thick you could barely see the other side. Jack sat this game out; he'd already blown his wad for the day.

"Hey, Jack."

Wilson glanced at David, and then he turned away.

"I saw the headline," David said.

"I'm finished, washed up. I wish we never hatched that crazy plan."

"What do you mean, Jack? It was working. The dance was working!"

"I'll never be able to face my Indian friends again."

"Well, maybe they'd feel differently if they knew what this was really about."

"I told them before the dance we were going to help the Earth Mother. The idea of it appeals to them, but only in an abstract way. The National Guard is what they will remember about yesterday. These people have families. They don't want trouble."

"The cancer is very real, Jack. My wife is one of the victims."

Wilson turned toward David. "I'm sorry."

"Don't you see what happened? Yesterday was history repeating itself. That scene with the National Guard was a replay of identical scenes one hundred years ago. Nothing has changed. The Indians possess an ancient power, and the government doesn't want you to have it."

Wilson stared into the smoke and shadows.

David continued, "Wovoka was given a special gift. He knew how to use the gift, and he knew how to teach other people to use it. If you really want to honor Wovoka, you should keep this gift alive. From where I was sitting in Atlanta, you definitely know how to use it."

"I'll never be able to get the Indians back again."

"Well, you know what? Maybe the Indians don't have an exclusive on this mojo. Maybe it's time to bring some other folks into the picture."

— — —

David sat down in front of his new computer, a Mac Micro with a thirty-six-inch plasma monitor. The big monitor reminded him of sitting in front of the giant screens in Room 99. He was connected to the CDC by a blindingly fast fiber-optic line.

"Gloria, how are you today?"

"I'm fine, thank you, Mr. Peters."

"How's the weather in Atlanta?"

"Seventy-five degrees, mostly sunny." A view of the Atlanta skyline flashed onto the monitor.

"Gloria, please bring up the ghost dance video stream."

The dance came up on David's monitor.

"Gloria, please calculate a rate of change for the ghost dance video stream."

"The ghost dance video stream is changing at a rate of 2 percent per hour and decelerating."

"Damn. We have got to get another dance going." David sprang out of his chair and marched into the kitchen.

"We need to get another dance going."

"What sort of dance?" Julia asked.

"A ghost dance, just like the Indians were doing."

"The government doesn't seem to like those."

"Well then, we'll disguise it as something else."

"Like what?"

"I don't know. We need to do something that is completely legal but has the same effect as a ghost dance."

"I've got an idea," Julia said. "How about a square dance or a contra dance?"

"That might work. And we tell everybody we're going for *The Guinness Book of World Records*. That would account for the size and duration of it."

"Sounds like fun," Julia said.

"I just need to run it by Jack Wilson."

— — —

"I know you've never done this before, Jack, but I want you to keep an open mind."

Wilson's braids hung in front of his cowboy shirt. His feet ached inside his boots. He hadn't worn them in years. Directly across from him stood a cherubic white woman who was apparently his dance partner. The dance pairings just sort of happened. The music started, and Wilson's partner launched herself into synchronous orbit. Wilson pitched and yawed and do-si-doed. But after the eighth promenade, his feet hurt so much he had to stop.

"I just don't think this is going to work," Wilson said. "It's entertaining, but there is no connection to the Earth Mother in square dancing."

"Okay, I can see that," David admitted. "We'll try something else."

— — —

Throbbing bass shook the sidewalk outside the Big O nightclub. *Boom boom, chicka-la, boom boom, chicka-la, boom boom ...* David and Wilson slipped inside.

"This music has more of a heartbeat feel to it," David shouted. He and Wilson pushed their way through the sweat and flesh and parked themselves off the end of the bar. The dance floor was awash in pheromones. Complete strangers gyrated against one another, spinning, sliding, bumping, and performing various versions of the foreplay shuffle.

A large-breasted Latino girl materialized next to Wilson. She smiled and fondled one of his braids. "Wanna dance, cowboy?"

Wilson didn't know what to make of her.

David nodded toward the dance floor. "Go ahead, Jack. It's research, remember?"

The girl led him toward the mayhem by his braid.

Wilson reluctantly stepped onto the Plexiglas dance floor. Lights flashed, and the floor shook. The girl's breasts whirled around like twin moons, the gravity of her body barely holding them in orbit. Wilson held his position on the corner of the dance floor like a mother ship. He swung and bobbed and spun in place, trying to work out some navigational coordinates. But the dance floor was just too crowded, and everyone seemed to be on different missions. When the song ended, he returned to Earth.

"This just isn't working," Wilson said.

"I'm getting that feeling too," David said. They left the Big O and headed home.

— — —

David gazed at the dance on his plasma monitor. Katie stood behind him, looking over his shoulder. "What's the problem, Dad?"

"I'm trying to figure out what kind of dance this is."

"They're not dancing, Dad. They're just being."

"What do you mean, honey?"

"They're not dancing because they don't know they're dancing."

David spun around and looked at Katie. She had a point. Dancing might only be a means to an end, a way to get people into a certain frame of mind. The dance might not be about dancing at all. "You're a very smart little girl, Katie Peters."

"I know, Dad. Sometimes kids are better at seeing things."

— — —

"Hey there, good lookin'." Sue's beer cans jangled.

"Hey, Sue."

"So did you find the Indian?"

"Yeah. I took him out dancing last night."

Sue practically dropped the coffeepot trying to conjure up that image.

"It was a disaster," David said. "We were trying to come up with a replacement for the ghost dance."

"You might have been looking in the wrong places," Sue said.

"I know. But then, this morning, my daughter made an interesting point: the dance might have nothing to do with dancing."

"How's that?"

"It might only be about moving in a circle and being in a certain state of mind."

"Hmmm." Sue wasn't sure what to make of that idea. She wiped down the counter. David glanced at the headlines on a nearby newspaper:

Global Warming Confirmed

"Well, *there's* something of interest to the Earth Mother," he said. "That could be the answer, right there. Sue, I think it's time to organize another circle dance."

— — —

Jamie carried a stack of posters under his arm. He found a vacant spot on the school bulletin board and tacked a poster to it. Marsha Reeves noticed him.

"What's your poster about, Jamie?"

Jamie ignored her.

"Look, I'm sorry. I know I was wrong about your dad. I don't know what got into me."

Jamie continued to ignore her.

"How's your mom doing?"

"She's okay."

"Please tell her I asked about her, will you?"

"Sure."

Marsha watched Jamie walk away. Then she took a closer look at the poster.

— — —

Wilson turned on his car radio. He was still tired from his late night dancing expedition. The radio announcer broke into the music with a special announcement.

"Here's something just in, folks. Tomorrow, there's going to be a kids' walk in Wirth Park at nine a.m. to highlight global warming. Organizers expect a large turnout, so be sure to get there early. Now for more music …"

Wilson gazed at the cloud formations. A smile spread across his face. He knew David was up to something.

— — —

"Dr. Miller, it's David Peters."

"Yes, Mr. Peters."

"I guess you heard about the trouble with the National Guard and the Indians."

"Yes, I did. It's sad that we would see a scene like that today. There are forces at work here, political forces, that are very powerful."

"Well, we've come up with a workaround. If you're not too busy, you might want to head out here early tomorrow."

Miller smiled. "I wouldn't miss it."

FIFTEEN

THE BUSES STARTED ARRIVING at 8:15 that morning. They stretched down Wirth Parkway as far as you could see. Julia and Sue directed traffic.

"Hey, check this out," Sue hollered.

"How on Earth did we get so many school buses?" Julia asked.

The first school bus opened its door, and Marsha Reeves stepped out. "I hope this isn't a problem," she said.

"Well—no," Julia stammered. "How many are you?"

"I think I managed to divert kids from six schools. Something like twenty-six buses, give or take."

Julia was stunned.

"I thought it was the least I could do."

A tear rolled down Julia's cheek. "God bless you, Marsha Reeves."

"Okay, kids!" Marsha commanded. "Off the bus and over to the big tree to receive your instructions."

David had staked off a large circle around the tree earlier that morning. He figured, as long as the inner radius of the circle stays the same all the way around, the energy should stay properly focused.

"And one other thing, Dad," Katie said. "You don't need to make a speech. The kids already know why they're here. Each of them needs to think about it his or her own way."

"Right."

The dance commenced with very little fanfare. There was no music, no drum, just thousands of little feet pressing against the grass like fingers on a harp. There were so many of them that they had to walk fifteen or twenty deep. The ring of life ebbed and flowed like an endless river. The adults watched from the perimeter and sipped lemonade.

A black Lincoln Town Car pulled up. Charles Miller and Jerome climbed out and walked toward the viewing area. Miller's eyes were fixed on the children. "David, this is the most beautiful thing I've ever seen," he said. "I hope you don't mind that I brought Jerome along."

"We wouldn't be here if it wasn't for Jerome."

Jerome nodded and smiled. He felt really good about himself. If fact, he felt really good, period. *What is this?* he thought. It felt as though he was inside some kind of good-vibe machine. He'd never felt like this before.

David scanned the horizon and noticed someone standing alone at the park's edge. He recognized the classic silhouette. It was Jack Wilson. David strode over to him.

Wilson wore a broad smile. "You are a clever man, Mr. Peters."

"Well, at least we don't have to worry about the National Guard."

"That's not what I mean," Wilson said. "The children. They have a closer connection to the Earth Mother than adults do. Their minds have not been cluttered up yet. They dance like innocents."

"So you think it's working?"

Wilson nodded. "Oh, you have no idea. Our Indian ghost dance didn't have one tenth of *this* energy. This is like a nuclear power plant of love."

David stood speechless.

"The Earth Mother is smiling. Oh, she is smiling!" Wilson exclaimed.

"I'll be right back," David stammered. He ran over to Miller and Jerome.

Jerome had a huge smile on his face. Miller was on his cell phone. He closed the phone and put it back into his pocket. "That was Gloria. I asked her to call me if she recorded any significant changes in the ghost dance video stream."

"And ...?" David asked.

"We're up 50 percent in the past hour and climbing."

"I have to find my wife," David said. He pushed his way through the crowd until he found her.

"I feel better," Julia said. "I don't know why, but I really do feel better. It's like I had cancer an hour ago, and now I don't. Strange."

"Jamie! What about Jamie?"

"I'm right here, Dad. I just took a water break."

"How do you feel?"

"Different. Like I did before all the trouble started. It's really weird."

Miller pulled out his cell phone again and dialed Sanchez. "Bob, we appear to be onto something here. I want you to keep a close eye on the cancer stats from nine this morning onward. Let me know if you see any changes at all."

— — —

A month later, similar dances were arranged in Denver and Kansas City with the same results. The cancer clusters were virtually stopped in their tracks. The human swarms disappeared, and the CIA gave up on the killer bee project. Sadly for David, the dance—the one seen from the satellite—also faded away. Without the cancer cluster, it had no reason to exist. The public never knew about the cancer cluster, so there was no glory for David or for Jack Wilson. Wovoka remained in obscurity. Most modern Indians still didn't know his name. With Hadley's help, the honeybees slowly returned to Minneapolis, but the fascinating honeybee pattern David uncovered was gone. Just to make sure there wouldn't be any repercussions, the government quietly removed the old oak tree in Wirth Park. In place of it, they populated the park with a forest of younger trees, with nature trails among them. The wildflowers still flourished there.

David and Gloria spent many hours scanning the American landscape for signs of another dance. Not a single pattern showed up in the many yellow swarms they viewed from space. It appeared that the situation in Minneapolis was unique, brought on by a unique set of circumstances. Had the CIA not tested the VX gas, the chain of events might never have occurred.

— — —

"Good morning, Gloria."

"Good morning, Mr. Peters."

"How's everything in your part of the world?"

"Things are fine in Atlanta, but it is very quiet here in Room 99."

"I'm sure you'll see more glory days before long."

"Thank you. I appreciate your confidence, Mr. Peters."

"I can't believe I'm talking to a machine," David said. "Not just any machine either. The formerly out-of-work marketing guy is connected to a Cray XT7 supercomputer located in a top secret underground bunker. And speaking of marketing, I wonder how Raj Nabi is doing?"

David's computer chimed to let him know an e-mail had just arrived in his in-box. He checked his incoming mail. There, right at the top, was an e-mail from none other than Raj Nabi. It was a startling coincidence. *How strange*, David thought. *I haven't even thought about him in months.*

David,

I hope all is well with you. As you may have seen on the news, things are taking a turn for the worst in Pakistan. The conservative clerics are trying to push us back into the dark ages. They use hatred for the West as fuel for their fire. Most people here don't know the first thing about the West, so they are easily influenced by dogma. I think the clerics are just looking to expand their sphere of power. I wish there was something we could do. I just don't know what. I hope this finds you well.

Peace,

Raj Nabi

"Business as usual in the Middle East," David muttered. He put on his shoes and headed for Max's Diner.

— — —

"Hey there, good lookin'." Sue had something on the tip of her tongue she couldn't wait to share.

"What's on your mind, Sue?"

"I just had the weirdest thing happen. After our adventure a few months ago, maybe it won't seem *that* weird."

David took a sip of coffee. "Try me."

"Things were kinda slow this morning, so I got thinkin' maybe I'd call somebody I haven't talked to in a while. I looked through my little black book and came upon the name of my best friend in high school. The last time we spoke was six years ago at our class reunion."

"Yeah …"

"When I dialed the number, it didn't ring. I just heard a voice. It was her. She had the same idea and dialed me at the same time. After six years!"

David pondered. This was indeed interesting news, especially since the Raj Nabi e-mail that morning. "You're right, Sue. That is interesting."

"I mean, what are the chances of that?"

David sipped his coffee.

"It's like we're all hooked up to some kinda big machine," Sue added.

David gulped the last of his coffee and drove straight home.

— — —

The phone number was scratched on the back of a beer coaster. David had a childhood friend with the red hair named Clark Husted. David ran into him at a bar shortly after he and Julia were married. It had been fifteen years since that chance meeting, and the beer coaster resided in David's desk drawer ever since. David dialed the number.

After a few rings, a voice answered, "Hello."

"Is this the Husted residence?"

"Who are you calling for?" the man asked.

"Clark Husted."

"May I ask who's calling?"

"It's David Peters."

"Holy shit, David! It's Clark!"

"Hey, Clark, how the hell are you?"

"This is too frigging weird. I was just looking up *your* number! How many years has it been? Fifteen?"

"You were gonna call *me*?" David said.

"I was looking for your number when it rang."

"I don't believe this. It's the second time this has happened to me today."

"You must have your mojo working or something. How have you been, man?"

The conversation drifted to chitchat, but David's brain was in full investigative mode. Something very strange was going on. When he got off the phone with Clark, he called Julia.

"David, you won't believe what just happened," Julia said.

"What?"

"I was sitting in the faculty lounge, and my mind drifted to the author of a book we're using in class. I thought, *Wouldn't it be great if we could get this guy to come talk to the class?*"

"Yeah ..."

"Only seconds later, the phone in the lounge rang. It was the publishing company of that very book, making an unsolicited call to see if we want to have the author do a book signing here. How weird is *that?*"

David was reminded of the trick Wilson did with the car radio, foreshadowing the announcer's words. "You're not alone, Julia. It happened to me and Sue today too."

"What!"

"The same kind of thing. Something's going on. It's like we're entering a period of synchronicity."

"It could just be some interesting coincidences," Julia said.

"No, this stuff is beyond coincidence. We are part of something so big that we can't see it yet."

"For a change, I believe you. I just don't know how anybody will ever prove it."

— — —

"Dr. Miller's office calling for David Peters."

"This is David Peters."

"One moment ..."

"David, it's Charles Miller."

"Yes, Doctor. What can I do for you?"

"I want you to take a trip to NSA headquarters in Maryland. They want you to take a look at something."

"The National Security Agency? Me? This sounds intriguing."

"I'm going to let them fill you in when you get there. See if you can bring Dr. Wilson with you. I'll have our jet out there tomorrow around noon."

"That works for me," David replied.

"All right then. They'll be expecting you at the NSA."

— — —

The Citation leveled off at forty-one thousand. Wilson gazed out the window at the cloud blanket below them. It looked like a snowy field deep in February. David couldn't get his mind off the NSA. There was no place more secretive in the Western world. He knew what most people knew: that the NSA listened to virtually every type of electronic communication, usually covertly. He also knew the NSA had been tapping into telephone companies' records, looking for calling patterns that might lead to terrorists. Beyond that, it was just a black glass building in Fort Meade, Maryland.

A nondescript silver minivan with Maryland plates met the Citation. The driver was in his thirties, wearing a sport shirt and Levis. He could have been the coach of the neighborhood softball team.

"So, how long have you worked for the NSA?" David asked the driver.

"I'm not sure who you're talking about," the driver replied. "I'm with the General Services Administration."

"There might have been a mistake. We were supposed to go to the NSA. They're expecting us."

The driver looked at David and smiled. "You're David Peters, right?"

"Yeah ..."

"You're all set."

Oh yeah, David thought, *they always said NSA stood for "No Such Agency."*

The building looked like a black glass toolbox. It could have been mistaken for just another corporate monolith were it not for the heavily fortified front entrance. There were no trees or plantings around it; the glass walls looked as if they'd been pushed right up out of the ground. The van passed through several security checkpoints and finally pulled up in front of the entrance. Two people were there to meet them. Once inside, they passed through metal detectors and received digital name badges.

David was surprised to see how ordinary the NSA facilities looked—nothing particularly high tech about it. The offices and work areas could have passed for any American corporation. *Of course, it's behind the scenes where the interesting stuff goes on,* he thought. Wilson quietly took it all in, his sixth sense in high gear. A staff member led them into a small meeting room, where two NSA employees awaited.

"Mr. Peters? Pleasure to meet you. And you must be Dr. Wilson."

They shook hands all around, but David noted that neither of them actually mentioned his name.

"Dr. Miller at the CDC suggested that we get your opinion on something."

David and Wilson looked at each other.

"As you may know, NSA has been collecting telephone calling data from various sources as part of the Homeland Security initiative. Over the years, we've developed methods to recognize patterns in telephone traffic. These patterns help us identify potential terrorist threats both in- and outside the United States. We use a variety of algorithms to evaluate the call traffic. When looking at large volumes of data, we prefer to use a graphical method, which makes it easier

to see trends. I'll show you what I mean." He punched a few strokes on a keyboard. An image appeared on a nearby wall monitor. The image looked like a moving abstract painting, with slowly blending colors and textures. "Obviously, you've got to be trained to read one of these things," he added.

"I guess you would," David said.

"But in the past few weeks, something entirely new has been coming from our data. We haven't the faintest idea what it is." He pressed another key on the keyboard, and the image changed dramatically. A beautiful ring of white light appeared on the screen. The ring slowly rotated, picking up energy in the center and shedding it in rainbows around the perimeter.

Wilson was transfixed.

"Whoa ..." David murmured.

"This graphically represents the current worldwide calling traffic. We've never seen an image as organized as this. It had sort of a biological look to it, so we ran it by the CDC to see what they thought. Dr. Miller suggested we talk to you two gentlemen."

Wilson walked closer to the monitor, his eyes wide. "It's her again."

"Who?" David asked.

"The Earth Mother. She's trying to get our attention."

The NSA people looked at each other.

"We've seen something like this before," David said, "but it only involved the city of Minneapolis."

"With telephone data?"

"No, we arrived at it a completely different way."

Wilson turned toward the others, his braids framing his face. "This is bigger than Minneapolis, bigger than the United States, bigger than humankind."

— — —

"I know what Raj Nabi needs to do," David declared.

"What about him?" Julia replied.

"It's been right in front of me, and I didn't see it."

"Why does Raj Nabi need to do something?"

"Because he's the perfect guy for the job. He's a marketing guy."

"What does he need to do?"

"Show the world how easy it is to coexist."

"That's a tall order," Julia said.

"It will all start with Raj Nabi."

"Why him?"

"I don't know why. I just know. You're going to have to trust me on this."

— — —

Two weeks later, David caught the first sliver of news on his car radio while driving to Max's.

"The children of Islamabad, Pakistan, staged an unprecedented event today. Thousands of children organized themselves into a massive ring that encircled the center of Islamabad. The event appears to have been organized by the children themselves as a celebration of life. Warring religious factions stood aside as the children took over the streets of the city for the first time."

David bolted into Max's.

"Hey there, good lookin'."

"Sue, did you catch the news?" David panted.

"No, what news?"

"The kids in Pakistan are dancing!"

"So?"

"I mean they're doing a circle dance, a huge one."

"How in the heck did they …?"

David just grinned back at her.

"You got friends over there?" she asked.

"Yeah, the guy who got my old job."

"It sounds kinda dangerous for the kids."

"That's the thing. They say it's completely neutralized the tension. This could be the answer, Sue, the answer to a whole lot of things."

— — —

David and Katie stared at the news coverage on CNN. Dramatic aerial images of Islamabad filled the screen. "It's amazing how the kids over there took to the dance," David said.

"No, it's not, Dad," Katie replied. "It makes perfect sense to a kid."

A great ring of children paraded around the center of the city. Adults stood by and watched from sidewalks and windows and doorways.

"I wonder if we could get more of these started?" David wondered.

"You won't have to, Dad. Once kids see this on TV, they'll get the idea. They'll want to start their own dances."

— — —

The next dance appeared a few days later in Tel Aviv, followed by another in Amman. Baghdad was quiet for the first time in years as children encircled the city. There was a dance in Los Angeles, followed by one in Tokyo and another in Paris. Soon China, Russia, and India were in the act, as well. Within a month, dances had occurred in fifty cities.

— — —

At first, no one picked up on it. From an adult's perspective, the dances were about children, nothing more. But the children felt it right away. They stood shoulder to shoulder with kids they never knew before—Jews with Arabs, blacks with whites, Hindus with Muslims, rich with poor—and it felt okay. It even felt *good*. The adults looked on with trepidation, staying on their own sides of the street, but the children were already forming bonds with cultures they had never known before.

"It is human nature to be wary of those we perceive as different," Wilson observed. "It is an ancient behavior, burned into our DNA. At some point in our distant past, this behavior may have served a purpose, but in a civilized world, it only serves to separate cultures. Religions have been devised to legitimize this behavior. The Christians, the Jews, the Muslims: everyone is guilty of it. People speak of *their* god, as if to say, 'My god is the genuine article.'"

"So why are children different?" David asked.

"Children have not become fully aware of their fears yet. They have not yet learned to fear people whose skin is a different color than theirs, people who speak a different language or pray to a different god."

"But when those children get older, we could be back to business as usual."

"Maybe or maybe not. As we saw in Wirth Park, the dance has a profound effect on those who witness it."

— — —

David first noticed the *ring* on the back of a minivan. It reminded him of one of those magnetized "support our troops" ribbons, made popular during the Iraq war. The ring, however, had no message. It was just a plain white ring, reminiscent of the ring of light he had seen at the NSA.

Variations of the ring began to pop up everywhere: in music videos, on T-shirts, billboards, and graffiti. The ring quickly worked its way up the food chain to become the most recognizable totem since the Christian cross. The ring crossed cultures and languages and religious barriers. At the United Nations, a representative from Somalia first used a hand gesture to represent the ring by touching his index fingers and his thumbs together. Without any words at all, everyone knew what the Somali meant by that gesture. People made reference to the ring in conversation; the phrase "to put a circle around it" was synonymous with bringing divergent parties together, finding common ground. The term "circle of life" took on a new meaning.

Initially, the Vatican was ambivalent about the ring. The pope called it a passing fad, a substitute for true spirituality. But when millions of Catholics began to celebrate the ring as a symbol for all things good, the church had no choice but to acknowledge it. Jewish and Muslim clergy, as well, were put off that the ring didn't conform to the teachings of the Torah or the Koran. The ring undercut all faiths by exposing the bedrock that binds us all. The ring had no rules, no dogma, no ethnic or economic boundaries. It didn't play favorites. The ring's concept was so simple; there was no need for prophets to teach it. Children grasped it right away. Those in positions of power tried to harness the ring, but it was akin to harnessing air, since it existed anywhere and everywhere. No one owned the rights to the ring; it couldn't be copyrighted or patented. It wasn't invented by somebody. The ring was a perfect good, a universal symbol of belonging, of being at one with the world.

— — —

Sue wiped down the counter. It was one of the two days a week that she worked the dinner shift. She could turn those counter seats five times on a good night. Sue glanced up just as the glass front door opened.

A Middle Eastern couple entered. The woman was draped in a blue satin shawl with gold trim. The man, in his seventies, held the door for her. Following them with his Mona Lisa smile was Omar, his jet black hair swooping like a grand staircase.

Sue dropped her rag and primped her uniform. "Hey there ..." She cut herself short.

Omar smiled. "I wanted to take my parents somewhere special for their anniversary," he explained. "And my mother said to take them somewhere that is special to me."

Sue's eyes welled up. "Well, I guess you came to the right place then. God, it's great to see you, Omar. We've got the best seats in the house for you right over here."

— — —

Jerome loved the sound of Catherine's voice over the telephone. Confident yet sweet, it was a sound he felt he'd never tire of.

"You know what I like about you, Jerome?"

"What's that?"

"You're straight with me. Flight attendants get hit on a lot. I've heard all kinds of tall tales from men. It's like, whatever they *really* do isn't good enough. They have to make something up to impress me. And then you come along, a nice guy who has the guts to tell me he works a floor polisher for a living."

"It's just what I do," Jerome replied.

Jerome was sworn to secrecy about his other activities at the CDC, but it didn't matter. Jerome knew he was *the man*. It didn't matter that Catherine didn't know.

"I think it's high time we got together for a glass of wine," Catherine said.

Jerome smiled. "You name the time and place, and I'll be there."

— — —

Wilson wore a faint smile that refused to go away. His eagle feather hung like a badge of victory.

"Okay, Jack, you can't tell me something isn't going on. Come on, what is it?" David asked.

Wilson's eyes had a lightness David hadn't seen before. He raised his head like a great warrior. "They're dancing," he beamed.

"Who's dancing?"

"My people."

"The tribes?"

"Yes. For the first time in a century, they are dancing, just as Wovoka taught them to do." A tear rolled down Wilson's face.

"Wovoka was a hundred years ahead of the rest of us," David said. "No one knew how important his discovery was."

Wilson removed a faded envelope from his pocket and handed it to David. "Actually, there was one person who knew."

David opened the envelope and pulled out a yellowed letter scrawled in India ink …

January 24, 1925

Dear Wovoka,

My God has bestowed upon me the inspiration to write you this letter. It is intended to be both a compliment and an apology. I was personally responsible for the demise of American Indian life, as you once knew it. As the commander of the US Army, I was assigned the task of moving the tribes away from their native lands and onto reservations. Many whites believed this was the best solution for the Indians and for the new settlers.

Some days after the decisive battle at Wounded Knee, I had a dream. In this dream, I witnessed the true power of your ghost dance, and I saw how it could bring our cultures together. I kept this dream a secret for many years while continuing to fight the tribes across the West. I had a job to do, and there was great pressure from Washington to settle the western frontier.

I apologize to you, your family, and your people. I believe your ghost dance will one day find its place in the world.

Sincerely yours,

General Nelson A. Miles

United States Army

"Your great-grandfather died a few months after he wrote this letter," Wilson said. "My family kept the letter hidden because they didn't want to vindicate him. The things he did to our people are no less terrible."

"But he believed in the ghost dance. That's amazing."

"Yes. It would appear that your great-grandfather was one of Wovoka's biggest fans."

— — —

The florist shop had no line at all. The man with sympathetic eyes looked up from behind the counter. He recognized David. "Yellow daffodils," he recalled. Then, realizing how long it had been, it occurred to him that David's wife might have gone the way of so many others. He searched David's face for a clue. "We have some lovely remembrance arrangements," he added. "They're designed for the outdoors, will last at least ten days this time of year."

"That won't be necessary," David replied. "But you can give me two dozen long-stemmed red roses."

The man smiled. It was nice to hear some good news for a change. He gently wrapped the roses in tissue and tied the bundle with a yellow ribbon. "These are on the house," he said.

David smiled and shook the man's hand. No words were necessary.

— — —

The roses sat prominently on the passenger seat. The Honda purred. No more smoke. The car had even been cleaned, inside and out. But David still wore the tattered motorcycle jacket, and he still had two days' stubble on his face. Those rough edges could have many different meanings, he knew. It was all a matter of context. David glanced at himself in the rearview mirror. Sadness lurked just behind the contentment. The adventure was over. The magic had come and gone. It was out of his hands now.

David thought of Julia and how he still loved her in spite of it all. Even if she did have an affair, it didn't matter. There are more important things in life, such as life itself. The Indians knew it. The children of Islamabad knew it. And David knew it. Albert was right. Everything *is* connected.

ACKNOWLEDGMENTS

WRITING A FIRST NOVEL is a challenging undertaking. I decided to add to this challenge by not telling anyone I was writing a novel. My friends and family hadn't the faintest idea I was writing, much less writing fiction. For nearly a year, they thought I was going to the office to take care of business, when in fact, I was involved in something quite different. Of course, this charade does have its advantages: if things didn't come to fruition, I was off the hook, and they were none the wiser.

Eventually, I came to a point in my project where the forward momentum overpowered the urge to throw in the towel. I decided to let a few close friends and my children in on my secret. It was especially gratifying to share the news with my daughter, a budding literary talent in her own right. Several friends—a few of them published authors—read pieces of the novel while it was being written. Their comments and criticisms were invaluable. Thank you to everyone who inspired me to keep the fires burning.

Foster, Anna and Cooper Lockwood
May Louise Lockwood

Spencer Bailey
David Beilman

Dennis and Judy Bosch
Jonathan Deitcher and Family
Martha Finch
Bill Gottesman
Douglas Grant
Al and Barbara Gross
Jim and Melinda Hamilton
John W. Hennessey
Eric Johnson
Stephen P. Kiernan
Nina Lynn
Steve Mann and Susan Taylor Mann
Donna Miller
John Paluska
David and Samantha Stetson
Margaret Strouse
Nuna Teal

Tip o' the hat to Sherman Miles

— — —

While this story is fictional, the iconic Wovoka and Nelson A. Miles were real people. Some of the ideas attributed to them are my own, written in the hopes of being true to their spirits.

Todd R. Lockwood, March 2011

NOTE

1   Eric Davalo and Patrick Naim, *Neural Networks* (Basingstoke, Hants, U.K.: MacMillan Education, Limited, 1991)

ABOUT THE AUTHOR

Author Todd R. Lockwood's life reads like the diary of a renaissance man. As a teenager, he took to serious portrait photography, something he still does today. His black and white portraits are known for their emotional candor and breathtaking detail. In his late twenties, he began composing and performing music, and that led him to build a world-class recording studio where he hosted such artists as Phish, Alice Cooper and Odetta. In 1990, he founded the Brautigan Library, America's only library devoted exclusively to unpublished writing. Throughout all of these activities, a writer was lurking. Lockwood has penned three novels. *Dance of the Innocents* is his debut release. Todd R. Lockwood lives and writes in Burlington, Vermont.

www.ToddRLockwood.com